WOLFEMAN
M C
BOOK ONE

Angera Allen

1

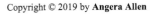

Angera Allen www.authorangeraallen.com

Editor Ellie Mc Love at My Brother's Editor - Formatted by Jessica Hildreth Cover Design by Clarise Tan at CT Cover Creations - Cover Photo Wander Aguiar Photography - Proofreader: Jennifer Guibor | Kim Holtz | Michelle Kopp

Quick / Angera Allen. -- 1st ed. 978-0-9986829-8-3 Ebook 978-0-9986829-9-0 Paperback

DEDICATION

This book is dedicated to my girl, Kim Holtz aka AmyKim. It all started at Book Splash 2016, when we found out that we lived near each other and we thought a lot alike, becoming instant friends. And wow, what a journey we've had. I really hope you know how much I appreciate you and your friendship.

We have come a long way from you printing my books out and handwriting the grammar errors, to using Word document. As I said above, we think alike, so you being able to take my words and unscramble them is a blessing in disguise. You make my words flow better by rearranging them and making them complete before I send them off to editing where Ellie makes them shine.

I love our endless phone calls, where we sit for hours talking about the details of the book and where I'm going with the story, or even planning out the next six books. Our mutual love for Mexican food, more specifically our love for tacos, has bonded us even more! I don't know if I'm happy you got me hooked on coffee, but it did help when I needed to stay up endless hours finishing these last two books. Tell your boys, that includes your hot hubby, I'm sorry for keeping you from them.

And last, your love and dedication to my words – that is why I'm dedicating this book to you.

Thank you!
Cheers, my dear friend

1 | Withdrawal

Quick

Ruby Malone.

My little firecracker.

Jesus Christ. I can't stop thinking about her.

I grip the bridge of my nose, applying pressure before rubbing my eyes. It's only been two fucking days.

Two.

Fucking.

Days.

A groan escapes me as I grab my beer, downing half of it in one swig. I try to focus my eyes as I look around the bar. Thank the gods above no one is around to see me sulking. Well, except Maze, the bartender, who has been moving around stocking the bar.

"Fucking pussy," I murmur to myself. Yeah, I've been hit with the motherfucking voodoo pussy. I'm ruined for any other woman. I huff, taking another long swig, almost finishing the beer. Who am I kidding? I can't even jack myself off – I'm so fucked in the head. And it's only been two motherfucking days since she left – *two!*

I shake my head, pissed off with myself. I need to get past this and get it together. She's still married. She can't just pick up and leave.

Fuck!

My heart constricts just thinking of never seeing her again. It's only been two days since she left to go back home with Izzy.

"What the fuck? You havin' a fight with yourself?" a voice booms from behind me.

I look over my shoulder to see Shy, club president and my

best friend, making his way over to the bar. I just shrug before finishing my beer, slamming it down.

"That bad, huh?" Shy chuckles as he takes a stool next to me. As soon as he's seated, Maze walks over.

"He's been sulking for over an hour. I couldn't take the negativity, so I've been leaving him to his own accord," Maze says, placing two fresh beers along with two shots in front of us. "Maybe you'll have better luck," she chuckles, making her way back to the other end of the bar.

"Brother, what the fuck?" Shy questions, but it's more of a statement by the look on his face.

"Don't even give me shit. You had it just as bad when Ginger was away. Fuck, maybe even worse, so don't fuck with me," I say, looking straight ahead as I fidget with the bottle label.

"You like her that much, huh? I thought she would be out of your system by now. It's been what—"

I cut him off before he can finish. "Two motherfucking days. Brother, I'm trying, but... *fuck!*" I yell in frustration.

"Do you think she's the one?" Shy blurts out, shocking me.

"Jesus Christ," I breathe out. I turn my head to face him and say, sounding defeated, "I think she *is* the one."

"Are you sure?" Shy teases and I can tell he's goading me.

This time I turn my whole body to face him as I place my forearm on the bar and lean forward so only Shy can hear me. "I told her my real name. So yeah, she is *the one*." When I'm finished talking, I lean back waiting for his response.

Nothing.

Shy can mask his face like no one I've ever seen. You can never tell what he's thinking. I'm about ready to say something when he says, "Huh."

I about lose my shit. "What do you mean, *Huh*? You know how big that is for me and how *no-one* can know it. I've been freaking out about it. I've never told anyone, let alone a woman, my real name." I stare at him with wild eyes. Feeling like I'm going to crack, I grab my beer and take another long swig.

"Brother, believe me, I know how big of a deal it is about your name. I'm just shocked. She's a good girl, and I wouldn't be worried about her knowing your name. But, did you tell her your full name and everything about you? And, I have to ask, why did you tell her?" Shy asks in a calm, soothing voice.

I'm anything but calm and soothed when I answer him. "Fuck no, I didn't tell her everything or my full name. No one knows that shit. I'm not fucking stupid. And I don't know why I told her. She wanted to fuck, and I wanted to talk about *us*. What fucking guy does that?" I groan.

I don't want to see the look on his face, so I drop my head to the bar. "I sound like a fucking pussy. I don't know what's wrong with me. I've never felt like this. Fuck!" I yell, lifting my head up off the bar.

I look over to see Shy smiling as he takes a long pull from his beer.

"It's like what you've been telling me all these years about how you knew when you heard Snow's voice for the first time. You hadn't even seen her face, but you knew. Well, I saw that wild fucking hair flying around and that goddamn marshmallow jacket of hers, and it hit me." I punch my chest. "At first I thought I just needed to fuck her, but then she opened her sassy little fucking mouth and those fucking eyes," I finish, turning to face the bar again as Shy stares at me, assessing me, thinking like he always does before he talks.

I hear a chuckle beside me. "Brother, tell me what we're trying to figure out here? What's the problem? What's got you all fucked up? I've never seen you this down or troubled. Do you want her or don't you? I don't see where the problem is here?"

"I want her. It's like she tapped into the old me and the new me, mixing them all together, and it's really fucking me up," I answer him truthfully.

"Jake," Shy says my real name. I snap my head around, making sure no one is in earshot.

Shy turns to face me, and says, "Jake, you can say your name. No one knows where you are, and sure as fuck, no one here is going to come after you. It's been years, everyone thinks you're dead, and even if they did... look at you!" He points to me before pointing to himself. "Fuck, look at us! We are completely different people. We look completely different. Yes, you are still Jake Reeves, and I am still Micah Jenkins, but we're so much more now. It's not bad that the girl you love knows your name. Shit, Snow calls me by my given name all the time. She should know the old you and the new you because it makes you, you."

My brain's on overdrive, and all this information is giving me sensory overload, it's all too much. I sit there in shock, face to face with my best friend, my brother, shit, my savior, and most of all, he's the president of the club I've sworn my life to. Only two things keep circling around in my brain – one, he just said my full name out loud and two, he said the *girl I love*. Fuck yes, I'm in shock.

"Look, we've talked about you seeing people from our past. You were going to see your good friend in LA, but we had to rush back. We can speak your name if we want to, but now everyone knows you as Quick. It isn't that we *can't* say your name anymore, it's just we don't. Same as me, I don't go by Micah anymore." He pauses, assessing me before he continues. "All I'm saying is you are and will always be protected. We can handle any threat that comes after us. Don't use that as an excuse, or stress out about it. I think you're tripping about how much you care for her and are using any excuse to freak out."

I'm still frozen, not saying a word. These past few years have been about keeping me hidden, not letting anyone know my real name.

He continues, "My only question now is why are you sitting

here? You can't compare my situation with Snow to this. I bitched and moaned because I *couldn't* go get my girl. Brother, you *can!*" Shy crosses his arms over his chest. "*So again,* what's the problem we're trying to figure out here? Because, it seems to me you have all the answers, but you're just sitting here feeling sorry for yourself. You need to go get your girl."

I'm shocked. He just handed me my ass on a silver platter, putting me in my place.

I cough, clearing my throat before I speak, "I thought we agreed to keep my true identity hidden from the Crows?"

Shy shrugs his shoulders. "I'm not saying go announce to the world you're alive or your real name, but telling your girl or anyone important to you, shouldn't be stressing you out so much. If the Crows find out your identity, or where you're at, believe me, we'll handle it. Just like we did all those years ago." He reaches an arm out, gripping my shoulder. "Brother, we're in this together. Don't let the past and future dictate your life, just live. I want to see you happy, like really happy, and Ruby seems to do that for you."

Keeping his hand on my shoulder, he reaches for his shot with his free hand. As I grip my shot, I reach out, clasping his shoulder, and say our little motto, "Nut-up, brother."

Shy laughs. "Exactly. Nut-the-fuck-up, *brother.*" We both hammer our shots back, slamming them down, grabbing the second one, slamming it back as well.

"Thank you," I choke out.

"Anytime. I owe you my life. Do you know how many times you've talked me off the ledge?"

"Are you fuckers going to kiss it out or what? Fucking get a room if you are," Dallas says with Mac laughing next to him as they walk up to the bar signaling Maze to bring us drinks.

"You jealous, Dallas, my boy?" Shy teases, releasing my shoulder, turning to face the bar.

My mind starts swirling around with what I should do or

what I need to do to get my little firecracker back. The three of them start talking club business, but I grab my phone and start to text Izzy. It's time to start a fire.

When I hear them talking about Ruby's aunt, I stop texting and listen to Dallas. "Her aunt owns and runs one of the biggest escort services in California. Her club is well known, but from what I hear, needs some help with a couple of issues. Issues we can help with and it so happens that one of her biggest clients is none other than the Sons of Saints," he says, looking over at me.

"Sons of Saints?" I question, making sure I heard him correctly. Dallas is our treasurer but most importantly our intel and all-around, go-to guy. He's a fucking Brainiac– smartest dude I know and completely lethal in combat. He's a silent but deadly motherfucker. He looks like the boy next door with his pretty face and baseball cap.

Shy looks over to me with a brow raised. "Seems like there's more than one reason for you to head down to Los Angeles. It's time to be reborn, brother. It isn't coincidental this just popped up, or that Whiz is president down there, it's all meant to be."

I just stare at the men I've come to think of as family while having flashbacks of my life so long ago. Whiz was like a father to me, took me in and watched out for me after my folks died. Now he's down in LA and president of the SoCal Chapter of the Sons of Saints.

Jesus Christ. Here we go.

"Well, it looks like I need to make some calls," I say, grabbing for my phone.

"I think it would be a good move, but we need to get all the intel and bring it to the table. We all need to be on board and vote on it," Shy says before emptying his second beer and slamming it down.

Anxiety stirs in my belly. I'm going to be resurrected and I don't know if that's good or bad, probably a little of both. I slam the rest of my beer before standing up.

"I want Chain and Jammer with you at all times once you leave here," Shy orders.

I turn back toward him. "You want me to take the two new prospects with me? I'd rather ghost in and ghost out."

"You're not leaving here without someone with you no matter what intel we find out," Shy demands.

I huff but don't say anything. Instead, I grab my phone and dial a number I know by memory but haven't dialed in years.

"Guess who, motherfucker?" I chuckle into the phone as I make my way to my room at the clubhouse.

2 | Reborn

Quick

"Well, I'll be goddamned. Are my old eyes deceiving me or can it really be *Jake motherfuckin' Reeves* standing in front of me?"

"Your eyes must be deceiving you, old man, because I don't see no *Jake motherfuckin' Reeves* anywhere," I laugh, extending my hand to greet my old friend as my prospects make themselves scarce.

"Well fuck, the last time I saw your punk ass, you were Jake Reeves. Who the fuck are you now?" He laughs, pulling me in for a hug, patting me on the back.

I reply, "Good to see you, *Logan Goddamn Jackson.*" I use his real name instead of his road name, Whiz.

We pull away from each other, still embraced, patting each other on the shoulders. I say in a more serious tone, "I go by Quick now. Jake Reeves died a long time ago," letting anyone in earshot hear.

Logan studies me a second before looking around the bar. "Shit, Jake, you ain't got shit to worry about here. Don't know those boys." He nods toward my guys. "But these are my guys, and they don't know you. *And,* you know I don't go by Logan anymore either," he ends with a chuckle, turning toward the bar to grab his beer.

Still feeling uncertain about being here, I look around the bar only seeing two of his men here. They both look at me with curious eyes darting from my guys then back to me with their club president, so I nod my head politely and move to follow my old friend. The last thing I want is to cause drama or bring more attention to me. I'm hoping this wasn't a big mistake coming to see him.

"Sit, man. Let's get you a drink." He motions to the pretty

bartender to bring us a round of drinks before turning back to me. "Fuckin' A. Where have you been? Everyone thought the Crows got you or that you were dead. It wasn't until Sweet Cheeks broke down and told me she helped you but that you took off. I asked her where and she said she woke up and you were gone," he says, taking a drink of beer.

"Yeah, I've been underground for all these years and sorry for being short over the phone. It means a lot that you came to meet me," I explain, hoping he won't keep pushing for information, but knowing my old friend, he will.

"Fuck, you took me by surprise for sure. It shocked the shit out of me hearing your voice. How are you?" he asks.

Whiz is the only person, besides my family, I've missed and kept tabs on since I left all those years ago when I cut all ties to my life as Jake Reeves.

I see that he's truly concerned, so I relax, taking a swig of my beer before I answer. "Shit got bad. I had to cut all ties to my life. I'm sorry I haven't been in touch. I've been trying to get settled," I say, honestly.

Whiz's face becomes serious. "Well, it isn't like I'm an easy person to get ahold of – I mean fuck – I moved across the country – too much drama with all those clubs in that area. Black Crows have about run our chapter out. When Johnny died, Bret asked me to come down here as road captain, and within a few years, I was voted in as president. Life's been good away from all those motherfuckers. Plus, there's no snow here and lots of half-naked pussy running around." He pauses a second to take a drink of his beer before continuing.

"Ronny kept giving me shit, always asking where you were. Then one day he just quit asking, I thought the Crows took you out. When Sweet Cheeks finally told me everything, I kept that shit to myself and told her if she liked breathing to do the same," he explains as we both take a long pull from our beers, letting what he said sink in.

I chuckle. "You were one of my closest friends, kind of like a big brother to me. Through all the years bouncing around cities, you were always my home base. I've kept tabs on you and what you've been doing. I just couldn't make contact, then when I was able to, shit just got busy."

Whiz turns to face me, leaning forward, resting his arm on the bar. Raising an eyebrow, he asks with a stern voice, "So, what's really going on? Why did you want to meet here and not at my clubhouse? After all these years with no word, and bam, you want to meet up? Kinda has me curious." When he's finished talking, he leans back, crossing his arms over his chest, his face as hard as stone waiting for me to answer.

"Like I said, I couldn't make contact for a while, I would have come sooner, but I was kind of locked into something. I've joined a club myself actually." I pause to see his reaction.

Whiz uncrosses his arms with a huge grin spreading across his face. "Fuck you!" he bellows, hitting me on the arm. I nod, smiling. "Well, fuckin' A! I turned you to the dark side after all. Fuckin' finally! You never wanted to be tied down, what the fuck happened?" he asks, crossing his arms over his chest again, giving me his full attention.

I laugh at his reaction. He was always trying to get me to prospect for his club back home, but I didn't want to be tied to one city, and he knew it.

"Wait! You're not a fuckin' Crow, are you?" he asks loudly, getting a few heads to turn our direction.

"Fuck. NO!" I exclaim.

Whiz relaxes, grabbing his beer. "Thank God. I would've fucking kicked your ass out of here. No matter how good of friends we were," he says with a half chuckle and serious look on his face.

That was the last reassurance I needed to know he still hated the Black Crow MC as much as we did. Right then, I knew he was the same old Logan, and I could trust him completely.

"Well, I'm glad you feel that way. It makes me feel a lot better about having this next conversation with you," I say as I glance over, waiting for his reaction.

He turns to the bartender. "Can you get us two shots of whiskey and two more beers please, Sugar?"

The bartender is on it, heading toward us with two beers in her hands. We both finish the ones we have just in time for our shots. We salute then slam them back before downing half our beer, just like the old days.

"I'm a Wolfeman," I blurt out, placing my beer onto the bar.

Whiz's eyes get wide while he's still chugging his beer. "Goddamn... You've been with them all this time? How the fuck did you keep *that* from the Crows? I mean, I heard rumors of what went down, but I never thought..." He trails off, not finishing his sentence.

"You're the first person I've even spoken to about this, and you'll be the last. We've been friends for a long time, and I'm trusting you to keep this between us. But, *yeah*." I give him a look hoping he understood what I was saying.

He raises an eyebrow, waiting for me to elaborate, so I continue. "*Yeah*, they still don't know who did it. They thought it was Shy, but after seeing him, they knew there had to have been someone else there. I was working the bar that night, so they figured I either knew who did it or I did it, but they still didn't know for sure." I take another drink of my beer to give him a few minutes to let that sink in before continuing.

"Ronny was harassing a bunch of people that knew me, and when they finally caught up with me, they beat me pretty bad. Crows kept asking me who did it and when I wouldn't give up who did, they were planning to kill me." I pause, thinking back to that night, and I chuckle. "But thank fuck for a big group of people that came into play, and saw what was happening. There were too many witnesses to just kill me, so they left me for dead," I say, taking a deep breath, glancing over to see Whiz's shocked face, I keep going. "Sweet Cheeks wasn't linked to me – shit, no one knew I was fucking her on the side. She was one of your club girls. I knew I could trust her to help me, so I got ahold of Shy, and they came to get me," I explain.

Whiz still hasn't moved, he just sits there staring at me with his mouth open. I laugh, giving him a few minutes to absorb what I just told him, but after a few seconds, he responds, "Holy. Fuckin'. Shit, my brother. Why didn't you come to me?"

I shake my head, swallowing my beer before replying, "No, it wasn't your problem. I didn't want them coming after your club for my shit. I needed to disappear, and I did. Hell, you know I'm good at doing that."

Whiz's face lights up with so many questions he starts to ramble, "But how? I mean, what happened? Motherfucker... it was you? Jesus Christ!" He pauses, lowering his voice. "Crows and Wolfs rivaled over that shit for a few years. I mean, rumors still go around about how a Wolf took down two Crows. No one thought it was you, brother. How did they not see or find you with them?" he asks, still looking shell-shocked.

"When they had it out, I was in New York City. Shy took me in and gave me protection throughout all the chapters for saving his life. Later, I prospected for a year while living in the city watching Shy's ol' lady. When he started his new chapter in New York City as president, I was named road captain," I say proudly with a shit-eating grin.

He smiles. "Well fuck... where's your cut, brother? Fuck, are you trying to be like me or what?"

I laugh smacking his arm. "I learned from the best, old man, and look at you now, president an *sheeeit*."

He sits up, pushing his chest out proudly. "Fuckin' A, brother. I'm building an empire out here."

We both grab our beers and salute, taking a long drink.

"Jake motherfuckin' Reeves is road captain of the Wolfeman

MC. I don't believe it. Where's your patch, brother?" He looks at me with questioning eyes and a smirk on his face.

I whistle, and within seconds, my prospect, Chain, hands me my cut. I instructed him before we got here if I whistled it would be for him to bring me my cut. If I snapped my fingers, I just needed him, but to leave my cut with Jammer. I didn't know how this was going to turn out, so I came prepared. I could have just worn my cut in, but I wanted to see if he was still my old friend before he saw my club colors.

I slip on my cut, giving Chain a nod, and he slips back into the shadows. He's going to be a good brother.

"Well, fuckin' A, Jake, you look good in a cut, brother."

I laugh, taking my seat again.

"I can't believe it. You're a motherfuckin' Wolfeman," he says to himself, shaking his head in disbelief before turning to me again with a big ass grin. "Fuck, I mean Quick." He throws his head back with a laugh. "Goddamn. You've been busy. Quick! Great fucking name. I'm proud of you, shit I'm glad you're alive," he says, gripping my shoulder.

"Thanks, me too. I've come a long way, but I love my life. It's cold as fuck in New York right now. You're definitely living the life here," I say, grabbing my beer for another drink.

"Fuck, wait a minute." He shakes his head in thought. "Damn, now that I think about it, Wolfe has mentioned a Quick in his ranks. Well fuck me, I guess you have known where I've been this whole time and what I've been up too, seeing as I've been working with them."

I smile. "Yeah, they knew how close I was with you. Shit, you're the reason I got to know all of them with all those parties at your clubhouse. When I left, I told them I wanted to keep eyes on you to make sure the Crows didn't fuck with you."

Whiz just sits there shaking his head with a big shit-eating grin.

Before I take a drink, I try to lighten the mood by saying, "Bet your old ass is loving this weather."

"My balls are loving me now, being all sweaty and shit, compared to being shriveled up nuts half the year," he says, as we both laugh, knowing it gets cold as fuck on the East Coast.

"So, what now? Are the Wolfs good with the Crows? You just come to SoCal to be resurrected from the dead or is there a reason you're here?" he asks.

I lock eyes with him, lowering my voice, I say, "Well, the Crows haven't bothered us in years. Crows and Wolfs never got along and still don't to this day. They stay in their territories, and we do the same. We don't know if they're still looking for me or not, but they definitely don't know where I am. No one knows me as Jake – he's dead. When I moved to New York, only a handful of people knew where I was, and I became Quick. I hope you can keep this little conversation a secret. That's why I wanted to meet with you here first. I wanted to get this conversation out of the way without any extra ears. I don't trust anyone, and no one knows me by anything *but* Quick. I don't want any of your brothers talking about a Jake Reeves, or for it to get out that I was here," I finish, leaning back with a stern face, letting him know I'm trusting him.

"Quick, you got my word. I kept Sweet Cheeks' little admission a secret even when everyone was asking if I'd been in touch with you. I got your back. You could have told me all those years ago, and I would have protected you. I don't want or need the Crows invading my turf looking for you. I have to deal with them in our other chapters over there." He pauses, taking a drink. "I don't know if any of the other brothers will recognize you. It's been years, and you sure as fuck don't look the same. Plus, I've built this club with new and younger members. When Bret got sick, handing the gavel down to me, I was pretty much the oldest fucker in this group. So, you have nothing to worry about, and you know the Sons of Saints hate those motherfuckers. We've always supported the Wolfemen, so we're all good."

I knew the Sons of Saints have always been good with the club, and still do some deals with us. Shy told me it was a good decision to bring Whiz and his club into the fold. We're not discussing any business opportunities just yet. I need to see how well the club is running and get more intel.

I shake his hand. "Well, I'm glad I'm back from the dead. I've missed you, brother. I just wanted to get this little chat down memory lane over with before we head over to your clubhouse. It's just me and my two prospects here. I'll be down here quite a bit and look forward to hanging out like old times. You have any bikes around? I need to ride."

"Brother, does a bear shit in the woods? Of course, we have extra bikes. Let's head back to the clubhouse. Maybe then you'll tell me why you're really here. Don't get me wrong, I love that you're back from the dead, but I'm sure there's a reason why," he says, finishing his beer.

Finishing my beer, I think of Ruby and laugh. "Oh yeah, I have a little Firecracker I need to light up down here."

3 | Surprise
Quick

"You sure this is the place and that she's coming home?" Whiz says next to me as we sit on our motorcycles across the street from Ruby's aunt's house.

"Yeah, she was coming from the airport so who knows how long it will take her with traffic. My friend just texted me, letting me know she dropped her off at the airport and was headed back home," I answer him, grabbing my phone to check the time.

After the bar earlier, Whiz and I went back to his clubhouse where he introduced me to his club as Quick the Wolfeman's road captain and longtime friend. No one seemed to question it as they welcomed me and my prospects. We all sat around bullshitting when I got the text from Izzy. I gave Whiz a nod letting him know I wanted to take a ride just the two of us. Before heading out, I let him know I needed to check in on my girl, which leads us to right now sitting in front of her house.

"So, I take it, *she's* the reason you're really here?" Whiz adjusts his bandana after taking his helmet off. I nod my head, placing my helmet on the handlebar.

"Fuck, it feels good to ride, it's been a bit with the snow back home," I say more to myself than anything. It feels good to be in just a t-shirt and cut. Whiz doesn't say anything.

"It's hot as fuck today," I continue my rant while Whiz situates himself on his bike. Riding next to him brought back memories of the earlier years when we would ride together. He's a good ten years older than me, but you wouldn't be able to tell, he doesn't look his age. Southern California has definitely been good to him. Looks like he's been lifting weights and the tan makes him look even younger. I'm happy for him.

I see him tilt his glasses down, giving me a look to explain myself and quit sidestepping the details about my girl. I smile. "Yes, that pussy of hers is the reason I'm down here. She's got me all jacked up feening for more." I shake my head. "You just wait and see, we call her Firecracker." I laugh, thinking about my little firecracker.

"Goddamn, I never would have thought Jake Reeves settling down in one town, let alone a club *and* an ol' lady. When did you meet her?" he asks with a smile.

I return the smile. "Well, this is really going to fuck you up..." I pause. "Last week."

I wait for his reaction, but he just stares at me with his mouth half open. "Last week?" he questions in shock.

I smile big and say, "It was one hell of a weekend, brother."

Still looking at me like a deer in headlights. "Fuckin' A, she must have some million-dollar pussy. I don't see me settling on *one* pussy. Especially, here with all these naked ladies." He pauses for a second to think. "Me... Fuckin' only *one.*" Whiz shakes his head. "Hell. No!" He laughs, shaking his head. "There are too many willing beautiful ladies around here." Tilting his head back, pointing to the sky, saying, "Thank you, God, for inventing bikinis."

We both laugh as a black Mercedes-Benz GLE pulls up to the address Izzy gave me. We've been texting since Shy pulled my head out of my ass and I texted her. Izzy came back with her to make sure Ruby's soon-to-be ex-husband didn't manipulate my girl or harm her since he flipped out after she served him divorce papers when she was in New York meeting me. That was last weekend, and I can't get my mind off her, which means my dick is hard all the time. I'm a crack head needing his fix. Our phone calls and her sexting me every day isn't helping. I told Izzy I was coming down for a few days to remind Ruby why she needs to move to New York and of course Izzy agreed.

"Fuckin' A... *is that* your girl?" Whiz asks, sliding his sunglasses down to check her out.

"Uh-huh," is all I could say as I watch her get out of the Mercedes. *Fuck me, that hair. It's always been that fucking hair.* I can't take my eyes off her and Lord have mercy, she's in short as fuck shorts with a tight little tank top. I bite my lip holding back a groan as my dick stands to attention.

"Fuck yeah. See, now you know why," I state. I look down her body, my mouth salivating seeing her tan legs and tight little body. She looks the complete opposite from when I first laid eyes on her back home, but goddamn she looks even better.

Nerves flare up, and doubt starts popping into my head. *What if she doesn't want to see me or she tells me to leave.* I start to panic when she lifts the rear hatch of the car open and bends over. Whiz whistles getting her attention.

I shoot him a death glare from behind my glasses, but he just laughs looking back over to her. She looks around, lifting her hand to block the sun to see who whistled as I sit here frozen, holding my breath.

Come on, baby. Come to me, Rube. Please, baby, show me you missed me.

I can only imagine what she's thinking with two dudes sitting on motorcycles watching her bend over. *Christ.*

But when I pull my glasses down and give her a smile, she drops the shit in her other hand and looks across the street. I continue to sit on my bike, watching her as she starts to walk toward me, hips swaying so perfectly, and her wild hair flying all around her face.

"Goddamn, she got a sister? Fuck!" Whiz murmurs next to me.

Halfway across the street, she screams, "It is you – Quick!" as she runs to me with a huge smile.

I chuckle, standing to get off my bike. I just barely have time to catch her as she launches herself at me with a squeal, wrapping her legs around me.

Laughing, I squeeze her tight. "That's my firecracker. Miss me, baby?"

"Oh, my God." Ruby pulls back, gripping the sides of my face before she kisses me hard and deep.

After a few minutes, Whiz laughs with a couple of coughs before Ruby lets go of me. "Quick. Oh, my God. You're actually here?" She places kisses all over my face as I laugh.

"Shit, I guess coming back from the dead is worth it," Whiz teases, and I turn to flip him off.

Jesus, just having her in my arms, I feel whole again, like I can finally breathe. I've been so twisted up and being so far away has gutted me.

"Rube, this here is my old friend, Whiz. He's the president of a local club called—"

"Sons of Saints MC," Ruby cuts me off, finishing my sentence which shocks both of us. I go to set her down, but she locks her legs around me and smiles. "Not yet. Don't let me go yet."

I laugh. "I'm not going anywhere, but how do you know the Saints?"

"I know I would have remembered you sugar – you know – if we…" Whiz teases, poking fun at me.

Ruby releases her legs standing up to face my old friend. "Whiz, right?" He nods his head. "We've never met and no offense but, Whiz, how the fuck did you get that name? I mean do you… *Whiz* on people or something?" she asks, sounding serious.

"Ruby, show some respect, and stop with the names," I demand, but laugh, missing her feisty little mouth.

"Well, at least I know where you got the name Firecracker, but no, I'm smart with numbers and shit like the whiz kid," he chuckles. *"But* I'm not going to lie… I have *whizzed* on a few people too."

She tilts her head back with a full belly laugh, letting all her hair fly around her, making my dick pulse harder against my jeans.

"That *is* a good name then. I love biker names and how they acquire them. I know it's not polite and against *the rules,* but with a name like Whiz, I just had to ask." She pauses to think. "Oh, I know them from the club. My aunt's strip club that is, not the clubhouse," she says, looking between the two of us. "I'm sure I've seen you, but we've never met." She steps forward, extending her hand to him. "It's nice to meet you Whizzz," she says, dragging his name out, making us laugh as he shakes her hand.

Whiz looks shocked. "It's my pleasure, Firecracker. Which strip club are you talking about?" he inquires, looking very interested.

"Club DazZelle," Ruby answers him as she moves back over to me, shoving her hands into her pockets.

Jesus Christ, this girl has ruined me. I need to be inside her like yesterday.

Whiz's face lights up like a fucking Christmas tree. "No shit?"

I see his head is whizzing with questions, but I need to fuck my girl more than he needs information.

"Can you leave? How long do you have before you have to pick up baby girl?" I demand, ready to get her on the back of the bike and back to my hotel to fuck.

She smiles, licking her lips. "How long do I have you?"

I pull her to me. "You've got me for a few days," I say, placing a kiss on her forehead.

"Well, I can give you a few hours, and we'll figure everything else out later. Let me go get my stuff," Ruby says, full of excitement.

I give her a kiss and swat her ass as she turns to head back across the street.

As we both watch her jog back to her car, Whiz murmurs, "We have so much to talk about, my brother. Her aunt's Madam Zelle. Mistress Z. Motherfuckin' Giselle."

I don't take my eyes off my girl and say with a shit-eating grin, "Oh, did I forget to mention that?"

"Fuckin' A, you did. What's your plan?" he asks as we both stare at her hurrying along.

"I'm going to take her to my hotel and fuck her senseless or until she has to pick her daughter up," I reply, feeling my cock twitch, eager to be enveloped by her warm pussy.

"Sounds like a plan. I'll ride with you 'til the clubhouse, just come back when you're done. We'll chat then. Motherfuckin' Madam Zelle. The brothers are going to freak the fuck out." Whiz laughs as we just sit there in awe of my little firecracker.

As she starts to head back over to us, I turn to him with an ear-to-ear grin. "Brother, you have no idea. We've got lots to discuss. I see lots of good things in our near future."

"Does Izzy know you're here? That little bitch tricked me, didn't she?" Ruby says, bouncing over while I grab the other helmet I snagged from Whiz's prospect.

"Yeah, you've said every day how you wished I was here, well bam. I'm here, baby." I kiss her head before placing the helmet on. I swing my leg over and start up the bike. Whiz is already geared up ready to go, waiting on us.

I reach out for her hand, and when I see her just staring, I yell, "What? What's wrong?"

She grabs my hand, moving to step on and yells, "You're hot as fuck on a bike. Jesus, I'm wet."

I growl, swatting her leg as she gets on.

Everything is right in my world right now. I don't know what will come of us but fuck if I don't want to savor every minute that I got.

Ruby scoots up next to me, wrapping her arms around me. I grab her hands, moving them down to cup my rock-hard cock. She squeals from behind me as she begins stroking it.

"Are you two fucking lovebirds ready to roll?" Whiz yells next to us, laughing.

"Let's roll, brother," I reply, and we both take off.

4 | Getting My Fix
Quick

After Whiz branches off, we keep going. The hotel is only a couple of blocks from the clubhouse, but it feels like hours. I am so ready to be inside my girl, my cock's straining against my jeans, throbbing like it has its own heartbeat. I have to move her hands up to my chest so I won't ejaculate in my pants.

Pulling into the hotel, Ruby starts to move her hips, making me groan.

"Someone misses her cock, doesn't she?" I say over my shoulder once the engine is killed.

Ruby giggles. "You have no idea. You ruined me – all those dick pictures just made it worse."

Once the bike and our shit are secure, I throw her over my shoulder and head to my room.

"Well, be ready for some fireworks because this firecracker is getting lit up," I tease.

As I unlock the door, she slides her hand down the back of my pants, gripping my ass. I launch her onto the bed shutting the door. She pops back up as I'm kicking off my boots, lifting my shirt over my head.

"Holy shit, Quick!" Ruby exclaims seeing the new ink I got done this week.

"What? It's not even close to being done. It's just the outline," I explain, flexing my chest where the head of a wolf sits bearing its teeth.

"It looks like it's mad at me for wanting to touch it," she says, reaching out tracing the lines.

"It's our Wolfeman MC insignia. I needed a distraction this week, and I've wanted to get it done," I explain, feeling self-conscious all of a sudden. I have a million tattoos, so I don't

29

understand why this one would make a difference, but I catch myself holding my breath for her approval.

"I love it. I like all your tattoos," she says, moving closer tracing my other tattoos with her fingertips, as she bites her lip.

"I've missed you so much," she moans breathless, caressing my body.

I reach for her tank top, lifting it up over her head, before pushing her flat onto her back. Grabbing her legs, I pull her to the edge of the bed so I can yank her *short as fuck*, shorts off.

"Jesus Christ, I want you so fucking bad. I flew six hours to be inside you," I groan.

"Please. Quick, hurry," she begs, while I slowly kiss my way up her legs.

"Fuck!" she grunts, leaning up on her elbows. "I need you right now. Hard and quick. We have hours for that other shit. I want you inside me now," she snaps.

I stand up, laughing. "Damn, Ruby Rue. Okay." I strip off the rest of my clothes as I watch her scoot to the middle of the bed, grabbing her tits.

Fuck yes. My little firecracker needs me.

I slowly climb onto the bed, slithering up between her legs kissing her belly as I slip two fingers between her folds and sure enough, she's soaked and primed for me.

"We still good with no sleeve?" I ask, praying she says we're good because I don't think I could ever fuck her with a rubber again after feeling her silky walls suck my cock dry.

"I said yes, as long as you hav—" I cut her off, slamming my cock fully inside her, knowing damn well I haven't fucked anyone.

She screams out, as I moan, "Fuck, yes." My eyes roll back from pure ecstasy – her pussy's like a goddamn instant high, so fucking warm and tight.

"Holy Shit, Rube," I say like a starved man. I flatten my

body over hers, demanding her lips. When I pull out, she gasps, gripping me around my lower back, digging her nails in.

Fucking heaven.

I start to slowly slide back in, keeping my face inches from hers. I don't take my eyes off her, slipping my tongue out, grazing her lips before sucking in her bottom lip. I slowly pull out. "Do you feel my cock?"

"Yes," she pants.

I slowly enter her wet pussy with a few pumps in and out as it milks my cock.

"Hmm. Do you feel how fucking hard I am for you?"

"Yes," she breathes out.

I pump a few more thrusts as she purrs with desire.

"You want more?" I start to pump faster. "Goddamn, I'm rock hard... only for you, baby."

"Yes. Fuck me," she begs, slipping her fingers into my hair trying to pull me down, but I resist, liking the pain of her pulling my hair harder. I start to thrust faster, rocking my hips.

"Mmm. Fuck, right there," Ruby murmurs, I kiss her with urgency, sucking her tongue and diving mine deep into her mouth. I break the kiss, breathless. Leaning back on my knees, I grab her legs, spreading them wider as I push them toward her so I can pound her with long deep strokes hitting her cervix.

I groan. "Take my cock."

"Fuck. Yes," she purrs.

I'm not going to last much longer.

"Grab your legs and keep them spread," I demand as I slide one hand up her belly to grip her hip while the other hand massages her clit. Ruby loses it, crying out harder. I grip her waist a bit harder, pinning her as I start my assault. Leaning forward, I pump faster, increasing my thrust, matching my flicks to her clit.

"That's it, baby, take all of me," I encourage her, feeling her walls contracting as she screams my name. I watch as my cock glides in and out, pounding her pink pussy rigorously. "I'm. So. Fucking. Close," I grunt breathlessly. Seeing her cum coating my cock as it glides in and out has my balls tightening up.

Oh, God. Ah, just a bit more. Jesus.

I close my eyes as I feel my climax at the brink. I grip her waist jackhammering into her with animalistic noises coming from deep within me. *Fuuuck.* The slapping sound gets louder, the harder I hammer into her.

"Rube. Fuck baby. Oh, yeah. This is my pussy." I open my eyes and see her tits bouncing all over from me pounding her.

I'm about to lose it. "Come, Rube. Fuck. Come again," I say with urgency.

"Quick. Yeah. Ah. Fuck..." she cries out as another orgasm smashes through her.

The wet suction sound between us gets louder as our bodies slam together. "Milk my cock with that pussy. Fuck yeah, cum all over my cock, baby," I groan, watching my dick slide rapidly in and out of her pussy.

"Fuck my pussy. God, I love your cock. Harder. Mmmm. Yes, Quick," she purrs, demanding more.

A deep low groan forms in my chest hearing her talk dirty. Fuck, it has me turning wild like an animal, releasing a roar, I explode inside her. I feel crazed, out of control, pounding into her as cum continues to spill from my cock.

I can't stop. *I need more.*

She feels so fucking good with her walls contracting around my dick. I slow my hips and continue to pump short thrusts into her pool of ecstasy. Leaning over, I capture her mouth breathlessly.

Pleasurable moans of our release sound from both of us. When I thrust up, she giggles.

"Quick," she murmurs into the kiss.

"Hmm." I thrust again, feeling my cock stir. It's her. I can't get enough of her. She's my motherfucking drug of choice.

She giggles. "Quick."

"I've missed you," I say, placing kisses all around her mouth. "Jesus Christ, that was so out of this world amazing. My dreams don't have shit on the real deal," she says, breathlessly.

"You've been dreaming about me, huh," I tease, shifting us so she's lying on top of me.

My cock jumps and begins to harden again as I grab a handful of hair, pulling it away from her face. "Goddamn, your hair is so fucking sexy," I say, trying to tame it into one hand.

She giggles, laying her head on my chest and starts to outline the new tatt. It's raw and in the early stages of healing, but I'm not moving her.

We lay there in silence for a few minutes. I begin to think she's fallen asleep when she suddenly says, "I'm really happy you're here. I…" She pauses. I can't see her face on my chest, so I wait to give her time to express how she's feeling. "I just needed to feel and see you. I know it's crazy but—" she stops, pausing again.

"Rubes, look at me, baby." When I lift her head, I see she has tears in her eyes. "What's wrong, baby? Don't cry."

I flip us again so I'm on top of her looking down. I caress her face, moving all her hair as I wipe the tears away.

"I've been staying strong with Izzy here. I know I can do this but having you here just solidifies I'm doing the right thing. But, I feel like I'm waiting for the other shoe to drop. Brody hasn't signed the papers or flipped out on me yet. I don't know if it was because Izzy was here or what, but I'm just waiting for something bad to happen. I feel it. Having you here makes me feel so much better and safer.

I lean down, kissing her softly. "Rubes, seeing you today confirmed a lot for me too. I want this just as much as you do. I mean, I flew here without even knowing if you would want me here or not. I just had to see you either way. I know you have a lot to figure out and I'm okay with that. I think you're worth waiting for. I'm here for you. Just tell me what you need from me."

She smiles up at me. "Well, you already took care of one thing I need from you, but I think I'll be needing that again for the next few hours."

I laugh. "Oh, you're going to be getting a lot of that," I say, slipping my dick back into her cum filled pussy.

Ruby's eyes roll back with a gasp. With her head in my hands, I place small kisses around her face before dipping my head into her neck as I slowly begin rocking into her.

"Ruby, this little session is going to make our last night in New York look like nothing. Like I said that night, I want you to know how much I want you and how special you are to me, so I want to do the whole 'slow and deep' thing again. I want you to feel how much I want you." I bend down, kissing her neck. "How much I need you," I say close to her ear as I rock my hips up going deeper this time. Ruby bites her lip with a moan.

Jesus Christ. I'm gonna come again. I can't get enough of her.

Leaning down, I suck her collarbone, if I could draw blood, I would. I crave her skin, just the idea of my lips sucking her sweet soft skin has my dick rock hard. I love marking her. I move over to her shoulder, sucking and kissing as I increase my hip motion. I feel my pelvic bone rubbing up against her clit.

She gasps, "Oh, Quick."

"Yeah, baby, feel me," I breathe.

I'm watching her every move while memorizing her face. When I close my eyes, I still see her naked body from our last night when I kissed every inch of her. *Goddamn, she's beautiful.*

"Mine," I whisper against her lips before kissing her slow and soft as moans escape both of us.

Ruby slides her hands through my hair, intensifying the kiss. I have so many emotions running through me as my cock pulses inside her. Sliding my hands under her shoulder blades, I grab ahold of them from behind, pinning her firmly against me as I start to pump long, hard, puncturing thrusts slamming her upward.

"Ah. Yes, don't stop. Yes. Right. There," Ruby pants against my neck as she grips my back.

"Jesus. You feel like heaven. I could fuck you all day," I murmur into her ear before sucking her neck.

Sweat builds up between our bodies. I keep rocking up into her tight pussy, feeling her body tense, knowing she's close.

"Lift your legs up and around me, lock them behind me, baby," I moan breathlessly.

She does what I say as I ram deeper inside her. Hitting her just right as her walls constrict around my cock.

"Yeah, baby. Fuck yeah," I grunt.

She starts panting 'yeah' over and over again, in between sucking my neck and biting me in return.

I can't hold it much longer with her lips sucking my neck.

"Faster. Quick. Please," she begs, clawing her nails into my back heatedly.

I rise up with Ruby holding on as I shift my knees, giving me more leverage to thrust fast, hard jolts into her pussy, hitting her clit just right. The bed starts to rock against the wall as we both build up our climax.

As I feel her close to coming, I say out of breath, "Hold it. Don't come yet, baby."

Her eyes pop open, looking up at me.

I lean down to give her a quick kiss. I'm breathless, grunting with each thrust, my voice thick with desire. "I'm close. So, fucking close. Wait for me."

I increase my pace as sweat rolls down my face and chest. I close my eyes, feeling my balls tighten up. "Almost, baby."

Ruby whimpers underneath me, "Your cock is so fucking big I can't hold on. Fuck me, Quick."

That does it. I lose it when she talks dirty.

I lift up onto my knees, hammering into her to the finish. "Now, Ruby," I grunt with each thrust. "Fuck, yeah, now, baby."

We both cry out. I grip her hips pumping every last drop of me into her.

My body begins to tingle all over as I start to shake, the orgasm is so intense I can barely hold my body up. I try to move off her, but her legs are still locked around me with her nails still digging into my back.

Lying there trying to catch our breath, I kiss up her neck to her ear.

"Fuck, now I know why people like doing that shit. Jesus Christ, that was intense. I just had a full body orgasm." I breathe heavy into her ear.

She releases me, lowering her legs. I slide out of her and move us both to our side, so we're facing each other. I push her hair out of her face, seeing her eyes are still closed.

"Are you talking about making love?" she whispers with her eyes still closed.

My heart jumps at the word love, but I guess that's what it's called.

"Yeah, I guess. I've never had sex like this until you," I say honestly.

Ruby's eyes shoot open. "What do you mean you've never had sex like this?" she questions, looking surprised.

"Before I met you, I would never do slow and deep. Shit, I wouldn't do anything slowly. I've hardly ever seen a girl more than once. Like I said to you when I saw you walk out of the airport, with that hair of yours flying around, something inside me clicked. I've never really believed in love, I mean I see people in love all the time, but I've never had it happen to me. I can't say it's love but fuck me, it's something. I couldn't even make it a week without flying out here. So yeah, this slow and deep shit has my body jonesing for more. I want this."

Tears fall from Ruby's eyes. I reach for her, pulling her to my chest. "Don't cry, Rube. I'm here to make you happy, not cry," I say, running my hands through her hair.

"You have no idea how happy I am. These are happy tears," Ruby murmurs into my chest.

We lay there for a few minutes until her phone rings.

I don't move as she exhales, "It's Bella."

I release her so she can move off the bed to grab her phone. As she answers it, she moves back to the bed. I jump up and head to the bathroom to clean myself off and run a warm towel for her. When I return with a towel, she's smiling as she talks to her daughter. My heart skips, or maybe it's a tug, but something happens because I halt in my tracks.

She must sense me or maybe because I stopped walking to stare at her, whatever it is she turns her attention to me. "Hold on, Bug. Are you alright Quick?"

I blink.

"Quick?" she says, sounding more concerned.

I shake my head and walk over to her, bending down to the floor. I spread her legs and begin to clean her. She tries to shoo me away, but I push her onto her back. "Continue your talk," I order her as I continue to clean between her legs.

"Bella, I'll be home soon. Yes, I know Momma's car is home. I'll be home soon. Okay, love you, Bug," Ruby pauses, holding the phone to her ear. "Hi Auntie, yes I'm with a friend. I'll be home soon. Thanks." Ending her call, she tosses her phone aside.

Ruby lifts up onto her elbows, looking down at me. I'm still wiping between her legs, trying to pull it together and figure out what's wrong. I have this strange feeling in my chest, and I'm not sure how to act.

"You okay? You've wiped that spot like three times. I think I'm clean," she says softly.

I drop the washcloth, gripping her legs, spreading them wide.

I'm entranced by her pussy as I glide my hands up and down the inside of her legs.

"Quick? Seriously, you're kind of freaking me out. Are you alright?"

Still, I don't say anything. I want her so fucking bad. The *need* I feel for her and how much I *want* to be with her starts to freak me out. I rise up on my knees, moving in between her legs. I continue sliding my hands along her inner thighs up to her crevice, spreading her pussy wide.

"I'm fine," I state, still not making eye contact, just staring at her pussy.

"Do you need to go?" I ask, rubbing my thumbs up and down her folds, down to her ass.

"Yes, soon," she answers breathlessly.

"Okay, just let me know," I say, sliding my thumbs back up, swiping over her ripe clit.

"Quick," she murmurs.

I lean down and lick her from her asshole to her pussy. Slowly sucking her folds as I run my tongue inside before moving to her clit.

"Jesus Christ." Ruby falls back, gripping her tits.

I grab under her knees, lifting her legs, spreading them wide. I lick around her asshole again before I make my way back up to her pussy, teasing her entrance. Her panting starts to increase before I dip my tongue inside repeatedly, making her moan.

From between her legs, I say, "I want to meet your daughter."

Ruby pops her head up. "What?"

I continue my assault, sliding my tongue from her pussy to her nub, sucking it into my mouth, flicking it with my tongue.

Breathless she says, "Shit, what did you say?" before falling back, moaning.

Sucking her clit harder, she starts shaking, and I know she's about to come. So, I repeat in between sucks, "I. Want. To. Meet.

Your. Daughter." As I slip in two fingers and slowly start to finger fuck her.

She cries out, "Yeah. Ah. Oh, God. Right there. Yes. Don't stop."

I continue until she's thrashing around on the bed, coming on my fingers. I feel crazed like I need to possess her. *Fuck what has she done to me?*

"Fuck me," she begs.

She's soaked with both our cum dripping from her pussy down to her ass.

"Move up the bed a bit. I want you to grab your knees and keep them to your chest. Don't move." My voice is hard and demanding.

She doesn't hesitate, scooting back, grabbing her legs. I palm my cock with one hand as I stand above her. After a few strokes, I'm hard as ever. Releasing my cock, I grip the back of her thighs and lean down to suck her pussy again. I suck her clit and feel her legs start to shake.

"Hurry, Quick," she gasps.

I put a leg on the bed while stroking my cock, slapping her pussy with it, gliding it up and down her folds lubing it up. I slip the tip into her pussy and pull out. Ruby is purring like a wildcat demanding me to hurry.

I slip two fingers into her and start finger fucking her again as I put the tip of my cock at her rear entrance. Once she sees my intention, she whines and begs me to continue. I slow my fingers, using the moisture from her pussy to lube her ass. Slowly, I slide my dick in just past the tip, making Ruby's moans get louder.

"Fucking so goddamn good," I grit out between my teeth. Slipping two fingers back into her, I work my cock into her ass and finger fuck her at the same time. Christ, she's perfect. I'm not going to make it much longer. She's so goddamn tight.

I start moaning, "Oh, God. Yes," over and over fully seated

in her ass. I start to slowly pick up speed continuing to double penetrate her pussy and ass.

"More. I need more. Please," she says breathlessly.

I do as she asks and give her more. *Fuck, it's the best fucking feeling ever.* My balls tighten up as I pump into her a bit harder, adding a third finger pushing her over the edge. She cries out as her orgasm crashes over her, making her butt clench, clamping down on my cock. *I can't breathe...* "Oh, fuck. Yes. Oh, fuck. Fuu-uuk..."

Two more pumps and I bust a nut in her ass.

I feel light headed as I fall forward. She releases her legs, allowing me to fall onto her, smashing her beneath me. Both of us are exhausted and out of breath.

After a few minutes, I pull out of her ass, staring down at her. I feel her chest rise and fall. Out of breath, I murmur, "I want to meet your daughter."

She stops breathing and her chest stills.

"Are you sure?" she replies after a few seconds.

"Yeah," I breathe out.

She laughs nervously. "Well, I guess if anything makes you run – it would be this, so fuck it. Let's get it over with."

Slightly shocked she agreed, I lean up and rasp out, "Are you sure? What about Brody? What will he say?"

Ruby runs her hand through my sweaty hair. "Relax. You're a friend of Auntie Izzy and Momma. Just no fucking or lovey-dovey shit in front of her. You're a friend. All the other shit we'll work out later, that is if you stick around and can stand the test. Plus, Momma has lots of friends."

Seeing her so calm, kind of relaxes me but my heart is racing. *Am I really doing this?*

"Are you sure you want to introduce him to her so soon?" my aunt asks, leaning up against the kitchen counter.

"Why not? It isn't like I'm saying we're together. He's just a friend of Mommy's," I reply calmly, but I'm anything but calm. I'm freaking out.

"What are you going to do if Brody comes by?" she questions.

"He won't come by without calling, and if he does, we'll deal with it," I explain.

"I can't believe Brody wasn't the one waiting at your door. With Izzy gone, I thought he would be here already trying to get you to change your mind," she says, opening the refrigerator door to grab a water.

"He doesn't know she left yet. He thinks she's here until Sunday," I say, thankful that Izzy lied to him the first day we got back and had to deal with him. He wasn't happy that Izzy was here and Bella was so excited to see her he couldn't yell at me like I'm sure he wanted to.

Brody never verbally manipulates me unless we're alone. I know he's biding his time waiting for me to be alone. He leaves to meet the band again next week. I only have to hide from him for a few more days.

"Well, that's good. Hopefully, he stays away while your *friend* is in town," she smiles, walking by me to head into the living room where Bella is watching cartoons.

"I hope so too," I breathe to myself.

My phone rings from my back pocket, so I dry my hands before answering it. "Hi, babe, you on your way over?"

"Hey Rube, I'm outside but need you to come out here," Quick says, sounding stressed out.

"What do you mean, outside? Why don't you just come in?"

I question, heading toward the front door.

"I'll explain. Just come outside," he pauses. "Please."

I open the door and see a taxi cab sitting in front of my house. Shutting the door, Quick steps out of the car. As soon as I see his face, I know something is wrong. "What happened?" I rasp out.

"I have to go back home. I got a 911 text. The club needs me to come home now," he says, pulling me into a hug.

"What happened?" I ask, concerned.

"I don't know. They didn't say. It's our way of letting members know there will be a lockdown, and everyone is needed at the clubhouse. I called the clubhouse and Dallas just told me I was on the next flight home, but that was it."

My heart is racing with all the what-ifs running through my head.

"I wanted to say goodbye, but I need to go right now to be able to catch my flight. I didn't want to meet baby girl and then turn right around and leave. I'll come back as soon as I can. I'll text you later," Quick says, leaning down capturing my mouth for a deep and soft kiss.

"Okay. I hope everything is okay." I'm sad he's leaving but more worried why he's being called back. I wonder if Izzy knows anything, but she just got back home so probably not.

Quick's looking at me with matching sad eyes. "I'm leaving Chain and Jammer, our prospects, to handle some stuff and watch over you. They're instructed to step in if Brody gets out of hand. Whiz and the boys will be keeping an eye on you as well, but don't worry, you won't see them. If you need them for anything, I'll text you their numbers. I'm serious, if Brody decides to be a punk ass, they have your back, and you let me know," he explains.

"I'll be fine. Brody won't do anything stupid," I say, trying to make him feel better.

I know him and Izzy have this plan to keep someone with me

so I don't have to deal with Brody alone, but I'm a big girl and know what I want. I want Quick. I want to move to New York. I want to be near Izzy. I really want this fucking job but most of all, I want a fresh start.

I've already started working for the label, and I love it. Luc and Mia have been amazing and have been helping me get set up with the company even though I am still in LA.

"Ruby, I wish you could just come back with me. Fuck, I hate leaving you, I want you with me," Quick says, hugging me tightly.

"I know... soon. I'm trying to get all my ducks in order," I murmur against his chest.

"Okay, I gotta go, babe. I'll text you when I get back," Quick sighs, tilting my head back to kiss me.

Quick deepens the kiss as I entwine my fingers in his hair wanting more, making us both moan.

"Momma, you kissin'?"

Fuck!

We both freeze and Quick's body goes stiff as a board against me. I turn to see Bella holding her princess doll. "Go back inside right now, Bella Bug. I'll be in soon."

Bella stares for a few more seconds before shutting the door.

"Fuck, well *that* will be fun trying to explain to her," I say with a laugh.

Quick looks worried. "I'm sorry—"

I cut him off, "Don't be. It's not a big deal."

He hugs me again, nuzzling his head into my neck, kissing me. "Fuck, I already miss you, and I haven't even left."

"I know," I whisper back.

Quick hugs me tight before letting me go. "Bye, my little firecracker."

I stand there watching him get into the cab taking off. I wait until the cab turns the corner before I head back inside.

Yep, this is going to suck.

5 | She's Pissed

Quick

Everything has been one big ass cluster fuck since I got off the plane. I come home to find out Gus, one of our prospects and head security at BB Security, was in the hospital, and Izzy had been kidnapped. It's been a week from hell.

A full week of evading Ruby's texts and ignoring her questions about Izzy – I haven't lied to her, but I haven't given her anything either. I turn the questioning back on her about Brody and their encounters. He flipped out the other night, and she won't tell me why. I'm sure she's keeping the bad parts from me because she doesn't want to worry me, just like I don't want to worry her. I guess we're both evading questions.

But, that all came to an end today when I got a text from her telling me she knows about Izzy, and she's pissed off at me for not telling her. My heart dropped when I received the text. I showed the guys, but they only laughed. When I called her, she didn't even answer, so I've been sitting here texting her.

Quick: Firecracker, please don't be mad at me. We've been busting our ass around here trying to find her. Gus being in the hospital just made it worse. Please forgive me.

Nothing.

Quick: Baby, it's killing me, that you're not talking to me. Yell. Flip out. Cuss me out. Anything! I can't handle all this bullshit AND worry about you not talking to me. I need you.

Nothing.

"What's wrong with you?" Maze asks from across the bar as she hands me a new beer.

I finish the one I have and hand it to her before grabbing the new one. "Ruby's not talking to me. Snow told her about Izzy, and Ruby's pissed she didn't hear about it from me," I explain.

45

Maze's face turns to a frown. "Why'd you lie?"

I snap back, "I didn't lie to her, I just didn't answer her questions. I told her I was dealing with club business."

She leans onto the bar. "Why didn't you just tell her?"

I'm starting to get irritated that I have to defend myself. "I did what Shy told me to do. The club didn't want anyone to know, and I didn't want to worry her until we knew something," I say honestly.

She asks, "Well, did you tell her that?"

"No, she hasn't talked to me since she found out." I take a long swig of my beer.

"Well, maybe you should text her and let her know. She'll come around," Maze says, pushing off the bar, heading toward the other end. I look back down to my phone and still no response from her.

Fuck it. What will it hurt?

I grab my phone and pray that this time she'll reply.

Quick: Rube, I'm sorry. I truly am. I was told by Shy, my president, not to tell you until we knew more. I was also worried about telling you because I'm not there to comfort you. We've been busting our asses. You're my everything girl, and I don't want you hurt. Please forgive me.

I set the phone down, and say a little prayer. My stomach has been in knots from all this shit. I let my boy down by not being there with him when it all went down, I'm letting my girl down by not telling her, and I'm letting Izzy down by not being able to find her. I'm losing it!

When my phone beeps, I almost drop the damn thing as I fumble to unlock it.

Ruby: Fuck you. She IS my life. I deserved to know.

Quick: Ruby Rube, I completely agree. I'm sorry, please forgive me.

Answer the phone. Please.

Ruby: No. I'm still too mad.

Well, at least she's replying to my messages.

Quick: When are you coming?

Ruby: Fuck off.

Quick: I miss you so much.

Ruby: Eat a dick.

I chuckle. *There's my firecracker.*

Quick: God, I love that feisty little mouth of yours.

She replies with a bunch of middle finger emojis.

Quick: I can't wait to see you and hold you. I'm not doing too well with all of this. I feel like I let everyone down. You. Izzy. Gus. Fuck, I need you.

Nothing.

Quick: I'm losing it.

Ruby: Quit texting me.

Quick: Never. You are mine.

She replies with a girl emoji with her hand over her forehead. So, in return, I send her a bunch of heart emojis. She isn't getting rid of me that easy. She just needs to get here so I can hold her.

"Quick, get over here, we need to go over this again," Shy yells from the office.

I slam my beer, feeling a little bit better now that she's at least replying to my messages. Now I just need to go get our girl, Izzy, and bring her home safe. This morning Frank, Luc's uncle, stopped by and told us he knew where Izzy was being held, we've been working out the plan to get her back since he left. Until I know for sure what we're doing, I'm not letting Ruby know we found Izzy either. I just need to go get Izzy and make sure she's safe. That way Ruby has no reason to be mad at me anymore.

"Is Gus still resting?" Shy asks when I walk into the office.

"Yeah, do you want me to go wake him?"

"No, not yet. We've got to lock this down before we bring him in. Everyone is meeting in five minutes. I'm just concerned with our plan solely depending on Ghost. I mean I get it, she is one bad bitch but what if it doesn't work? We need to have a Plan B in place," Shy explains.

I nod my head agreeing but knowing Ghost, and what she did for Ginger, the bitch will get it done. Ghost works for Maddox's security. She got the name Ghost because you don't see her coming. Her real name is Andy, but I've never heard anyone call her that, except Chad, and she wants to kill him most of the time. We've been indebted to her since she saved Shy's ol' lady. She pretty much single-handedly saved her life.

"If they let her in with Frank, she'll get it done. The girl doesn't know failure, but if they don't let her in with Frank, I agree, we need to have a Plan B," I say.

Dallas walks in with his hat on backward, a big grin on his face and as always, his laptop. "Got it! You were right. I can get a bomb inside for the distraction. It can also be our Plan B if Ghost can't get in, but we need to do it now."

Shy jumps up and moves around the desk to see what Dallas found. For the next five minutes we listen to Dallas' plan. Everyone arrives, so we go over everything again locking in all the small details. We call Frank to come in and tell him what's going to happen and once he's on board, everything starts falling into place.

I move to the bar to get a drink while everyone prepares themselves. I scan the room watching everyone. It's kind of my thing. The clubhouse is full with a lot of different groups of people. Some you wouldn't even think would be linked together. But we're all tied together because of Luc Mancini, the owner of Spin It, Inc, and his best friend Beau, who owns BB Security, where Gus is his number two.

Then we have the girls – Alexandria, Ginger, and of course Izzy, who all DJ for Spin It, Inc. I actually call them the Spin It girls. I chuckle to myself as I watch them. Alexandria is Luc's daughter – and is with Maddox. Now Maddox is a DJ too, but he's also linked to Luc's mafia side of the family somehow, but I don't know all that shit yet, it's on my to-do list.

Focus, damn it.

I shake my head, focusing on Maddox's group of men. Maddox has his own security team of badasses. We've worked with them before when there was an issue with Ginger. I look back at the girls and see Ginger waving her hands around explaining something to the bartender, Maze. I smile. Everyone in the club calls Ginger, Snow. She's Shy's ol' lady and daughter to the president of the Wolfeman original chapter, Wolfe, whose chapter is here as well.

Since Gus is prospecting for our club, it makes us one big happy fucking family. I lean back against the bar surveying the massive group in front of me. Between the two chapters and two security teams, we make one deadly motherfucking team. I wouldn't want to fuck with us, and that isn't even including Frank's mafia ties.

Happy with my assessment of our group, I slam my beer. Out of the corner of my eye, I see Frank trying to approach Luc again. I try to keep my eyes averted but maintain a visual on them. Something is off with Frank, and it's making me feel off. My gut never lies. Watching them right now is like watching twins that don't speak to each other. Frank moves and talks just like Luc does and watching Frank watch Luc – it's kind of creepy. It's like Frank is obsessed with Luc, never taking his eyes off of him. I know Luc feels and sees it, but he just ignores him.

He's probably only dealing with him because Frank's the reason we found Izzy. It's one of Frank's "associates" that has her, and they're planning to auction her. Frank's helping us get her back, which is good, but he's definitely up to something. He says he's doing it for Luc but the way he's watching Luc, it's like there's another reason behind it. I have a feeling we're going to be doing some digging of our own on Frank once this is all over with.

My phone beeps and I almost fall out of my chair.

Ruby: I just heard. Please bring her back to me. Please.

I look down the bar at Snow who has her phone out too. Of course, it would be Snow who is keeping her in the loop.

Quick: I will baby. I will.

Ruby: I'm still fucking pissed off at you. You didn't even tell me you found

her.

Quick: I know. But in my defense, we're all in here finding out details. Ginger has time to text you. I'm a little busy being involved with the recovery of Izzy. Give me a break. I'm bringing her home.

Ruby: I know. Sorry. Just still so mad and scared.

Quick: I'll bring her home.

And I add in a bunch of kisses and hearts.

Fuckin' pussy. I'm officially pussy whipped.

6 | On My Way

Ruby

"Ginger, are you positive she'll be okay. They have her?" I exclaim anxiously inside the limo. Ginger and Alexandria have come to pick Bella and me up at the airport.

"Yes, she's at the hospital, still unconscious, but she's alive and safe," Ginger says, hugging me.

"Momma, is An-tee okay?" Bella asks from her car seat.

"Yes, Bella Bug. Auntie's in the hospital, but she'll be okay," I try to keep my voice from cracking. I had to fight with Brody to sign the release paperwork so Bella could fly with me out of state. He wanted to come with me, but I told him hell fucking no.

Just as we thought, the Sunday after Izzy left, Brody was knocking on my aunt's door. He demanded we sit down and talk without Bella there, but I told him no. I wanted to keep Bella close so I sent her to her room to play. I knew Brody wouldn't try to fuck me or do anything crazy with her in the house.

Things only got worse when Bella let slip, pointing to a taxi cab, "Momma kissed him." He lost it. I had to explain Jake was a friend. I didn't want to use his biker name or say he was in a club because I can only imagine him going over the edge with that kind of information.

We fought all week long about everything. He doesn't know anything about Jake except his name. He thinks he lives in LA. When I found out about Izzy being kidnapped, my life came crashing down. I lost it and made all the arrangements to come out to New York, bringing Bella with me. I didn't know how long I would be here, but one thing was for sure, I wasn't waiting at home to hear what was going on.

Ginger is letting me stay at her place since she barely uses it now that she is always at the clubhouse with Shy. Mia, Alexandria's mom, is going to help me with Bella.

"Mia's going to head to my place and wait—" Ginger says, but I cut her off.

"Can she come to the hospital? I want to keep Bella with me until I know more. I want to go straight to the hospital and see Izzy."

Alexandria pulls out her phone. "I'll call her and let her know to stay there and wait for us."

"Momma, I want to see An-tee," Bella says, looking like she's going to cry.

"I know, Bug, but Auntie won't be able to see you for a while. Only grown-ups are allowed where she is. You'll have to sit in the waiting room with everyone else while Momma goes in to see Auntie," I tell her, rubbing her leg trying to comfort her.

Ginger warned me Izzy wasn't looking too good and was in ICU. I knew kids weren't allowed, but I didn't care at this point. I just needed to see Izzy. It took me longer getting here since I brought Isabella. I had to get a letter signed from Brody since we are legally separated. He fought me, but I knew he couldn't keep her since he's headed back out on tour. I wasn't leaving there without her. I can't afford to fly back and forth. I needed Isabella with me, and I need to be here for Izzy. I think he finally gave in because he thinks Quick lives near us in LA, so he thinks me coming here will keep me from him. Plus, when it comes to Izzy, he knows there is no compromising.

Once we arrived at the hospital, the driver let us all out. Shy, Maddox, and Luc were standing outside with Mia. I was trying to keep calm and not freak out Bella, but it was hard. I needed to see Izzy and the closer I got, the more frantic I was to see her.

After the hellos and getting Bella settled with Mia and Luc, I rushed to see Izzy. Ginger and Alexandria stayed close and warned me the boys were in there, meaning Quick was here. I didn't care. I just wanted to see Izzy.

That was until I threw open the door to her room and saw Quick standing there. I completely lose it. "Get the fuck out! Now!" I point at Quick. I don't know why that's the first thing that comes out, but everything hit me at once.

I'm about ready to flip out on Gus but stop when I see the look on his face, and he says, "Not here."

I turn back to Quick, who is grabbing my elbow and shoving me out the door. Maddox and Shy pass us when I'm about ready to unleash my fury. Quick swings me around, smashing my face into his chest. Once I'm pinned against his enormous chest, with his vise grip arms around me, holding me tight, I give up. I let the tears go and all the shit I've been holding in so Bella wouldn't see how upset I am. I've been holding in all this anguish and anger that I haven't let myself feel. Being in Quick's arms, I quit fighting it and sob.

"Fuck you. I'm so fucking mad. I could have lost her forever," I cry in his arms as he tries to comfort me, gliding one hand up and down my back, and the other arm keeps me securely pinned against him, not letting me go.

"Shhh. I got you. Shhh. She's going to be okay," Quick says, calmly.

"Why?" I question. When he doesn't answer, I push away from him so I can see his face.

"Don't you dare lie to me again, Jake Reeves. So help me God," I threaten him by using his real name.

Quick pushes my hair away from my face, wiping my tears away. "We still don't know who did it. We're working on it and trying to figure it all out," he says, truthfully.

My lips quiver. *God, he is so beautiful.* I can see the pain and worry in his eyes. I bite my lip and just stare at him.

Quick's lightning fast, smashing his mouth to mine with a painful groan. We embrace as our tongues dance with one another.

Quick breaks the kiss leaving our foreheads touching. "I'm

sorry. I just needed that, and you in my arms. I promise I won't keep anything that is in my power from you, but club business is something I can't promise."

I pull away. "If it has to do with Izzy, it is my business."

Quick slides his arms around me, pulling me to him again. "Yes, I understand."

"I need to see her," I demand.

"Be prepared and no flipping out in there. Okay?" he says, sounding worried.

I nod my head and walk away from him, heading back into the room. When throwing the door open again this time, I come face to face with Gus who looks horrible. The look in his eyes breaks my heart. When he reaches for me, I protest, hitting his chest at first, but he does the exact same thing Quick had just done, hugging me so tight I can't move from within his grasp. I'm furious with him for telling them not to tell me. Ginger told me it was Shy and Gus who made the decision to not tell me, and Quick had to obey the orders.

Gus murmurs, "I'm sorry. We should've called ya. It was my call, not his."

I'm so mad and angry that I want to flip out on him but looking into his tear-stricken eyes, I can't fight him. Gus' tears drop onto my forehead, and I join him as tears run down my face. "She's all I got, Gus. Don't you ever keep her from me again."

He pushes my hair away from my face, "Not gonna happen again. I promise." He kisses my forehead before letting me go to Izzy.

Shocked, I place my hand over my mouth, holding in a gasp as I look down at my best friend. Her face is black and blue with tubes and wires all over her body. I start to cry again.

I don't care what's happening around me as the men leave us girls alone. All I care about is my best friend. I can't take anymore, collapsing down into the chair next to her bed. I grab her hand in mine and say a prayer asking God to help her. She has to be okay.

7 | Meeting Bella

Quick

After stopping in to see Ghost, we head down to the main waiting room so we can get updates on the men we took. We're still trying to figure out who took Izzy to begin with. As I turn the corner, I'm overwhelmed with all the people. I thought everyone was at the clubhouse, but Wolfe and his whole chapter now including the women are here, along with Luc, Beau, and his team. Maddox, Gus, Shy, Dallas, and I move into the crowded room.

Everyone is conversing, and I'm standing with Mac, Dallas, and Shy when I feel something tugging on my leather cut. Before I can look down, I see Dallas' face go blank. When I feel another tug, I look down to find little Miss Bella staring up at me. I look around and notice Mia and a few other women talking. She hasn't even noticed Bella walked over to me.

Crouching down, I get to eye level with her. She's a tiny little thing with big blue eyes and hair just like her momma. It's pulled back in two cute little pigtails. With a big smile, I say, "Well, hello. What's your name?"

She hugs her baby tight, but says, "Bella."

I smile. "Hello, Miss Bella. My name's Quick." I extend my hand.

Bella stares at me a few seconds before she shifts her baby doll into one hand so she can shake my hand. I feel all the men watching from behind me.

"You kissed my momma."

Everyone goes quiet, and I swear you could've heard a pin drop.

I chuckle. "Are you sure it was me?" I raise my pointer finger, tapping her nose.

57

She giggles, answering, "Yes. Taxi guy."

I hear a few chuckles and chokes of laughter, including me because she must think I owned the taxi cab I was standing next to. I try to explain, "No baby girl. I went in a taxi to the airport. Someone else was driving it."

She just looks at me weird like I'm making a joke because she starts to laugh. I stand up, tapping her nose again, but she grabs my hand to hold it, and my heart constricts, and I feel all warm inside.

I reach down to pick her up, and she squeals in laughter. This little girl could ask me anything, and I would give her the world.

Mia must've heard her squeal as she comes over. "Bella, are you playing with Quick?" teasing her, she tickles her making her laugh. Mia tries to take Bella from me, but Bella wraps her tiny little arms around my neck and says, "No."

I laugh and tell Mia it's okay, I have her and notice everyone is watching us. I look at them and ask, "What?"

But before anyone can say anything, Bella yells over my shoulder, "Momma, don't cry."

I turn around to see Ruby crying as she watches us. Worried something's wrong with Izzy. I walk toward her with Bella's arms still wrapped around my neck. Gus must feel the same thing because he beats me to Ruby.

"Is it Iz? What's wrong?" Gus demands, sounding a bit frantic.

She shakes her head to Gus, "No, Izzy's fine. I'm just..." She trails off, looking at me holding Bella.

I take another step closer to her, asking, "What's wrong? Why are you crying? You know I can't handle you crying." Reaching out with my free arm to pull her into my chest for a group hug, with Bella saying again, "Momma, don't cry."

"I just..." Ruby stops, pulling away to look up at us. "Just seeing you two and Izzy. I'm just emotional," she says, wiping her tears away.

Ruby reaches up to grab Bella, as I lean forward to pass her, but Bella turns her body toward me, gripping my neck tighter and says, "no" again.

Ruby gasps, "Bella Bug, come on, let Quick go, he needs to go."

I interrupt her, "No, I don't need to go anywhere. I'm actually going to take you two home. She's fine – I got her."

Ruby's face is frozen with shock, and she's completely speechless.

I shift Bella in my arms, placing her against my chest with her head laying on my shoulder. I start to rub her back and try to figure out if Ruby's mad. I ask, "Are you okay? I just want to make sure you both get settled into the suite okay. I don't need to stay, if that's what you're worried about?"

She shakes her head, snapping out of her shock and says with a smile, "No. No, that's fine. I'm just in shock. She's never said no to me except maybe with Izzy or my aunt."

"Ruby, sweetie. We're all going to head back to the house," Mia announces as she and Luc walk up holding each other.

I start to say, "I can take them—"

But Ruby cuts me off, "No, we need to go with them. They have Bella's car seat," Ruby explains.

"Okay, well, I'll go with you too. Baby girl is sleeping on me anyways. Let me tell Dallas what I'm doing so he can watch Gus and take my truck," I say, turning before anyone can change their minds. I'm going with her no matter if she wants me to or not.

Finding Shy, Maddox, Mac, Gus, and Dallas all huddled together, I make my way over there with a now sleeping baby girl in my arms. They all stop talking when I approach, and all eyes are on the sweet girl in my arms. It's Shy who speaks first, "Goddamn, I thought out of all of us you would be the last motherfucker to have a kid in your arms."

Everyone starts to laugh, making their own cracks, but I fire back, "Ha-ha. Fuck all of you." I turn to Dallas and Gus. "You two good? I'm gonna ride to the suites and make sure Ruby's all set up. Gus, I can come back and hang with you once I'm done..."

Gus stops me before I can finish, "Nah, take ya lass and get some rest. Bring Firecracker back in the mornin'."

Dallas speaks up, "Yeah, I'm gonna stay here with Gus while y'all get some rest. We have Brant with Ghost, and I think the girls are staying too. So we're covered here."

I reach in my pocket and grab my truck keys, tossing them to Dallas. "Alright. I'll see you tomorrow." I grab Gus' shoulder. "She's back, brother. She's safe."

Gus leans in giving me a hug with Bella between us, and says, "Thanks, brother."

Breaking the hug, I give each guy a handshake half hug, as men do. I turn to walk back over to Ruby, who's talking to Luc, and one of the guys says from behind me, "Take your family home and be good."

I flip them off, hearing them all bust up laughing.

Fuck them.

Once we're at the building Luc owns, where most of the DJs and security live, we make our way up to Ginger's place. She hardly stays here anymore since she lives with Shy at the clubhouse. She told Ruby and Izzy they could move in if they wanted. Izzy has an apartment across town, but it's a one bedroom, as this one is a two bedroom.

The ride to the suite was quiet. No one wanted to wake up Bella. I think everyone is just over exhausted with the last forty-eight hours of no sleep and the rescue. Shit, I'm exhausted.

I have baby girl in my arms as Ruby opens the door for us. She moves around the place, getting everything set up for Bella. I stand in the living room, swaying my body from side to side while rubbing her back. Never in my life have I held a kid like this – like *ever,* but it just feels so right. It's like she's my own kid, and I've been doing it all my life. My heart feels like it's expanding with how much love I have for this baby girl. I'm caressing her back, moving my hand in a circle as I sway from foot to foot. When I sway around, I find Ruby crying again with her hands over her mouth.

"Rube, don't cry. Why are you crying?" I walk over to her, pulling her into my chest, hugging her. She wraps her arms around my waist, squeezing me back.

She pulls away, wiping her face, and says, "Here, follow me. Let's put her down so we can talk."

She grabs my hand, leading me to a room where I put Bella onto the bed. I kiss her forehead before pulling the covers up over her. I move so Ruby can finish tucking her in, as I back out of the room clutching my chest.

These women have ruined me, and I couldn't be happier. I feel it finally. I've wanted to feel what Shy feels for Snow for so long. I've always been in awe of their love and devotion. When my parents died, I felt like I died too. Feeling what I'm feeling for these two girls, they've brought me back to life.

Ruby turns to see me rubbing my chest, and asks, "Do you need lotion?" I'm confused by the question, but she finishes with, "For your tattoo? Is it in the peeling stage?"

I laugh. "Aw, no, it's good."

We head back to the living room, stopping in the kitchen first. Ruby grabs us two beers from the fridge, handing me one before going to the couch in the living room. I start to follow but stop. Placing my beer on the kitchen table, I take my cut off, placing it on the back of a chair. As I pick up my beer, I feel her eyes on me.

"Are you okay? It's been a long emotional day for all of us," I ask.

She doesn't say anything, just stares at me while taking a sip of her beer. I sit down next to her on the couch. I know she's probably still mad at me, but I need to be near her, touching her, so I put my hand on her folded leg.

"Are you not talking to me again?" I ask softly, looking at her staring at me. I sit there watching her, waiting for her to speak.

She takes a long swig of her beer, closing her eyes as she tilts her head back, almost finishing it. When she's done, she pulls the bottle from her lips staring at the label when she finally speaks, "It's been one fucking roller coaster of a ride these past few months. I decided to end my marriage and move out. I fly to see my best friend while my soon-to-be-ex gets his divorce papers served. I meet you. Izzy comes home with me. Then you come to see me, only to fly right back home. Brody finds out I kissed a taxi guy. Fighting with him about it while worrying why you pulled away from me."

I start to explain, but she puts her finger on my lips.

"Let me finish. I knew in my gut that something was wrong. With you. With Izzy. Fighting with Brody. My life is upside down right now."

When she starts to cry, I say fuck it and pull her onto my lap so she's straddling me and I say, "Rube, don't cry."

She puts her hand up, covering my mouth, so she can finish. "Life is shit right now but watching you with my baby. I can't even describe to you what that does to me. Brody, her own father, doesn't even do that. He has always dealt with her but always and I mean – *always* hands her off to me."

My blood starts to boil, and I try to tamper it down, knowing I can't kill him, and it won't make anything better if I flip out.

She continues, "He picks her up and hugs her, but he doesn't have that touch. She hasn't even really met you, and she didn't even want to leave your arms. And you... it was like you've held her all her life – it was so natural," she explains, wiping her eyes.

I sit there caressing her thighs, giving her my full attention.

"In my heart, I know I'm doing the right thing. I want to be here. I want to work for Luc. I want to be near Izzy. I want you in my life – our life. So, yes, I'm a little emotional right now because my life is completely turned upside down. But, watching you two together made all the fucked-up shit worth it because, in the end, I know it will all be okay," she rants. Throwing her arms out to her side, tilting her head back, exhaling. "I will have all this freedom."

I can't take it anymore, leaning into her, I kiss her exposed neck pulling her against me. I say between kisses, "I want all of that too. I want us, baby."

Ruby wraps her arms around my neck, and says, "I'm sorry I flipped out on you. I know it wasn't your fault, but dealing with—"

I cut her off, kissing her. I slowly slide my hands up under her shirt, lifting it up over her head, breaking our kiss.

"Never apologize. I'm sorry for not telling you. Obviously, I've learned from this, and I think Gus has too. Anything to do with Izzy or Bella, you *are* on the need to know, not it's club business." I kiss her again.

Ruby cups my face running her fingers through my now scruffy beard. I'm usually trimmed-up but this week has been a long one with no time to shave. I explain, "I'm sorry. I've had no time to shave or do anything remotely normal for almost two weeks."

She keeps toying with my facial hair. "I like it," she says, pulling my club cap off my head, raking her fingers through my long hair on top. "It's really long," she giggles. Moving my bangs down over my face, they go past my lips.

I laugh, "I've been kind of busy. I haven't cut my hair since before I met you," I tell her while she glides her fingers through it making my cock pulse under her.

"Rube, you keep touching me like that and I'm gonna fuck you real quick," I groan.

Ruby smiles. "I could do with a real quick fucking right now. I need to feel you inside me."

"Goddamn, Firecracker. I've missed you," I groan, tugging

on her jeans. Ruby stands up, pulling her jeans down, sliding a leg out. I undo my pants shoving them down enough to free my cock.

Within seconds, Ruby's back on my lap placing me at her entrance before sheathing my cock with her wet warm pussy.

We both express our pleasure – Ruby gripping my shoulders, moving her hips back and forth.

I unclasp her bra, freeing those beautiful tits of hers, engulfing one in my mouth. She picks up speed, as I grip both breasts, sucking and nipping them.

Ruby pants, "Fuck, you feel good." Tilting her head back, she lets go, thrusting above me.

"That's it, my little firecracker. Ride my cock. Fuck. I'm gonna come, baby."

I lean back against the couch, gripping her hips, thrusting up so hard you can hear our bodies slapping against each other. We both grunt breathlessly, chasing our climax.

"Oh, God. Quick. Fuck," Ruby whimpers as her body starts to shake.

I rasp, "Fuck yeah, Rube – come for me, baby." Feeling her pussy clench my cock, I almost lose my shit but flex my leg muscles, clenching my ass, I pump faster, holding her hips. Ruby cries out a muffled cry as she comes all over my dick. Needing more, I grab her waist, flipping us on the couch and laying her under me, slamming deeper inside her. I cover her cries with my mouth, kissing her, muffling both our guttural moans.

Breaking the kiss, I keep our faces inches apart from each other. "Goddamn, Firecracker, I'm gonna cum baby. Fuuuck yee…ass." Pumping furiously, I explode inside her.

After a few more thrusts, I grab her limp body, flipping us back to a sitting position with her on my lap. When she giggles, my cock slips from inside her, letting all our juices drain from her pussy on to me. Once I catch my breath, I grab her ass, lifting us off the couch and carry her to Ginger's room. I walk slowly, shuffling my legs as my pants fall to my ankles. I place her on the bed before I head into the bathroom to clean up.

"Quick, we can't sleep together. Bella can't see us like that yet," Ruby murmurs.

Exhausted, I reply, "I know, Rube. I'm just gonna stay with you for a bit, and then I'll get one of—"

She interrupts me, "No, I meant you can sleep in here, and I'll sleep with Bella tonight. I don't want you to leave."

My heart skips a beat knowing she doesn't want me to leave. After I clean her up and discard the washcloth, I climb into bed, pulling her to my bare chest. I'm exhausted. "Whatever you want, or think is best."

Ruby turns in my arms facing me, and says, "She's young. Plus, Brody's hardly ever home, so she doesn't get the whole break up. I've explained it to her when we moved out, that Daddy and Momma were going to have our own places. I'm sure she will have questions – lots of them, but for now, I'll sleep with her." She kisses me, snuggling into my chest.

My heart slows, and right at this moment, everything in my life is right again. Having her in my arms, knowing she is safe, I let my body relax, and within minutes, I pass out.

8 | I'm Hungry
Quick

"Qwak."

I'm sleeping on my stomach, completely comfortable when I feel someone poking my arm. When I peek one eye open, I see a little head peering over the bedside. Pushing my hair out of my face, I blink a few more times trying to wake up. Then I roll to my side coming face to face with a very happy, very awake little girl and I smile back.

"Qwak, wake up. I'm hungry," Bella pouts.

When I hear her try to say my name, I laugh, sliding my arm under my pillow and say, "Well, good morning, Miss Bella. Where's your momma?"

Bella climbs on the bed with her baby and mimics me, laying on her side with her arm under the pillow. She says softly, "Momma's seep'n. She tired. I'm hungry."

Jesus Christ, this little girl is going to ruin me. I want to squeeze her when she talks in that sweet baby voice.

Laughing, I ask, "Do you want me to cook you some food?"

She nods her head yes.

Realizing I don't know what little kids eat, I chuckle again. "What do little girls like yourself eat?"

With the sweetest smile, she says, "Momma makes me cereal or eggs."

Now I can do that.

"Is that a woof?" She points to my chest tattoo with our Wolfeman insignia across it.

I look down to my chest and back up to the eager little girl and say, "Yes, it's a wolf." Not really knowing how to explain to a three-year-old what that means, I roll to get out of bed.

She sits up, clenching her baby and says, "It's scary."

Grabbing my t-shirt I wore last night from the chair, I smile at Bella and say, pointing to my chest, "He will protect you from bad things." Bella just keeps staring at it. I chuckle, throwing on my shirt walking over to the side of the bed she's sitting on. "He might look scary, but I promise you he'll always protect you and keep you safe."

Bella smiles up at me, and I feel a tug on my heart. I reach my hand out for her. Bella stands up on the bed and puts her arms out for me to pick her up.

Fuck me. This little angel just stole my heart, right there next to her mama.

I laugh, picking her up and carry her to the kitchen where I place her in the middle of the island.

"Don't fall off there," I say, worried she might fall and add, "Move to the middle or maybe I should put you down. I don't want you getting hurt the first time I'm watching you."

Bella giggles, scooting to the middle with her baby. "I help Momma cook. I wanna help you."

I smile, scratching my head my hair falls from behind my ear, so I pull it back into a small ponytail, making a mental note to get a haircut.

I pull out eggs and bacon, placing them on the island next to Bella. She just sits there watching my every move while playing with her baby.

Since I know nothing about kids, I ask Bella a series of questions. "Miss Bella, do you know how to drink out of a cup like this?" I show her a small glass. Ginger doesn't really have kid shit here either.

She shakes her head. "I have a sip cup."

What the fuck is a sip cup?

"Well, I don't know what a sip cup is, do you have one here?"

She nods her head, pointing to a bag on the kitchen table.

Walking over to grab the bag, I ask my next question, "Are you potty trained?"

Her face lights up, nodding her head excitedly. "Yes, I go potty in big girl potty now."

Thank fuck. Otherwise, I would've been in trouble. I need a crash course in little girls.

Handing her Ruby's bag, I say, "Here, get your sip cup, and I'll put milk in it for you, yeah?"

For the next few minutes, I ask Bella about her baby, if she likes cartoons and what she likes to do. I've learned her baby's name is Molly and she loves Mickey Mouse Playhouse. She asked me if she could do my hair and play dress up. I ignored that part and kept asking her random questions.

I'm leaning against the island eating, while she's still in the center of the island eating her food. I guess it's her turn to ask questions, because she asks, "Can I ride in your taxi?"

I laugh, almost choking. "Baby girl, I told you last night it wasn't my taxi. I paid that guy to take me to the airport. I drive a big truck and ride a motorcycle."

She tilts her head to the side like she's thinking about something important and says, "You kissed Momma?"

Oh shit.

I fill my fork up with food lifting it to my mouth, I reply, "Yes, I did," before shoving it into my mouth.

She smiles big with her crystal blue eyes going wide, and before she can ask another question, I explain, "I was leaving town, so I took a taxi over to your house and gave her a goodbye kiss. I do not drive a taxi. I ride a bike."

Like I hadn't just told her I kissed her momma, she says, "I ride a bike too."

Hearing laughter behind us, we turn to see Ruby leaning against the wall. Bella squeals, "Momma, Qwak made breakfast."

Panicked, I ramble, "I didn't know what she usually eats. She woke me up hungry. I–I…"

Ruby's laughter rings through the kitchen. "It's fine. She's pretty bossy and will tell you what she wants."

I nod my head.

Ruby continues, "She talks *a lot* for a three-year-old, but it's usually just her and me, so I talk to her all the time."

I say nervously, "Are you hungry? I made coffee and plenty of food." Hoping I didn't do anything wrong or overstep with Bella. I feel like a little kid. I don't know what is wrong with me. It's not like I kidnapped the girl or anything. It's all just so new, and I don't know what to expect.

Ruby rounds the island coming to stand in front of me with a smile. "Are you okay? I hope she didn't ask too many questions. You look freaked out," she questions, reaching her hands up, giving me a big hug. I just stand there frozen, not saying a word. I don't even hug her back. Ruby turns to her daughter. "What did you do to him? Did you freak him out?" she asks, half laughing and half serious.

Bella giggles. "No, Momma, Qwak rides a bike, like me. He kissed you bye-bye and later we're going to play dress up."

Ruby turns to me with questioning eyes. "Is that so? Well, he does have amazing hair."

I place my hands on her hips, needing the connection to pull me from my stupor. I clear my throat. "Yes, I told her *maybe* later we would play dress up."

Ruby stretches her arms out as Bella squeals with excitement scooting to the edge of the island to her. "Okay, let's go put some Mickey Mouse on for you so Momma and Quick can have some adult time while Momma eats her breakfast."

Ruby carries Bella to the living room, putting her on the couch and turning on cartoons. I stand there staring at the girls that have stolen my heart.

Beautiful and mine.

When she returns, she stands in front of me again, looking worried. "Are you okay? What's wrong? Is she too much? I'm sorry for all the questions."

I feel like I'm in a trance, I shake my head, realizing she must think I'm freaking out about being alone with Bella. I smile down at Ruby and say, "No, I'm fine. Really, she's cute as shit and talks *a lot* but..." I pause, shoving off the island to stand up, shifting from one foot to the other nervously. "Fuck, Rube, I was more worried I would say something wrong or give her something she shouldn't have. I don't know a fucking thing about kids." I throw my hands up, exasperated.

Ruby's face relaxes, laughing at my rambling ass.

"What?" I ask seriously, putting my hands on my hips looking down at her.

"Babe, she's old enough to tell you what she wants. My girl's smart for her age. So, unless you give her drugs or alcohol, I'm sure you'll be fine," Ruby teases.

I turn to pace around the island. "I just don't want to fuck up around her or you."

Ruby walks over to me, pushing me back against the fridge out of Bella's sight. Before I can say anything, she pounces on me, smashing her mouth to mine. I let her devour me for the split second that it takes me to snap out of my panic attack. I groan into her, grabbing her waist and lifting her up. She wraps her legs around my waist as I move to the counter to set her down.

Ruby wraps her arms around my neck, fisting my hair. I break the kiss moving down her neck but remember where we are and pull back.

"Goddamn, Firecracker," I grunt.

Ruby smiles a seductive smile. "I needed you to quit freaking the fuck out, so I did what needed to be done."

I smirk at my woman.

"Seriously, you're amazing with her, and she likes you. Don't over think it. She's three going on thirteen. You'll be fine," she explains softly.

I run my hands through my hair, tucking the long strands behind my ears. When I see the blaze ignite in Ruby's eyes, my cock pulses. I growl, closing my eyes taking a deep breath trying to calm down because I'm hard as fuck and I really want to be balls deep in my girl. But, I'm too worried about doing something wrong and fucking up with the kid. I take another deep breath before opening my eyes, only to see Ruby smiling back at me.

"You need to quit looking at me like that or I'll carry your ass back to the bathroom and fuck you really quick," I warn.

Ruby bites her lip with a sexy as fuck smile. "Promise?"

I raise an eyebrow challenging her. *If she thinks I won't, she's got another thing coming.*

She giggles. "Let me eat first *and then* we'll sneak off for a quickie. Yeah?"

I grab her hips, giving her a soft kiss as I lift her off the counter, placing her on the ground. "You got five minutes," I warn her.

Thank you, Lord! My little firecracker is back!

She laughs while I hurry to make her a plate of food.

9 | Recovery

Quick

It's been a couple of weeks since Izzy was released from the hospital. Life as I used to know it has completely changed. The Malone girls have completely taken over my life, and they now consume every ounce of my heart.

With Ruby and the girls running around trying to get everyone settled, Izzy and I have been watching Bella. Mia has stepped in a few times, but she loves being with everyone in the mix so we try to include her as much as we can. That little girl has got me wrapped around her finger. Shit, she has everyone wrapped around that little finger of hers, including my whole club.

Thinking of the other day when I took Bella over to the clubhouse, I chuckle to myself. This kid had everyone laughing with her million-and-one questions – *Why this... why that... how come... I don't get it.* The little shit doesn't stop jabbering.

I definitely got over thinking that I'd corrupt her because this kid's doing a pretty good number on me. It's been the best damn couple of weeks of my life. I only stayed at the clubhouse a couple of nights, when I had some club business to take care of. Otherwise, I've been staying with them.

Izzy agreed to move out of her place when Ruby announced she was moving here for good. Once she looked at the place Luc had available in his building, it was a done deal. Most of the suites are fully furnished since he uses a handful of them for entertainment performers, instead of putting them in a hotel. Luc told her whatever furniture she didn't want, could be moved to a different suite, just to let him know.

My brothers from the club and the security guys helped me finish moving Izzy's stuff this last week. With her parents and the Spin It girls, they had her moved and organized within no time. It's been hectic but shit's getting done.

Ruby was ecstatic about this because she didn't really want to fight with her ex over big shit and he can have almost everything she left behind. She took what she could when she moved out a few months ago.

What I'm excited about and *I think* is the most important thing... is that it's a three bedroom. I've had to sneak quickies here and there since Ruby sleeps with Bella, but *now* baby girl has her *own* room.

Thank Fuck!

Ruby has been running around crazy since she got here. In the first week working for Luc, Ruby recruited two new singers, so he's on a mission to keep her here. He handed over Izzy's manager's position to Ruby since Alex has more or less turned into a DJ herself and isn't managing the girls anymore.

Izzy and Gus are staying at Gus' place, which is in the same building. Ruby had to go to the old apartment to finalize some stuff and then to the office to handle some of Izzy's events and rescheduling.

So, today it's just me and baby girl here at the place. I've been sitting on the floor, letting her fuck with my hair. She has a box full of hair shit that she likes to put in my hair. She jibber jabbers to herself while I watch TV. The kid loves to play with my hair.

The first time I let her do it, Izzy was here egging her on, they had a field day putting girlie shit in my hair. When Ruby came home, she almost fell over – she was laughing so hard. I almost went and cut my hair off so they wouldn't want to play with it anymore.

"Qwak, why you take your hair out?" Bella says pouting, as she comes from her room where she's been playing. I took the stuff out as soon as she said she was going to go play with her babies.

I am still sitting on the floor in the living room. I smile at her and explain, "I'm sorry, baby girl. I thought we were done." I quickly add, "Momma will be home soon." Hoping she won't freak out.

"Yay, I miss Momma," she says with a smile, sounding sleepy.

She looks tired, so I turn on the Disney Channel and motion for her to come sit on my lap. Already glued to the show playing, I pick her up, placing her on my lap facing the TV. Stretching my legs out, I reclined back against the couch with her leaning back against my chest, drinking from her sip cup. Yep, my heart just melted. The kid loves to cuddle and is so affectionate just like her momma.

Within minutes, she's asleep, and I take her sip cup from her. If you would have asked me a year ago – shit, a few months ago, if I'd be sitting here babysitting a little girl, I would have laughed in your face and said you'd lost your fucking mind.

Hearing the door open, I turn to see my little firecracker come in, looking exhausted, but once she sees me sitting here with baby girl in my lap asleep, her whole face brightens with a huge smile.

"Hey," I say softly, not wanting to wake the kid.

Ruby drops her purse and stuff on the table in the entryway before coming over to us.

"Hi, babe. It looks like you're having a relaxing day. She wasn't too much for you today?" Ruby crouches down, moving loose strands of hair away from Bella's face before leaning in to give me a kiss.

I reply, "No, she was great. Always an adventure with her. How was your day?"

"Good," she replies. I can see the exhaustion across her face. "Let me go put her down, so we can have some adult time," Ruby says with a smirk, grabbing Bella from me.

I wiggle my eyebrows. "Mmm, some alone time. I like the sound of that."

Ruby laughs, shushing her tired little girl in her arms. I relax back into the couch, flipping back to the channel I was watching before Bella wandered into the living room.

Ruby stops at the entrance of the hallway and says over her shoulder, "I need to take a quick shower too."

I loud-whisper, "Okay, babe," jumping up, knowing an invitation when I hear one.

I walk into the kitchen, throwing back my beer, finishing it, giving her a few minutes to get Bella to bed and into the shower. I walk back over to the TV, turning it off when I hear a phone beeping. I move to the entryway as it sounds again.

I grab Ruby's phone from the table and look at it. I can see the beginning of a text flash across her screen. It's from her ex, Brody.

Brody: Fuck you bitch. I'm her father. I want to see her. I'll...

My blood boils seeing him call her a bitch. She told me he wasn't happy with her moving here and that the lawyers are involved now. But I didn't know he was threatening her.

Another text pops up.

Brody: You fucking slut. You will never take her from me. I will...

Motherfucker!

I hate that I can't see the full text. I need to quit looking at this goddamn thing before I flip the fuck out. I take her phone with me into the bedroom. I hear the shower running with steam starting to billow from the room.

I lay the phone on the dresser, stripping my clothes off in seconds. The rage inside me intensifies the closer I get to the shower. The need to protect her consumes me. I've never felt so possessive of something in my life since my parents. The need to fucking claim her – make her mine, is all that fills my mind.

Fuck, no one talks to my woman like that.

I take a deep breath before opening the shower. She doesn't hear me come in with her head under the shower. When I see her naked body leaning back with her eyes closed, her hands pushing her hair back so the water can cascade over her face and down her body, I pause. She's goddamn magnificent. *Fuck me.* I move in front of her, wrapping my arms around her waist. She gasps, pulling her face from the spray of water.

"Quick, you startled me, I didn't hear you," she giggles, placing her hands on my chest.

I don't say anything as I stare at my firecracker. She's been burning the candle at both ends with so many responsibilities lately and now this shit with her ex on top of it.

She stares up at me with the most beautiful hazel-golden eyes I've ever seen, so loving and filled with desire.

"Quick, what's wrong? You have this look in your eye..." She trails off as I step closer to her.

I close the gap between us, moving her back halfway under the water again. She tilts her head back, letting her long hair cascade with the water down her back. I lean down, kissing her exposed collarbone, all the way up her neck. Gripping her waist, I rock my hips against her, with my erect cock slipping between us.

Ruby moans, wrapping her hands around my neck. She murmurs, "Baby, what's wrong?"

I grunt against her neck, "Mine."

My hands tighten their grip around her, just thinking of that cunt threatening her has every muscle in my body tensing. *I need to protect my girls. Mine.*

I growl, cupping her ass, lifting her up, she wraps her legs around my waist. I slam her against the shower wall, pinning her. She gasps. Within seconds, I'm seated inside her thrusting, long, hard thrusts. I lean us hard against the wall gripping her ass cheeks tighter, digging my nails into her flesh as I ram faster. My breath quickens, grunting with each slam.

Ruby's panting, making guttural sounds as her climax builds. I feel her walls tighten around my cock.

Breathless I grunt, "Mine" before sucking her neck and biting down.

"Yes. I'm…" Ruby cries out, coming all over my cock. I glide in and out of her as hard as I can, faster, and deeper. Slamming us against the wall, I feel my balls tighten with my orgasm at the brink of exploding. I grunt, breathless, getting louder with each thrust. My legs start to cramp from exertion, pumping a few more times. I climax, throwing my head back with a roar, filling her with everything I have, marking her.

I drop my head back down against her as I slow my hips but not pulling out of her. I try to catch my breath. I feel her chest rise and fall against mine and I know she's breathless too. I loosen my grip from her ass cheeks, knowing without a doubt that I have left my finger imprints. She lowers her legs

"Baby, fuck I needed that. Shit, that was intense," she rasps while lowering her legs still trying to catch her breath.

I'm still leaning into her with my hands up against the wall. I push off the wall, locking eyes with my little firecracker's lustful eyes.

"Okay, you're freaking me out," she murmurs, cupping my face leaning in to give me a kiss.

I growl, leaning into her deepening the kiss, but she pushes me back, breaking us apart.

Looking into my eyes, she demands, "Quick, you better start talking before I lose my shit."

I tilt my forehead down connecting with hers and take a deep breath, closing my eyes for a brief second before standing up saying, "Let's dry off get some clothes on and we'll talk in the living room."

Hearing my voice come off so harsh and the look in her eyes

tells me she took my words wrong. I lean down, placing a quick kiss on her lips before exiting the shower and grabbing two towels. I hand her a towel, drying myself off, heading into the bedroom. As if on cue, her phone chimes again but this time it's ringing, not a notification.

She looks to her phone and then to me, knowing damn well it wasn't there when she got in the shower. I lift a brow, nodding my head toward her phone. She grabs it and lets out a long dreadful breath.

"It's Brody. I need to answer this," she says, moving to leave the room.

Before she answers it, I demand, "Do not leave this room. I want to hear what he has to say."

She freezes, shocked by my demand and I'm sure by the tone in my voice, but she doesn't leave. "Brody," she says, sounding irritated. I'm sure with both of us, keeping her eyes locked with mine. I move closer, hoping that I can hear the cunt bastard.

And sure as shit, I hear him screaming at her, "I want to see my fucking daughter."

This cocksucker. I clench my fist as I try not to yank the phone from her.

"Brody, you need to chill the fuck out. I told you I wouldn't be back down there for a couple more weeks," she says calmly.

"Ruby, you knew I was coming home this week. I haven't seen my daughter in almost a month," he demands, adding, "*And* I signed that consent letter for you to take her to New York to visit, not—"

She cuts him off, switching her tone becoming enraged herself. "I'm fucking moving, Brody, *with* Isabella. You need to get that through your head. You are only home a total of three months out of the year. The lawyers already told you that the courts would not rule in your favor. I have a great job here and a place to live, with a great support group."

The feeling of pride washes over me hearing her stand up to

the cocksucker. I move behind her, wrapping my arms around her waist for support. When he starts threatening her, I go to reach for the phone, but she breaks free from me, firing back into the phone, "Fuck you. You should have thought about that before cheating on me and sharing me with your fucking best friend. I'll have Isabella back before you leave again. I'm done..." She hangs up the phone before he can reply.

Her face is red with wild eyes as she turns around facing me. Turning her phone off, she walks up to me, slamming her phone against my chest before walking past me. She spouts off, still pissed, "I take it *that's* what you want to talk about."

I stand there in shock and to be honest, *turned the fuck on* hearing my little spitfire mouth off. I chuckle. Clenching her phone, I watch her move around the room, slamming dresser drawers, muttering to herself.

Fuck me... my feisty bitch... Mine!

Sensing I need to give her some time, I toss the phone onto her bed and get dressed. When I'm finished dressing, she's in the bathroom combing her hair. I move up behind her watching her face through the mirror when she looks up, meeting my eyes, I smile and ask in a deep calming voice, "Firecracker, you ready to talk to me?"

Ruby's eyes flicker back and forth from being angry to upset. I move closer, wrapping my arms around her shoulders, engulfing her against me. She reaches up, grabbing my arms with both hands as she holds on for dear life. When her lower lip starts to tremble, I turn her into my chest, hugging her tight.

"I got you, Rube. I'm here, baby," I murmur, kissing the top of her head.

Ruby tilts her head back to look up at me. "I'm sorry."

I'm shocked hearing her say those two words. I shake my head like she didn't just say them. I need out of this fucking room before I lose control.

"Fuck!" I snap.

10 | About Me

Quick

I need to get us out of the bedroom for this conversation. Otherwise, I'm going to end up balls deep again, fucking her senseless. My need to claim her after that dick's little temper tantrum has me primed and ready to go. I break our embrace, grabbing her hand, leading her to the kitchen.

Ruby, surprised by my outburst and sudden demand to leave the bedroom, asks, "Quick, what's going on?"

I sit her down on one of the bar stools at the island in the kitchen, moving myself to the other side so we're across from each other. I roll my neck, letting some tension release before leaning forward, placing my hands on the counter.

"Okay," I say, pausing to take a deep breath. "Now we need to have this conversation, and you need to understand some things about me." I lift a hand up, flipping out my pointer finger. "One, I don't ever, and I mean ever, want to hear you apologize for that piece of shit."

Ruby's eyes widen as she leans onto her forearms, resting on the counter, not saying anything.

I raise my next finger. "Two, I'm sorry for earlier, but when I was coming to join you in the shower your phone buzzed. I grabbed it to bring to you and saw parts of his texts. They…" I pause, pushing off the island, running my hands through my damp hair. I start to pace, trying to hold in my rage. "I flipped out seeing him talk to you that way and I didn't even see the whole text." I turn back to face her. "I've never felt this way for someone. This feeling of possessiveness filled my body, and I lost it."

Ruby's eyes tear up at my admission toward her. I grip the

counter holding myself back from walking around the counter to devour her.

"Third," I continue lifting up another finger. "If we are in this together – and I hope to fuck we are – Rube, you need to quit taking on the world for everyone else and let someone take care of you too. Baby, you got that fire in you, and I love that, but sometimes you need to let me protect you." I pause. Letting that sink in. When her tears start to slip down her cheeks, I know she heard me. "You and baby girl are my life now. You are *my* girls to protect. And, by God, I will not let *any* motherfucker threaten you like that. No one will talk to *me* or what is *mine* like that, *ever!* Do you understand me?" I ask her, practically yelling at her.

She nods her head, wiping her cheeks as more tears run down her face. Seeing her upset tugs at my heart, but we need to finish this conversation first before I can hold her in my arms. I close my eyes for a brief second, taking a couple of deep breaths, to control my anger toward that rat bastard.

"Lastly, don't keep shit from me. It will just piss me off. I need to know what's going on in that pretty little head of yours. I don't want you to be afraid to burden me with your problems. Let me help you. If I see you overdoing it, like you've been doing, I am going to step in and get involved. I know your divorce is between you and cunt face, but don't think for one fucking minute, I'll let him threaten you like that. I'm your man, not some bitch like him, that gets off on bossing you around. Don't let this easy going, funny as fuck, façade fool you. I'm one mean motherfucker when I need to be."

I'll kill the fucker before he hurts my girls.

"Okay." I clap my hands, feeling a lot better now that I got everything I needed to say off my chest. "Now, talk to me. Tell me what's stressing you out – got you mad, sad, or whatever the fuck. I want you to unleash all your burdens on me. If I see you holding back, I'll find out.

Feeling good about my little rant, I fold my arms across my chest and wait for her to speak. Thinking about what she's going to say makes me want to sink my cock inside her and take away all this negative shit.

Looking down at her fingers, Ruby rasps, "You have no idea how much your words mean to me."

My chest swells with pride, hoping she truly understands how I feel about her. With her eyes still lowered, she continues, "I–I feel like–like such a burden with all this baggage. I hate Brody so much for making my life hell." I bite my tongue not wanting to interrupt her, calling him every name in the book for making her feel this way.

Mother. Fucking. Cock. Sucker. Whore...

Clearing her throat, nervously wringing her fingers together, she says, "Being with you here and seeing you with my girl has been the best ever. I'm scared he'll take it away from me, you, my new job, Izzy, everything. I'm just so scared. He has so much money, he'll bury me in lawyer fees. Izzy and Luc are helping, but they don't know Brody. In his eyes, I am and always will be his."

I growl, clenching my teeth, making her look up at me with sorrow in her beautiful eyes.

Not looking away, with tears in her eyes, she says, "I've always been afraid to leave him, or get anyone else involved because he throws his money around. His new celebrity status has his head even bigger. Having Izzy back in my life, I feel whole again. She *is* my soul sister, and a piece of me has been lost without her. I love it here. Even with everything that's happened with everyone out here, I still feel safer here with you than I ever did with him. I don't want that for my baby. I'm doing this mostly for her. I–I..." She stops mid-sentence, covering her eyes to cry.

"Motherfucker!" I blurt out, gripping the edge of the counter.

Startled, Ruby's eyes pop open looking at me.

I say through clenched teeth, "You will never have to be scared again. You have a lot of people here willing to fight for you and keep you safe. You have me first and foremost, but even if you didn't, you and Bella have embedded yourself into not only my club but the BB boys and the Spin It crew. You have three powerful groups of people that will protect you. He will never hurt or make you do anything you don't want to do again." I promise her with everything I have in me.

"He has an abundance of money and too many connections," she replies.

"Fuck him and his money. I have a shit ton of my own money," I blurt out.

Shit...shit...shit... I can't believe I just said that out loud. I never talk about it. Only my brothers know about my money. Hell, only a hand full of people know my full name.

"FUCK!" I yell as this feeling of panic builds inside me.

Ruby flinches at my outburst. I round the island, sitting on a stool next to her. I turn her to face me, entwining our legs. Looking down, I clasp her hands within mine and take a deep breath.

When I look up, I see her eyes wild with confusion. I hesitate for a second. "Look, Rube, we hardly know each other, yeah?" I pause, waiting for her to nod back before continuing. "Okay, well I'm hoping we can continue to pursue what we have going and get to know each other better. Yes, I know it's been a little on the fast side, but when you know, you know, at least that's how I feel," I explain as she nods her head with a smile.

"We've had so much going on that we haven't really discussed what's happening between us, but I'm telling you now, you are completely and totally mine. *And,* I am completely and totally yours," I stop, giving her a look so she knows how serious I am about this.

She smiles so big, showing me her beautiful white teeth. Before she can say anything, I add, "*And,* I don't share. I'm very,

very protective of what's mine. And, not in the 'let me yell at you' for some dumb fuck trying to put his hands on your shit. It's the 'I will beat the man to death' for putting his hands on you – kind of protective." That little comment gets me a sweet giggle with a smile that lights up her whole face.

I continue, "With that said, I need you to know I've done some bad shit and I'll probably do it again. Shit that you will never ever know about. I'm not always this funny, laid back, horny as fuck guy. I have other sides to me, sides you don't want to see, and a past that no one knows about."

She whispers my name, and I nod my head. "When I was Jake, I was a completely different person. I was mad at the world for taking my parents from me too soon. I was a spoiled little rich kid who got into fights all the time before they died. And after well, let's just say I turned into a mean fucker that hated everyone."

Taking a deep breath, I continue, "What I'm trusting you with right now, that nobody outside of my club knows is, I came from money, and I have a shit ton of it. I already had a heavy trust account from my grandparents on my mom's side. I was just out of high school and in college when my parents were killed suddenly in a car accident, and since I was the only living heir, I inherited everything my family had. The pressure of dealing with everything and the loss of my parents sent me over the edge. I couldn't take it anymore, so I took off. I didn't want to be found or known as Jacob Reeves Walton, so I shortened my first name and dropped my last name becoming Jake Reeves. Before the club, I never stayed in one city long enough to care about anyone or anything."

Ruby's face goes from blissful to complete shock. I smile, letting it all sink in. I haven't spoken about my parents in years. The pain is still there, but I feel a little lighter telling her about my family. I might have been a fucked up spoiled kid who caused a shit ton of problems, but I loved my parents just as fiercely, as they did me.

Ruby stammers, "Quick. I–I…ah—"

Shaking my head, I cut her off, "Don't, baby. It was a long time ago, and I don't talk about my past to anyone." Dragging it out, so she understands how important it is to keep my past in the past.

I smile, trying to relax my face and lighten up this heavy conversation. In a soft tone, I tell her, "Just know when I moved here, I changed my life to becoming part of a brotherhood. That brotherhood became my family, and I'll do *anything*, and I mean *anything,* for my brothers, their ol' ladies, or anyone that I care about."

Ruby's eyes sparkle with hope, making my heart leap. "So… you're saying you care about me?" she laughs, teasing me.

And that right there is why I'm falling for her. She doesn't push or ask too many questions. She just goes with it. Relief washes over me, and my heart swells.

I raise my eyebrow in amusement. "Damn right, I do. I've just claimed your ass whether you like it or not. But, how would you feel about being my ol' lady one day?" Her eyes widen at my words, and to be honest, I'm shocked hearing them myself.

She squeezes my hands that are still entwined with hers, drawing my attention to how sweaty they are. "I've been yours since the first day I jumped into your truck. But…" She pauses, causing me to hold my breath. "Being on the back of your bike is a whole new kind of love, baby," she says, leaning in, kissing me. I let out the breath I was holding and grab her behind the neck deepening our kiss.

When I hear her moan, my cock twitches beneath my jeans, wanting some attention, I break the kiss, leaving our foreheads touching. "What I've just told you about my past, the inheritance, everything needs to stay between us, okay? I just needed you to know I got you, Rube. All of your drama, baggage or whatever you need in life, I got you. No matter what, I will always protect you girls. Like I told Bella, this Wolf—" I pound my fist over my chest where my new Wolfeman tattoo is and grip the back of her neck. "This Wolf will die for you and do anything to make sure you're both happy, yeah?" I finish, crashing my mouth to hers, pulling her off her stool onto my lap.

She squeals, breaking the kiss, throwing her hands around my neck laughing.

My firecracker. That smile. Fuck.

Ruby smirks and says teasingly, "So... do I call you my sugar daddy?"

I laugh, standing up, holding her around the waist with one arm. With my other hand, I slip it under her ass, beneath her shorts, plunging my fingers into her wet core. "I'll give you something to call me, but I don't think it will be sugar daddy."

As I carry her back to the bedroom, I add, "I promise one day I'll explain it all to you but no more serious talk right now, horny Quick is back and needs some loving."

11 | Challenge Accepted

Ruby

"Firecracker! You finally fucking came to see me!" Maze screams from the bar as Quick, and I walk into the Clubhouse. The place is packed with people, looking around, I notice that there are other MCs along with some of our other chapters. I curl into Quick's side, hugging his waist a bit tighter.

When he squeezes me back, I smile, always my protector. As we walk toward the bar, I see Ginger standing with a group of women, some I recognize, some I don't know. I smile in their direction, excited to hang out without Bella attached to my hip, but sad Izzy isn't here with me.

I love my baby, but good Lord, I need a break. At least back home, I used to be able to go over to Club DazZelle and dance to relieve some stress. I've been in New York for a month now, and I've only been away from Bella while I'm at work or when we were moving Izzy. So I'm really excited to be out with Quick for some much-needed adult time.

"Who's watching Bella?" Ginger asks, pulling me from Quick's arms, giving me a hug.

"Gus and Izzy are home watching her tonight," I reply.

"Hello, ladies. Geez, I get a woman, and you forget about little ol' Quick. You know – your dance partner and your drinking buddy? Shit, now I don't even get a fucking hello," Quick pouts, throwing his hands in the air, faking a tantrum. I notice two new girls eyeing Quick with excitement in their eyes.

All the ladies yell, "Hello, Quick!"

Quick smiles big. "Now, that's a hello I like to hear."

Everyone laughs as Quick pulls me back to him, kissing my temple, whispering, "I've gotta go talk to Shy and the boys. Stay here with Snow, and I'll be right back." I nod my head in acknowledgment, when I see the new girls are still watching him closely, I turn to him, pulling his face down for a real kiss. Quick grips my ass, tugging me closer to him with a groan. "Firecracker, I'll be right back...behave," he says before disappearing into the crowd of bikers.

I watch him until I can't see him anymore, when I turn around everyone is watching me now. I blush, "What?"

Ginger laughs. "Firecracker – you just fucked him senseless with your eyes."

I smirk. "I actually did just fuck him senseless. I'm looking for round two."

Everyone laughs and like always, Maze screams, "shots" from behind the bar.

Let the festivities begin.

Everyone grabs a shot, and we salute to our normal, "Cheers Biatches," before throwing it back. After Maze hands me my vodka soda, I turn around, and Ginger introduces the new girls to me. It seems the club hired new dancers for their big parties. Trixie, and of course fucking Dixie, are two tall blond bombshell girls, with model bodies like Izzy. I smile, shaking their hands with a look letting them know my man is off limits.

He's mine, bitches.

They start telling all of us how they dance solo or together. Storm, not looking too impressed, decides to tell the girls about the time Izzy and I danced together and how the men came out on the stage with a dance of their own. Everyone laughs, remembering the men dancing around on stage. Lolli starts to explain how Izzy's been helping her with her stage performance when I hear someone calling my name.

I look over my shoulder and see Cash heading my way with Bear and Wolfe. Bear moves up behind his woman, Storm, giving her a kiss, pulling her into his massive chest. Wolfe greets all the women before moving toward the bar next to his daughter, Ginger, giving her a fatherly kiss on the cheek.

"Hi Cash," I greet him.

"Firecracker, good to see ya. How's Legs doing?" he asks with concern in his voice.

"She's doing really good. They're home watching my little one so I could get some much-needed adult time," I say with a smile.

Cash raises an eyebrow and says with a smirk, "You gonna dance for us tonight?"

I'm about ready to say no, when the two new chicks pipe up and say, "Yes, you should dance tonight."

Cash glances over my shoulder, looking for whoever interrupted us. I guess he doesn't like tall blonde bimbos, because the look that crosses his face when he sees them is fucking priceless. I stand there with my lips tucked between my teeth holding in my laugh, when he snaps, "Who the fuck're you?"

Ginger chokes on her drink. "Cash, be nice, this is Trixie and Dixie. The club's new dancers we hired for the big parties.

More like twit and twat.

When Cash looks back toward Ginger like he could give two shits who they are, I bust out laughing, unable to hold it in anymore. Ginger clears her throat with a straight face until Cash gives her a quick nod. With a half-smile, he turns back to me and says, "So, are you going to dance for us tonight?"

I shrug. "I haven't thought about it. We'll see how the party goes and how well you behave," I tease, making him smile bigger.

"You'll do what, if who behaves?" Quick says, walking up with Shy, Mac, and Dallas.

Fuck, these men are hot as fuck tonight, looking all kinds of badass in their leathers.

I turn, folding myself into my man's arms and reply, "Cash was asking me if I was going to dance tonight and I told him it depends on the night and if he behaves."

Quick chuckles. "Cash behave, like that will ever happen. The man is walking chaos waiting to happen." Making everyone laugh, even Cash laughs, nodding his head in agreement.

When "Simple Man" by Lynyrd Skynyrd, blares throughout the speakers, Lolli says to the girls, "Well, that's our cue to head up." When she slides off the bar stool to leave, I hear her mumble to herself, "I wish we could dance to this kind of shit" thinking no one can hear her with the music blasting.

When I tell her, "You can dance to this. Why do you think you can't?"

She turns to me. "It's just not a sexual song. If the song is this slow, it needs to be a sexual song, plus everyone always wants us to dance to faster, more 'fuck me' songs."

I'm about ready to tell her she's crazy, but Trixie the twit speaks up first, "It's too hard to dance to this stuff and how can you make this song sensual?"

These two dip shits are getting on my fucking nerves – fucking amateurs.

Laughing, I say, "You can make any song sensual you just need to listen to the beat, let your body take over."

The girls look at each other, then back at me like I've lost my mind. When Dixie, the twat replies, "Well, I guess you'll just have to show us, and we can let the men decide what they like better."

This bitch did not just challenge me...

Storm says, "Oh...*sheeit.*"

Lolli asks what I'm sure everyone is thinking, "Are you challenging Firecracker?"

Trixie smiles "It's all fun and games, but seriously I'd like to see her pull it off with this many men here. They want to hear fucking songs."

I smirk nodding my head letting her know I accept, while Cash bellows from the bar, "Y'all just fucked up. Firecracker kills it on that pole." And, that is why he's become my new best friend. Fuckin' love him.

I clarify one thing though. "It has to be just one of you performing since I'm solo tonight. We all know how the men would rather see two women than one," I state in a friendly voice, knowing my eyes are anything but friendly.

I'm trying to be chill, even though dip shit Dixie is eyeing my man behind me. I'm about ready to smack the bitch. I've dealt with twats like this being around my aunt's club. They get busted up or fired really quick with their high and mighty ass thinking they know it all. I feel Quick's grip tighten on my hip, breaking through the tirade in my head. I give them a smirk before turning around to look at my gorgeous man smiling proudly at me.

Damn straight baby. I'm the fucking shit.

Lolli says from behind me, "Okay, it's time to go up there, ladies." I hear everyone say goodbye to the two bitches and Lolli. I give Lolli a smile and tell her I'll be up there to see her set.

"Feisty as fuck, my little firecracker," Quick says over my shoulder. Everyone one laughs agreeing. Ginger busts up laughing. "Damn those sluts have some fucking nerve. I thought about putting them in their place but decided fuck that, let them get schooled."

"Angel, be nice. We just hired them," Shy says, sounding amused.

"First of all, we've discussed this. Why the fuck are you paying bitches to come dance for y'all. You just need to put some club sluts up there shaking their ass," Ginger says.

"Snow's right, brother, why do we pay for bitches when we got plenty of free pussy running around here," Mac says from the bar, shocking everyone because we all know he loves strippers.

Everyone looks at him, as his mom, Storm, replies laughing,

"Did my son, who pays for strippers all the time, just agree that paying for sluts is ridiculous?"

Mac turns to his mother, smiling. "Ma, I haven't paid for pussy since I was like ten. Just because they're a stripper, doesn't mean I pay them. I get my shit for free."

Everyone laughs except Storm as she shushes her son.

The rest of the night goes on without any problems, even when the president of the Hellman MC, Big Pete, approached us. I thought for sure there was still bad blood from when their secretary, Sam, kept grabbing me, until I overpowered him, bringing him to his knees. Big Pete was super nice asking how I was doing. I guess word got around that there was a challenge later tonight and I was one of the girls. Before he went back to his crew, he told me it was good to see me again, and he was rooting for me to win.

Maze kept refilling my drinks, getting me good and buzzed. I'm with Ginger upstairs looking for something to wear. Since I wasn't prepared to dance, I didn't bring anything, but luckily Ginger's my size. We settle on a very tight, very short black skirt with a black cami that matches my lace bra. It'll show my girls when I hang upside down.

I check myself out in the mirror to see how it all looks, I've teased my wild mane making it wilder, darkened my makeup, and I'm in all black with red – come-fuck-me – stiletto heels.

Ginger stands next to me dressed in all her leathers and Property of Shy cut. "Damn, girl you look hot as fuck," she says, smiling at me.

I smile back. "Let's hope it's enough. Izz will never let me live it down if this bitch beats me."

We both laugh.

I'm sitting upstairs in the club area that we mark off whenever we have big parties, so that way we always have a secure place to hang out while watching the entertainment. My girl's coming out here soon. I didn't think Ruby would dance without Izzy here, but she shocked the shit out of me. She's definitely fired up tonight.

I've been uneasy all night, and when the Hellman MC arrived, I went on high alert. They haven't been back here since the little incident with Ruby, laying out their secretary when she first visited last month. The fucker saw her dance up here and decided she was club pussy and got a little too grabby with her, so she took him to his knees using some self-defense move. My bitch single-handedly took his big ass down. If I hadn't already fallen in love with her, I would have right then.

The room is over capacity right now waiting for one of the bitches to come out. Thank fuck I didn't hire them or fuck them. I see the way they're looking at me, and for the first time in my life, I wasn't interested or egged on by it.

"You good, brother? You seem off today," Shy says, leaning into me so only I can hear him.

I take a drink of my beer. I don't know why I'm on edge tonight, but I am. "Don't know. Just feel off," I answer honestly.

I scan the room, only seeing Wolfeman and Hellman members around. It's been bugging me all night. I thought it was because of the Hellman's being here, but when their president, Big Pete, came up to us shaking my hand, asking how we were, I knew Big Pete didn't want any problems.

"You okay with her doing this? I mean do you feel different about your girl being up there for everyone to see now that you claimed her as your ol' lady?" Shy asks.

Earlier when I left Ruby, we had church, and I brought to the table about making Ruby my ol' lady. After a few members asked if I was sure and we discussed it, everyone voted in agreement welcoming her to the family, and I couldn't be happier. Now I just need to get her a vest and wait for the right moment to make it official. But thinking about what he just said, maybe it is because all these men are going to be watching my girl.

"Fuck, I don't know. I guess we'll find out. If I do lose it..." I pause. "I'll either haul her ass off the stage or knock a motherfucker out," I chuckle, looking over at my brother.

Shy tilts his head back with a full laugh. "This should be an interesting night."

Ginger's voice booms through the speaker. "Alright. Alright. Alright... I'm sure y'all heard by now about our little bet going on with these two beautiful ladies." The club erupts in a deafening noise as all the men get rowdy. Ginger yells, "Shut the fuck up."

I look over at my brother knowing he's hard as fuck watching his ol' lady order these motherfuckers around. Shy smiles and lets out a loud whistle and the room settles down a bit so she can continue, "Thank you, lover. Now, since you men will be the deciding factor, you need to know what you will be judging. The major decision is which song choice is better, who has more sex appeal, and last, which performance overall did it for you – if you know what I mean."

The men catcall, wanting it to start, so Ginger introduces the first person. "New to the Wolfeman stage *and* challenger, Trixie."

"Chandelier" by Sia begins to play as Ginger hops off the stage.

The men get rowdy when the lights flash onto the pole where the blonde bitch glides around the pole wearing nothing but a tight red dress.

I'll give the bitch this – she's good. She flies around the pole in a flag-like move, and the men go ape shit watching her twirl around.

But, not as good as my firecracker.

I look over and see all my brothers watching intently, calling out when they like a move she does, but they're still seated.

She moves to the floor with some leg shit and ends it with some slutty moves that I'm sure get the men hard as fuck. The men around the stage are hollering at her, throwing her money.

"Alright. Alright. Thank you, Trixie," Ginger says, trying to calm the men down, but when the song, "Another One Bites the Dust" by Queen rings through the room, Ginger turns around to the DJ wondering what the fuck is going on. When she sees who's behind her, she bends over laughing.

Shy shocks everyone as he comes out strutting his biker ass onto the stage, dancing up behind Ginger. Seeing our president busting a move up there, the crowd goes berserk, laughing and whistling egging him on.

This motherfucker. I can't help but laugh my ass off at my brother.

He grabs the mic, kissing Ginger, giving her another smack on the ass before pulling her into his side.

"You like that song, motherfuckers? Well, I played it for a couple of reasons..." He points to me. "I'm honored to finally say I'm not the only fallen brother. As the song says, another one bites the dust..." *Sonovabitch*

Everyone looks my direction, and I salute him with my beer before slamming it. Shy laughs, continuing, "The untamable has been tamed by this next little firecracker." Everyone heckles me, hitting me on the back,

Shy smiles. "Which leads me to this." Pausing, his face becomes dead serious, and in a threatening voice, he says, "If any of you motherfuckers touch her, you will get knocked the fuck out. *But...*" he drags out, returning his smile and becoming his playful self again. "By all means look, drool, fuckin' jack

yourself off *but* if one of you touch her, you've been warned."
Shy hands his ol' lady the mic planting a deep, wet kiss on her,
laughing as he jumps off the stage, heading my way with a huge
grin on his face. Ginger recovers from the kiss, fanning herself.

"Well, that was fun! Why don't we keep this party going?
Give it up for my girl, Firecracker."

The stage goes completely black, and then you hear it. "Babe
I'm Gonna Leave You" by Led Zeppelin rings loud, and slowly
the lights start to come back on lighting up my girl on the floor
touching herself.

Fuck me. My cock stirs to life instantly.

The room booms with whistles and shouts as everyone,
including the ladies, stand, moving closer to see her on stage. I
have to stand up to see her with so many people standing. She's
on the floor, slipping her hands up and down her body, gripping
her tits giving us a show, playing the part of the song, like she's
torn between leaving her partner.

My girl bends into a position lifting her backside up showing
the globes of her ass.

"I'll give you this, brother. Your bitch has some fucking
moves. Goddamn!" Mac says, standing next to me, staring at my
girl as he empties the remaining whiskey from his glass.

I chuckle. "You have no idea, brother."

When the guitar solo hits, she does a handstand up to the
pole, bending back, she slips the pole between her legs,
clenching the pole between her thighs, lifting her upper body up
off the ground onto the pole. When she's upright, she spins
around the pole before landing back down onto the ground in the
splits.

The crowd goes nuts, throwing money on stage, cheering her
on. She gets up, moving around the stage, when the next guitar
solo hits she flies through the air, flipping her body around the
pole as she moves up the pole, doing sexy as fuck moves one
after another.

How she flips herself into those fucked up positions, I have no idea, but my dick loves them. She dropped upside down, and I think every man in here wished her tits would've fallen out of her top. I know I was. *Fuckin' A.*

And that fucking hair cascading down her back as she shifts into the splits against the pole. Grinding against the pole like she's fucking it as he screams in the song, "babe... babe..." making me want to pound the fuck out of her.

I start to move to the edge of the stage, needing to be near her because when this is over were fucking. There will be no talking, just fucking. The crowd moves to the music, with their hands in the air singing the song. Who wouldn't like Led Zeppelin?

The song's almost over when she lowers herself to the ground with her eyes on me. Spreading her legs into the splits like I do when I'm fucking her, giving me a full view. She bends backward lifting her chest up, gripping her tits, giving me and everyone next to me a full view of what is mine.

My heart beats faster – *motherfucking mine.*

She's inches away from me when the lights go out, and the song ends. Everyone is on their feet, screaming her name. When I feel small hands wrap around my neck, relief fills me as I lift her off the stage wrapping her legs around my waist, just as the lights turn back on with Ginger bouncing on stage.

"That's my girl! Now that's how you do it..." She must realize Ruby isn't on stage anymore and calls out, "Wait! Fuck, Firecracker, where you going?"

Ruby tilts her head back laughing as she throws up a peace sign, letting everyone know we're out. I just laugh as men pat me on my back as we walk through the crowd. Ruby's laughing as people are stuffing money at her. It's time to fuck my ol' lady, my firecracker... mine.

12 | The Call

Ruby

The elevator dings on the second floor where Quick, Mac, and Shy all have a private room. Since we've hit the hallway, I've been devouring his mouth, gripping his hair as he carries me. Quick shifts me, grabbing his keys to unlock his bedroom door. Once we're inside, he drops us onto the bed with me on top of him.

"Goddamn, Firecracker, I love watching you dance," Quick says, breaking the kiss.

Placing my hands on either side of his face, I push myself up. When I look down at his beautiful face and see the admiration in his crystal blues, my heart skips and all kinds of feelings erupt in my chest.

Smiling down at him, I say, "Thank you. It felt fucking good." I sit up, straddling him, trying to tame my hair away from my face. With all this adrenaline running through me, I feel like I'm about to explode. Quick puts his hands behind his head, not saying anything, just watching me. I continue to try to explain how I'm feeling, "It makes me feel so alive and not because people are watching me. It's just – it's like I become one with the music, losing myself in the song. I feel carefree flying around the pole. It – it's like…"

"Like I feel on the back of my bike with the wind and freedom all around me," Quick explains.

I smile. "Exactly!"

"Rube, I can see when you dance that you love it. You can see it in your face how it makes you feel. You make me feel so proud to be your man watching you," Quick says, sitting up wrapping his arms around my waist.

I have a permanent grin on my face.

Quick slowly leans in placing a soft sensual kiss on my lips. I moan into his mouth, slipping my hands around his neck. Jesus, I want this man. I rotate my hips over his perfect cock, but when my bladder screams at me, I break the kiss laughing.

"What?" Quick says, smiling at me.

"Babe, I gotta pee," I giggle.

Quick laughs, releasing my waist, saying, "Get at it because I plan on fucking that sweet pussy of yours all night long."

I hop off of him to head for the door but turn back around to grab my brush, remembering I brought my purse and overnight bag up here.

Quick gets off the bed walking over to me, placing a kiss on my shoulder. "I'll get the music so it will muffle you screaming my name," he chuckles, moving to his stereo system. I laugh and head for the bathroom, shutting the door.

I feel the best I've felt in a really long time. When I look at myself in the mirror – I smile, finally liking what I see looking back – I see happiness. A girl that's happy. A girl that's free to do whatever she wants. A girl that has a man that supports her.

Taking a deep breath, I move away from the mirror with a huge grin on my face to relieve my bladder. When I'm done, I move back to the sink to freshen up when I suddenly hear Quick yelling at someone.

I panic, thinking there's someone in our room. I throw open the door, ready for whoever's out there. But all I see is Quick's naked back, with a phone to his ear. Looking around the room, I relax seeing his cut and shirt laying in the chair. When I see his body tense and his muscles flex, I instantly know who he's talking to, and all the happiness I was feeling, drains from my body.

Oh, God. No.

"Bitch, you might have my name, but you don't know who the fuck I am because if you did, you'd be scared shitless. But, if you keep threatening my girl, you'll find out real fuckin' quick though. I've seen your fucking pussy ass texts to her. Who threatens the mother of their child?" Quick seethes into the phone.

I can hear Brody screaming through the phone, "I don't give a fuck who you are. She'll always be mine, their my girls, and I'm coming for them."

Stifling my gasp, Quick laughs with a vindictive snarl. I've never seen or heard Quick act this way.

"I dare you, fucker. I dare you to come here and try and take what's mine. You have no idea what I'm capable of," Quick says in a low, sinister voice, so controlled making it sound more lethal.

Quick turns, sensing me move farther into the room. My eyes go wide when I see the look in his eyes – murderous. I cover my mouth, muffling my cry. Quick doesn't move to comfort me – he just stands there staring with his chest heaving, clenching his fists.

"Dare accepted, bitch—"

Never breaking eye contact with me, Quick interrupts him, "You might want to do more research on who I am before you show up here. I won't be held responsible for what happens to you if you do. That's my last warning." He hangs up the phone abruptly. I feel like that was a warning to me too, letting me know he'll do anything to protect me, even hurt Brody if he tries to take me.

I stand there with both hands over my mouth frozen, staring at him in complete shock. I don't even know what to do or say. Quick closes his eyes, breaking the stare, taking a deep breath trying to control his anger. The second he opens his eyes, he's on me so fast, I don't even flinch.

"Rube, I'm sorry you had to hear and see that, but I couldn't take him threatening you anymore." Quick's voice is low, raw and rough.

He hugs me tighter, as I pull myself together and ask, "What happened? Everything was so good and bam!"

Quick moves me to the bed setting me down, reaching over to grab his shirt, before explaining what happened.

"I was putting some music on when I heard your phone beep with a message. I saw it was from him, of course, he was talking shit in the part I could read, then he called your phone." He pauses. "So I answered it."

I look up at him not, saying anything.

His adrenaline is high, and his expression is still murderous – no doubt thinking about his conversation again.

"So, what did he say? I want to hear it all," I demand.

"When I answered, he asked who the fuck I was, I laughed saying his worst nightmare, and he replied, so you're Jake Reeves." Quick starts to pace, running his hands through his hair. "How did he know my name?"

"I told him," I blurt out.

Quick stops dead in his tracks and turns to me. "When? Why? Fuck!!" he roars.

I flinch at his words, answering him, "Bella told him about me kissing the taxi guy. He was threatening me, so I told him your name. I didn't tell him anything about you, not your road name, Quick, or that you're in a motorcycle club or even where you live. He thought you lived in Los Angeles until recently when Bella told him Momma's friend watched her, and he asked if that friend was you and I said yes. That's why he's been flipping out lately. He knows you live here."

Quick stands there looking shocked, but I can see his brain thinking. I stay quiet, and when he closes his eyes, to take taking a few deep breaths, I relax.

"Okay, Rube. I need to go talk to Shy, you wanna get dressed and come with me, or you can stay up here and wait for me to come back. It's up to you, baby, but I need to talk to Shy."

"Did I do something wrong? Are you mad at me?" I murmur.

Quick kneels down, grabbing my legs, moving between them in a soft voice he says, "No baby, but I need to deal with this and do some damage control. He's crazy and isn't going to go away. I will not let him keep hurting you, and I'm sure as fuck not letting him get near you."

I nod my head. "Okay, let me change. I need a drink. I can't be up here alone with my thoughts."

Quick leans in, kissing me softly on the lips, before standing up, extending his hand to help me up. My heart aches, he's so good to me, and I've caused him so much trouble. I hurry to get dressed just throwing on jeans leaving the black tank top on.

When I grab my Converses, he says, "Leave the red heels on. We'll pick up where we left off when we get back." I look up at him confused.

Quick squats down as I put on my shoes.

"I will not let him take away anything from us. Everything will be okay, I promise. I just need to deal with some stuff. Then we'll head back up here. I want to be balls deep in you more than ever, yeah?" His voice is so soft and loving, I get tears in my eyes and nod my head.

In the elevator, Quick pulls me into his side, holding me. "I don't want you to be alone anywhere down here. Always stay with one of our guys or Storm, Ginger, or even Maze. Never wander off alone. If you need to go somewhere, make sure your with someone you trust. There are too many unknowns down there right now. I've been on edge all night," he explains.

Walking back into the club, I see the party has taken a turn toward the wilder side. I glance around and see naked women sucking men off or getting fucked. Quick keeps me tucked into his side, moving us through the thick crowd toward the bar. When Quick whistles, Maze looks up from Tiny's lap. When she sees Quick's face, she straightens, tapping Tiny, pointing upstairs.

Quick moves us upstairs where it's roped off. There are

naked girls walking around up here too while some give lap dances. I look toward the stage and see one of the regular girls up there. When I see Ginger sitting on Shy's lap laughing, I let out a big sigh.

Walking up, everyone starts to heckle us, but once they see Quick's face Shy stops talking and gives Quick a nod. I don't see what he does back but Shy taps Ginger's ass to get up. Out of the corner of my eye, I see Mac folding what I'm sure is his cock back into his pants, pushing some girl off his lap.

Quick turns me to him, "I'll be back. Do not leave this area unless you are with Ginger or one of our guys." I nod my head. He kisses me before turning to Ginger. "Don't let her out of your sight. Like. At. All." His voice comes off rough.

Ginger nods her head looking at me, knowing I'm about ready to lose my shit. She walks over, throwing her arm around me, telling him, "We'll either be up here or downstairs at the bar with Maze."

Shy whispers in her ear before giving her a kiss.

Quick nods in response giving me a half smile before him, Shy, and Mac disappear into the crowd.

Ginger whips me around, looking all kinds of concerned. "What the fuck happened? I haven't seen Quick look that deadly in a long fucking time."

Tears fill my eyes, and I drop my head, I can't talk, the lump in my throat is preventing me from talking. Ginger pulls me into her arms, giving me a big hug. "I got you, girl. Everything's going to be okay. Let's head downstairs and have Maze get us fucked up."

Shy leads us through the clubhouse with people moving to give us room to pass. My heart's racing, it took everything I had to keep myself under control in front of Ruby. Talking to her cunt ex flipped a switch in me that hasn't been flipped in a very long time. When he called me by my first name, I froze for a second wondering how he knew or what he knew about me. But when he started threatening to take my girls – I saw red.

We stop at the bar where Worm's sitting. Tiny sees us and moves from behind the bar.

"Tiny, need you and Worm on watch duty. I need one of you upstairs where our girls are." Shy stops talking when Tiny points behind us.

We all turn to see Ginger holding my broken girl coming down the stairs. *Sonovabitch.* All I want to do right now is go to her and comfort her, but it'll have to wait. I need to handle business first.

"Fuck, okay. Tiny, I want eyes on them at all times. I'm sure they're coming here to get fucked up with Maze. Keep them here and make sure one of you is always with them. If you need us, we'll be in the chapel," Shy orders.

"You got it, Prez, anything you need just let me know," Worm says, moving to stand up.

"We got problems here, Prez?" Tiny asks in a low voice, looking around the clubhouse. Tiny, our SGT at Arms has been acting as our enforcer as well until we fill that spot, so naturally, he's always looking for that threat.

"Not sure yet," Shy says, pausing giving me a look, but I don't give anything away. "I'll let you know when we figure it out."

The three of us move as one, heading toward the hall of doors leading us to our clubroom where only members are allowed. We throw ourselves into Shy's office before heading in, shutting the door behind us.

Shy sits in his chair at the head of the table with Mac at his side. I start to sit across from them, but I can't sit down, so I start to pace.

"What the fuck, brother? I haven't seen that look in your eyes in a very long time. What's got you all fucked up?" Shy asks, concerned.

"It's Ruby's cunt of an ex-husband. He's been threatening her with texts and phone calls. Harassing her, trying to manipulate and scare her. She's been telling me she can handle it or that she is got it under control. Well, I've been paying attention lately and finally seen some of these fucked up texts he's sending her. Tonight she went into the bathroom, and her phone beeped. I looked at it of course and saw half of a text with more threats. Then he called – and I answered."

"Shit," Mac murmurs.

Shy looks to him and then back to me. "And?"

"He asked who the fuck I was. I told him his worst nightmare, and he said 'so you're Jake Reeves.'"

Shy sits up, leaning forward, placing his forearms onto the table, fisting his hands. I knew that would get his attention. I nod my head. "Exactly."

"What the fuck did you say after that?" he growls.

"We exchanged some threats. He threatened he was coming to get *his girls*. When he said, she will always be *his*... I fucking lost my shit, daring him to come and try to get them." I ball my hands together, pacing back and forth as the rage builds inside me.

"Jesus Christ," Mac says.

We both look at him, and he just shrugs. "What? He sounds like a fucking nut job."

My face hardens, and I narrow my eyes. "No. Fucking. Shit! Why the fuck do you think I'm losing *my shit*?"

"Reel it in. What happened next?" Shy yells.

"I told him he might know my real name, but he didn't know me and that I dared him to come find out. He accepted my dare. I laughed at him and told him he might want to do some more investigating before he came to find out because I wouldn't be held responsible for what would happen to him if he did. And, that it was my only warning I'd give him, then I hung up on him." I turn to start pacing again but stop, dreading this part, taking a deep breath. I blurt it out, "And, it was Ruby who told him my real name."

Both the men ask in unison, "Why?"

I tell them the story Ruby told me, about Bella telling him I was a taxi driver and that Ruby thought it would be better to give him my real name instead of my road name or the club name. How she's scared of him and how he throws his money around to bully people. I told them everything I know about the guy. I end it with how I told Ruby about my money and that I would protect her. When I finish, I slump into my chair across from Mac.

We all sit there in silence for a few minutes, letting it all sink in and giving me time to reel in my anger.

Shy looks to Mac. "Go get Dallas. We need him now. And Wolfe, if he's not *busy*."

Mac gets up without a word and heads out to find the guys, shutting the door behind him.

I drop my head into my hands.

"What do you want to do about this? Tell me what you're thinking." Shy asks.

I lift my head. "If I could, I'd take him out, but it's Bella's dad. I can't do that unless he does something to hurt them. Then all bets are off, and I'll kill the bastard. But no matter what, he needs to be dealt with. The fucker's got her scared shitless." I sit back in my chair, resting my hand on the chair arms. "I don't know everything about him or if he could hurt us with my real name. I don't think he really runs with people that would know the Black Crows."

Shy leans back in his chair, clasping his hands together in deep thought.

When the door flies open Dallas' hyper ass walks in fixing his pants. "Sorry, I was balls dee–" He stops mid-sentence once he looks up from adjusting his pants, seeing our faces. "What's going on?" He moves around the table to sit next to me.

Right at that moment, in strolls Mac and Wolfe, followed by Cash.

Wolfe looks around the room before giving Shy a nod, taking the seat at the opposite end of the table. He's president of the original chapter and founded the MC, along with his VP, Cash, who's always by his side.

Once everyone's seated, Shy announces, "We got a problem that could possibly turn into an all-chapter problem." He pauses leaning forward. "Seems Ruby, or Firecracker, has an ex-husband that's been harassing her and is now threatening her and Miss Bella." Cash's head pops up, hearing Ruby's name got his attention. I know he's fond of my girl. Shy turns to me. "Quick, why don't you explain what's going on."

I turn to my brothers and tell them about everything Ruby's told me and everything I've seen. The tension in the room rises with each detail I reveal. Our MC doesn't like men who hurt or manipulate women. I go into what happened tonight and the phone call.

Cash leans over dropping his fist on the table. "Where is the motherfucker? Let's go pay him a visit." Wolfe grabs his VP's arm giving him a look to shut the fuck up. Cash groans, not saying anything else.

"He lives in LA, and I think I've got that covered with Whiz from the Sons of Saints. The biggest problem, or could be a problem, is he knows my name, Jake Reeves." Now this bit of information has Wolfe sitting forward, looking furious, along with everyone else in the room.

"Do you think he knows your *real full* name? Or that you're connected to the club?" Dallas asks, looking around the room.

"I feel he would've said something if he knew anything else.

I think he was just trying to piss me off. I really feel no one knows my full name besides you guys. I've never spoken my family name since the day I came clean with you and the day I left. There is no way anyone knows me as anything other than Jake Reeves or Quick," I answer.

Shy and Wolfe silently stare at each other until Shy breaks the silence, ignoring Dallas' question, he asks, "Dallas, what do we have on the guy? You did a background check on Ruby when she first wanted to come here. What did we find? I know he's some kind of famous singer and he has a shit ton of money, but what else?"

Dallas replies, "I have all the files, but I need my laptop. They both were clean – well he's clean in comparison to us, but he is far from clean. We have a bunch of footage of him cheating and overall just an arrogant guy. He was a controlling prick before he was famous and now – *sheeit*, fucker thinks he's untouchable."

Cash's face mimics mine and when our eyes connect, my jaw clenches as I give him a nod. We both have the same thoughts. *Kill the fucker.*

"Dallas, go get your shit. We're not in church so bring it in here instead of us going to the office. I ain't in the mood to move rooms," Shy says, leaning back into his chair.

Dallas jumps up, and once the door is shut behind him, we all sit silently thinking.

"The blowback on this will be huge. We can't take him out," Wolfe speaks for the first time.

Shy agrees, "Yeah, he's too high profile if something happened to him and with his family's kind of money, they wouldn't rest until every stone is turned. We just need to figure out if he's a threat and silence him."

"He *is* going to get his ass beat for sure, regardless if he's a threat or not just for fucking with Firecracker," Cash says, more of a promise than a request. I nod my head in agreement.

Dallas flies through the door with his shit in hand, and we sit there listening while Dallas goes over all his information, and when he's done giving us the details, we're all quiet for a few minutes letting it sink in.

Jesus, the fucker is worse than I thought.

"Well, I kind of agree with you, Quick, about having Whiz and his boys send a warning. For one, they don't have any ties to us, and from what we know, he doesn't know your road name or that you're associated with the Wolfemen. Hopefully, getting his ass beat will silence him and keep him from fucking with your girl. That will give us some time to do some more research to see if he knows your real name and if he can hurt us," Wolfe speaks, and we all nod in agreement.

Dallas looks to me. "What the fuck are you going to do if he knows your *full* name?"

I look over to him, but it's Shy who answers, "We need to focus on him knowing about you being Jake Reeves since *that* is what links him to the Crows. They should be our biggest concern. If he finds out about Jake's fortune, we'll deal with that too."

I add sarcastically, "Let that bitch find out I'm a billionaire, it might put his punk ass in his place, and if he does, I'll handle it. I agree with Shy, our biggest concern is the Crows finding out about me."

Dallas' eyes go wide. "Motherfucker you're a billionaire, and you borrowed money for a coffee last week. What the fuck?"

Fucking Dallas. My brother. Always joking.

Everyone breaks out in laughter, relieving some of the tension in the room. Dallas pats me on the back. "Brother, just kidding. I'll start tapping into shit and see what's rolling around out there."

Wolfe leans forward. "Quick, stay strong, brother. We got you and your girl. Nothing's going to happen to either of those girls. We'll make sure it's all handled."

I nod my head feeling a lump in my throat.

"I just want the cocksucker to pay. My girl's scared shitless and feels *she's* the problem. This motherfucker has done a number on her, and that little baby girl doesn't even ask for her daddy. That should tell you right there he's a piece of shit. It needs to be handled." I slam my fist on the table.

Everyone in the room nods their head in agreement.

"Make the call to Whiz and put that shit in motion. The business with Quick's name stays here and doesn't leave this room, because the fewer people that know his real name, the better. We've been in here dealing with Ruby's cunt ex-husband, yeah?" Shy demands.

Everyone says, "Aye."

Shy stands up. "I need a fucking drink."

Everyone stands up, filing out of the room. When I pass by Wolfe, he slaps me on the shoulder. "Wolf for life, brother."

I reach back, slap him on this back. "Thank you. Wolfeman for life, brother."

When we reach the bar, we hear them before we see them. Ruby's laughing and Ginger's screaming at Maze about something. Cash laughs. "Your ol' lady's one of a kind. If you need anything, you call me. I'll go down there and handle it myself if it doesn't get handled properly."

I smack him on the back. "Thanks, brother, that means a lot to me. And you're right, she's one of a kind."

As all of us walk up to the bar, everyone moves to give us room to slide in behind the girls. When Ruby looks up and sees me, she smiles big.

My firecracker is back and fucked up.

"Firecracker?" I question, raising an eyebrow.

Ruby stands up and sways, grabbing the bar giggling. "It's Ah-Maze-Ing's fault. Sh-She g-got us dr-unk."

Everyone laughs, the shit show really begins when Ginger tries to get up, falling off her bar stool, but Tiny catches her before she hits the floor. Ginger straightens herself up, laughing and tries to stop to be serious but horribly fails when she faces all of us. Raising her hand up to speak like a fucking little kid, and says, "Um... it was" –she hiccups– "it was me" –hiccup– "I did it."

They both start giggling, grabbing each other, helping each other stay up. I look over to Shy laughing, looking just as amused as I am, so I yell, "Maze, line up some shots for us boys, we need to catch up, obviously."

Maze, who's been leaning up against the bar laughing not saying anything, raises her finger pointing to us acknowledging we need drinks. She pushes herself off the bar but doesn't move. Tiny lifts his hand above his head with five fingers up. We all watch him lower them slowly, while Maze stands there swaying. It's like she's trying to make herself move and sure as shit when Tiny got down to two fingers, Maze falls flat on her ass laughing uncontrollably. A few of the members stand up, leaning over the bar to see if she was okay.

Worm laughs. "These bitches have been drinking straight up whiskey since y'all left and the bottle's almost gone."

Tiny gets up to move around the bar, picking Maze up, tossing her over his shoulder with no effort at all, smacking her ass. Tiny isn't tiny, being over six foot. He's one big motherfucker. Maze looks teeny tiny laying over his shoulder. Tiny calls over his shoulder, "Night. If you need me, just holler."

Seeing our women start to go down, I grab Ruby just as Shy grabs Ginger pulling them apart before they take each other down.

Wolfe yells, "Where the fuck are the prospects? We need a fucking bartender."

Chain comes rushing up. "I got it!"

"Baby, are you still mad at me?" Ruby pouts, saying it loud enough for people around us to hear.

I look over to Cash who's still standing next to me. His jaw clenches, hearing her say that shit.

I lean down, giving her a kiss. "Rube, I was never mad at you."

She sways in my arms. "Good. Now let's go. I want to fuck."

Hearing a few chuckles around me, I laugh and say, "Your wish is my command, Ruby Rube." I kiss her nose before leaning down, grabbing her around the waist, throwing her over my shoulder.

She squeals, "Quick!"

I start toward the elevator while she begins waving to everyone, saying goodnight to people she doesn't even know. When I hear her scream for Ginger, I know Shy's not far behind me carrying his ol' lady too.

I hold the elevator door for him, and once all four of us are in the elevator, the girls try to talk to each other over our shoulders. Shy laughs, "The two fallen holding up their angels."

He referenced earlier when he spoke on the stage about us being the only ones with ol' ladies. I laugh, "Wouldn't replace it for anything." I smack Ruby's ass, and she moans.

Yeah, tonight should be interesting.

13 | The Evidence

Quick

"Speaking of my man. It's him calling right now," I tell Dallas, getting up from my chair in the office where we've been going over all the shit he found on Ruby's ex-husband.

"Nice," Dallas says as I answer my phone, putting it to my ear.

"Whiz, my man. Whatcha got for me?" I say into my phone.

"Brother, it's been handled, and your message was loud and clear. The only hiccup, some other dude showed up as we were pulling away but no encounter. He ended up taking him to the ER with no shields being called, and it's been forty-eight hours, so we're good. We covered our ass, so no links to either of the clubs," Whiz explains without details that he sent Brody a message from me, Jake, not Quick, to back the fuck off.

"Good. Thank you, brother. I owe you a marker, and you have my gratitude," I say, happy that it was handled without any trouble.

"I'll keep an eye on him and update you in a few days," Whiz says before we say our goodbyes, hanging up.

Tossing my phone onto the table. I sit back down across from Dallas, who's watching me, waiting for the details.

"It's been handled. He said someone showed up when they were leaving but no trouble. The person took him to the ER and so far, no police have been called. He'll keep an eye on him and let me know if anything changes," relaying what Whiz told me.

"That's good. Well, we'll know for sure once he reaches out to Ruby. Have you told Ruby yet?" Dallas asks, sounding concerned.

I take my hat off, running my fingers through my long hair. I've been trying to figure out how to tell her since I made the call to Whiz, but I've been worried she might not understand what I've done.

"I haven't told her, I don't really know how to bring it up. I – uh..." I pause. "I'm worried she might not understand. I don't know."

Dallas taps his computer, bringing something up on the screen, when he turns around to show me, my blood boils. "Maybe you need to show her everything you found on him. Explain why you want to protect her from him, and this is just one of the ways you do things," he says, while I stare at a picture of Brody with four bitches in a hotel room.

Dallas has found a lot of dirt on Brody, and I'd rather not show her all of this, but then again, I might have to. I need her to understand he's a piece of shit.

I nod. Dallas turns his laptop back around and says, "And, there hasn't been any activity related to your surname or even under Jake. We'll see if he decides to do anything after this little incident. Last known job for you was the bar in Myrtle Beach, so if he does go looking, that would be where the problems would start."

I lean back in my chair, looking up at the ceiling. "Well, he isn't going to find any links from Jake to my surname anywhere. Only y'all and a few others know the difference. Like I said the other day, I'm more worried about Ronny finding out and coming to look for me. If Ronny finds out because of Brody, I won't have to worry about Brody anymore, Ronny will take him out just to get to me."

"Don't you think you might want to let Ruby know about all of this? It could impact her and her family big time if the Crows come looking. They don't care about anyone or anything," Dallas suggests, shoving his laptop aside before relaxing into his chair.

Dallas has been here for me from the beginning. Shy, Mac,

and Dallas took me under their wing after Wolfe declared me under his protection.

I look to my friend, taking a deep breath. "Yeah, I need to sit her down and tell her everything, need to see how she reacts to the Brody incident first before I go telling her *all* my shit."

Yelling from the other room makes us both jump.

"Where the fuck is he?" a woman screams.

Ruby?

I'm throwing open the office door with Dallas on my tail.

"Chain, for fuck's sake, get the hell out of my way. I know he's here," Ruby yells.

I rush down the hall, panicking thinking something happened to Izzy or Bella but when I see her standing in front of the prospect with her hands on her hips pissed the fuck off in full firecracker mode. I know she found out about Brody.

"Ruby, what the fuck?" I growl, approaching them.

When she notices me, she turns her rage on to me. "What the fuck did you do? Tell me it wasn't you," she yells, holding her phone up to me.

I don't even look at her phone as I grab her outreached arm, tugging her in the direction I just came. Dallas is only a few feet behind me when I turn, almost running into him.

"Answer me!" Ruby screams, fighting to get out of my grasp.

I turn seething. "Calm the fuck down. Now!"

It only fuels my little spitfire, and she lashes back, "Fuck you. Tell me what you've done."

I look to Dallas. "Let's go. She needs to hear it all. I need all the information."

Dallas nods and follows us. Ruby puts up a fight, pulling back, yelling at me. About halfway down the hall, I turn picking her up around the waist, hauling her kicking and screaming into the office.

I put her down across the room from the door, pointing to the chair. "Sit the fuck down and listen to what we have to say."

Ruby opens her mouth to fight back, but the look in my eyes must tell her I've had enough, because she sits down huffing, crossing her arms over her chest.

Dallas takes a seat farther down the table from where we were sitting, not saying a word. I start to pace the room, trying to calm down. I'm so fucking pissed right now. She seriously just takes his side before even listening to me. I can't believe this shit.

"Did you do it?" Ruby grits out.

I turn to her with my hands on my hips, chest heaving and fury in my veins. "Yes, I sent him a message."

Ruby's face switches between a few different emotions not settling on one. She grabs her phone, opening it, sliding it across the table. "Well, you did a good job of that. Actually, you made him more pissed off. Now he's going to hire a private investigator. Was *that* the message you were sending?" Ruby asks, her voice filled with mixed emotions.

I don't even see Dallas get up or move next to me until he's reaching for her phone. When we both look down at the photo displayed on her phone, a mixture of things rush through my mind and before I can stop myself I'm blurting out, "He's lucky he's alive, and when did you and *Sam* start chatting?"

Ruby inhales deeply through her nose as my words rip through her, and she's on her feet in an instant. "*Sam* is the one who texted me, telling me it wasn't good and that Brody is livid. *Sam* is the one that's worried Brody is going to lose his shit and do something stupid. *Sam* is being a friend."

Hearing both of their names sends me over the edge and Dallas must sense it because he moves in between us. "Okay, both of you calm the fuck down."

Ruby puts her hands on her hips. "He had him almost killed for what? Because he talks shit to me?"

I'm enraged. I clench my hands together, crossing them over my chest trying to hold in my fury.

Dallas' usual friendly happy demeanor changes to something lethal. "Ruby, you need to sit the fuck down and listen to everything. You don't know shit about your ex and your supposed friend Sam."

Ruby turns her fire on Dallas, "So the club *was* behind this. Was it *club* business? Is that why he couldn't tell me?" Before either of us can answer, Shy and Mac come storming through the door, slamming it shut behind them.

"What the fuck's going on?" Shy demands, his voice a deep rumble.

Ruby sits down glaring at all of us. I turn to my president and say, "Ruby just found out about Brody. It seems Sam took it upon himself to send Ruby pictures of Brody."

"Who the fuck is Sam?" Mac asks from behind Shy.

Shy announces, "The fucker her husband shared her with, his best friend, I think?"

Ruby squints her eyes in anger, not saying a word. I know I should say something, but she told everyone about her business, not me. I'm too pissed off and yeah, a bit jealous he's contacting her. She's mine, and I don't want any of those fuckers near her.

"No shit?" Mac chuckles.

Dallas takes the lead. "Why don't we all sit down and discuss this like adults. Ruby, you don't know everything and seeing that you're completely involved, you need to know the details about what's going on."

Ruby and I stare at one another, I'm so mad and hurt she took his side, I spout off, "She'll just take his side. Why explain it to her?"

Damn, I sound like a spoiled little kid throwing a tantrum. Fuck!

Hurt sparks behind her eyes, but I'm hurt she came at me all crazy. I'm doing this for her sake and to claim her as mine but mostly because of her.

"Enough," Shy snaps, moving to his chair at the end of the table with Mac right beside him.

I don't move.

Dallas moves behind his laptop and starts typing away. "Ruby, why don't you move down here next to me so we can show you some stuff."

Ruby's stubbornness tries to defy him, but her curiosity wins as she moves down toward him. Dallas, not taking his eyes off his laptop, says, "Quick, stop being a possessive fucker and start explaining to everyone what we came up with today. Explain to Ruby what is going on, including your past."

Everyone's quiet, shifting their eyes to me. I take a deep breath, closing my eyes not wanting to make eye contact with her. I turn away to pace and start to explain. "Ruby, like I told you before, we did a background check on you when you started to come back around Izzy. After I met you, I had Dallas do a more extensive search on you. What you didn't know, is that we looked into your husband." I pause to take a deep breath. "What we found was not good. You already told us you were leaving him, so we let it go."

Ruby sits up and orders, "What did you find?"

I hold up a finger, still not looking at her, continuing to pace in circles at the end of the table. "We'll get to that, but you need to hear me out. Once I started having more feelings for you, we did more digging only to find more of the same shit."

"What shit," Ruby demands.

Shy, tired of hearing her, blurts out, "The fucker's been cheating on you for years. Him and that Sam dude have been pulling trains on bitches for a long ass time."

Ruby sucks in a deep breath. I turn around, unable to take it anymore, and the look on her face is complete shock.

Dallas takes this opportunity to step in, adding, "Ruby, when you're ready. We have emails, photos, and all kinds of correspondence showing proof of his adultery. The more famous he is, the more arrogant and power struck he's become."

Ruby's face stays frozen, not showing any emotions as she looks between Dallas and Shy. I move across the table into her peripheral view, wanting to see her face when I continue. "In the last three years, he's had four sexual harassment claims against him that were handled by paying them off. And he's had two assault charges that were taken care of before it ever made it to the legal aspect. So nothing was ever recorded."

Ruby's head snaps my direction when I mention assault. The fire in her eyes slowly diminishing with each word I say, as if she remembers something.

"When we found all this out, I had Dallas start monitoring him since you left him, he's becoming more dangerous, more violent."

Dallas asks in a gentle voice, "Ruby, does any of this sound familiar to you? Did you know anything about this?"

Ruby doesn't take her eyes from mine when she explains, "He blamed me for getting pregnant. He hated that I got pregnant. Thought the baby would take me away from him. He always said he needed me to be with him, that he couldn't be a star without me by his side." She pauses, wiping a couple of tears away before continuing, "He's never hit me, but he has yanked me around and has been forceful in other ways. He was more verbally abusive with me."

"Well, Ruby, this past month he's lost it completely, knowing you're with someone else. The last few concerts he's had since you served him divorce papers, he put a guy in the hospital and gave a woman a black eye while he was fucking her. Luckily, Sam was fucking her too and stopped him from hurting her any further."

Ruby covers her mouth, whispering, "Oh my God," as tears slide down her perfect face.

"So, you see Ruby, he's actually lucky our friends didn't just kill him," Shy explains.

Ruby looks to me. "Yeah, but you beating him up is only going to fuel his fire, making him want revenge."

"Not when I send him this little package of shit I've accumulated – a package I can send to the press and media. We have a lot of shit on him – it would ruin him. He needs to leave you alone," Dallas tells her, leaning back in his chair, folding his arms across his chest.

"Rube, I've only ever wanted to keep you safe. He needed to get his ass kicked not just for how he's threatening you, but for everything," I say, waiting for some kind of response from her before I head into my shit past.

When she looks over and nods, I know she understands he's a piece of shit. I look to Shy, and he nods his head, knowing what I'm about to say, giving me the push I needed. "Rube, we're also concerned because he knows my name and with his kind of money and resources, he could pull up some of my past – past that I don't want to be pulled back up."

With a confused look on her face, I move to sit across from her and try to explain, "After my parents died, I left behind a complicated life, changing my name which I told you about the other day. I moved around from state to state, picking up jobs bartending. I didn't really need to work since I have a trust fund, but new name, new life, new me. Plus, the last place anyone would look for Jacob Walton was a biker bar – let alone working in one." I pause, looking around the room. I can see my brothers are lost in their own thoughts of what happens next in my story. When I look back at Ruby, she's waiting, listening to every word I'm saying.

"I had been living in Myrtle Beach for a while, that's how I met Whiz. He took me under his wing, and we partied – hard. Whiz is the one that introduced me to these fuckers." I chuckle. "Like I told you before, I helped Shy out of a situation. That situation has to do with another MC, the Black Crows. Well, they came after me and hurt me really bad because I helped Shy. They almost killed me, but Shy returned the favor, saving me. That day I left Myrtle Beach – Jake Reeves died, and Quick was born. I went into hiding while the two MCs had it out. No one knows where Jake went after that or what happened to him. The Crows still have a vendetta with me. That's why no one knows my name."

Realization sparks in Ruby's eyes and she whispers, "And I told Brody your name. If he starts throwing it around, the Crows will come looking."

When I smile at her, she starts to cry. "This is all my fault. I'm so sorry," she murmurs, dropping her head into her hands.

I'm up out of my chair and around the table in seconds. Picking her up, placing her on my lap, kissing her head. "It's not your fault."

"It is my fault. What can I do? Can't we just tell him to shut the fuck up?" Ruby starts to ramble.

"Ruby, listen to me." Shy's voice comes out loud and commanding.

Ruby stills in my arms, both of us turning to look at him.

"Ruby, it isn't your fault your ex is a fucking whack job. We'll handle it, we just need to get the rest of your shit and move it here. We're going to send him parts of this package and give him our demands," Shy explains more calmly.

Ruby sits up, giving him her full attention, asking, "What kind of demands?"

Shy smiles. "Well, for one, he needs to sign the divorce papers the lawyers have negotiated. He needs to quit contacting you unless it regards your daughter, the lawyers have a visitation schedule all laid out and detailed. He needs to quit pursuing Jake. Otherwise, meaner men will come calling at his door."

"What happens if he doesn't?" Ruby asks softly.

"Well, your ol' man over there has endless amounts of

money, so I'm sure the lawyers will deal with that. You will never have to deal with him again if you don't want to. You just need to be prepared because if he doesn't stop asking around about Jake, and the Crows do come calling – they'll kill him to get to Jake," Shy answers, dead serious.

"Shy, I'm so sorry. I've done nothing but—"

Shy cuts her off, putting a hand up. "Ruby, stop, you're family now. You don't have your cut yet, but your man here has already made it law you're his."

Fuck. Great way to tell her. I wait for her to look over, but she doesn't. She just keeps listening to Shy talk.

"No one fucks with us or what's ours. We just need you to be prepared. We can't have you flipping out like you did today. You need to trust us and that we'll take care of you. You and your baby girl are under our protection now. We might live by our own laws, but they motherfucking work." He smiles.

Ruby nods her head as tears stream down her face.

"Okay, the last couple of things," Dallas chimes in with a smile. "One, obviously everything we're discussing here stays here and no more name dropping or shit like that. It's no one's business if anyone asks. The less you say, the better because hardly anyone but like six of us know about your man having money or his true name. The less attention we have, the better. Lastly," he says, getting serious. "That guy you call a friend, Sam... You need to cut all ties with him."

Now, this has my attention, because he hasn't told me this yet. Shy and Mac must be thinking the same thing as me, wondering what he's going to tell us.

Dallas continues, looking right at Ruby. "Yes, I hacked his shit too, something felt off, and I was right. The fucker has a couple of videos of you. He has pictures of you sleeping, like a straight-up stalker. I'm not sure if he's in love with you or more obsessed with you. I just know he's not right in the head either.

You should never, and I mean, never be alone with either one of them."

Hearing that last part has me tensing, as Ruby nods her head. "Oh, my God. He-he has videos, of me? What kind of videos?" Ruby asks, sounding nervous.

Everyone looks at Dallas, who turns to look at me. The second I see his eyes, I know. He has a video of them fucking. I take a deep breath closing my eyes, giving myself a minute to compose myself. Ruby must sense or understand the look we just had because she gasps, covering her mouth with her hand.

"No!"

The room goes silent.

"From what I can see, it looks like it was the night your ex shared you. I didn't watch the whole thing, but from what you've told us happened, I'm pretty sure it is. Unless you've been with him other times?" Dallas states calmly.

Ruby's hand is still over her mouth as she shakes her head no.

Dallas continues, "That's what I thought. From what I can tell without watching the full video, it looks like he took a few short videos from his phone. He hasn't done anything with them from what I can see, so they're probably for his own viewing."

Ruby has tears in her eyes as Mac curses under his breath. Slamming his hand on the table. "That fucker needs to have a talking to as well. Fuck that."

Shy speaks, "We'll deal with both of them accordingly. Brody and Sam being famous, makes it hard to just deal with them."

Ruby pulls herself together. "Thank you, Dallas, for letting me know. Just tell me what to do, how do I get those videos deleted and most of all, rid them from my life. I really hope all this will work to keep him away from me."

We all say together, "It will."

Dallas goes into depth about what information he has and

what we're going to send to him, that way Ruby isn't blindsided if he comes after her. Since our meeting the other night, we've all been working on what to say or do with Brody and how to go about it with Ruby. I've been too chicken shit to bring it up, so I guess her flipping out today was for the best. It forced all of us to sit down and go over every detail.

We discuss what she needs so we can put it in the demands. And figure out exactly how much stuff she has left down there, so we can get the move arranged. What started as a really fucked up fight ended with us having a plan.

The plan is to head down to LA right after Shy's birthday party that's coming up. Shy said the sooner, the better, and I couldn't agree more. It would give Brody enough time to get his shit together before we arrive and time for us to prepare for the trip as well. We end our meeting with Dallas, putting a tracker on her phone.

Now I can monitor all the calls and text messages. I won't let him hurt her anymore.

Mine.

14 | Waiting Game

Ruby

Since my little tantrum at the clubhouse, I've been shocked and a little overwhelmed. Going over all the stuff Brody's done these past few years is just insane. I knew he had a control issue with me and wasn't happy about sharing my time with Bella. He always made comments, like "if we had just a few more years together before having a baby." But for him to completely flip out and do the things he's done is beyond comprehension.

And, Quick is rich. That is just mind-boggling. I mean, I don't care if he is or not, but I have so many questions – the biggest one being what could have happened for him to leave it all? I know he'll tell me when he's ready, but it's consuming my thoughts. I'm itching to google his birth name, but after seeing what Dallas can do on a computer, I don't want to get caught snooping when I know he'll tell me.

My God and Sam… That motherfucker has videos of me. It took everything in my power not to text him or call him asking why. Dallas told me he would make sure they were deleted and lost forever. I ask him how if they were on his phone, but the guys told me it would be dealt with, so I let it go.

Dallas should be working for the government with how badass he is on the computer. The guy can hack any system and find out anything he wants to know. He sent over just part of, "the package" as he calls it. What he found on Brody is a shit ton of evidence, and all the fucked up crap he's done. Like hard concrete proof that could ruin him.

Brody, of course, stepped back from harassing me and got his parents involved. When I spoke to them, I was floored to find out they knew all about his bullshit. Brody cut all contact with me, only speaking to Bella or me through his parents. He's only spoken to Bella once and to be honest, I don't think he even cares. In his eyes, she ruined everything for him.

Who fucking thinks like that? It's his fucking child, not a fucking competition.

I guess now I know why they let me go so easy and didn't try to stop me when I decided to move out and divorce him. They knew what he'd been doing and me having Bella set him off. Thank God they love their grandchild enough to keep her from his craziness. I just wish they would've told me what had been going on the last few years of our marriage.

The worst part about all of this is, I can't vent to Izzy about any of this shit. She's still processing and trying to deal with everything that happened to her. I don't want to burden her with my drama while she's trying to heal. Plus, I can't tell her anything about what we talked about in the clubhouse and Quick's past. No one knows about it, and the last thing I want is to tell someone else.

I've been upset and feeling down. If it wasn't for me, none of these problems would be happening to Quick and the clubhouse. I said that to Quick when we got home that night, and he flipped out on me, telling me he has never wanted anything more than he wants us girls. I fell apart because he didn't just say me, he meant Bella too.

The bond they have already, in just the small amount of time we've been here in New York, makes me so happy. I just can't wait for this move and divorce to be over so we can get on with our lives.

We plan to leave after Shy's birthday bash this weekend. I'm not in the mood to party, but I'll hold it together. I know Izzy senses something is wrong, so I make sure to keep myself busy around her. She's been in the studio nonstop and staying with Gus at his place.

I'm pretty sure they know something happened between us,

they just don't know the extent of it. Knowing Izzy, she's probably trying to give Quick and I some time alone.

My phone rings, pulling me from my thoughts and see it's Quick. I smile, feeling my body heat with excitement – one thing's for sure, the man has me hook, line, and sinker. I love him.

"Hi, babe," I answer, cheerfully.

"Rube, just got out of our meeting, and I'm headed home, but I wanted to check in with you before I jump on the bike." Hearing him mention his Harley has my center throbbing.

I smile. "Hmm, that sounds fun."

He chuckles into the phone. "Firecracker, you miss being on the back of my bike?"

"Fuck yes, I miss it," I fire back.

"Well when we get to LA in a few days, I'll take you on a long ride along the coast," he says warmly igniting the fire inside me making me want more.

"Be safe but hurry home," I purr.

I hear his ignition roar to life, and I'm wet instantly.

"You feel that, baby. I'm coming for you." Quick growls into the phone, "I'm on my way."

I hang up totally giddy with excitement. I love the way he makes me feel. He has been practically living here with us, and Bella loves him. Speaking of Bella, I need to go check on her. She is a bit too quiet back in her room.

As I head down the hallway, I hear her talking to her babies. She loves her babies and is always playing dress up. I lean against the door frame watching my precious girl, playing with her back to me. She's putting two of her babies in bed, tucking them in like I do to her every night.

I giggle. "Whatcha doing, Bug?"

Bella snaps her head around to see me and smiles. "Hi, Momma. I put babies to bed. They go ni-night."

I'm laughing when my phone rings again. I answer it before the name pops up thinking it has to be Quick calling me back to say something sexy, he likes to get me all riled up before he gets home.

"Miss me already?" I answer with a laugh.

"You have no idea how much I miss you," a cold, deep, rough voice fires back.

Fear consumes me as I stand frozen in Bella's doorway. *Brody.*

I don't say anything. I don't know what to say.

"I know I'm not supposed to call or bug you anymore, but I wanted to talk to my girls." His voice is raw and void of any emotion.

I'm still shocked, not saying anything. I just stand there and watch Bella play with her babies.

"I know he isn't there. It's why I called. I wanted to talk to you alone. Do you know anything about your new lover boy? Well, I seem to be finding out a lot about him lately. See, I'm doing what he told me to do – I'm looking into him before I come to get what's mine."

I snap out of my stupor as rage builds inside me, overpowering my fear. He needs to stop this shit and let me go. "For fuck's sake, Brody, I'm not yours. We're over. Stop this madness, please."

"When we meet at the lawyer's, I want you to be alone. I want to show you a *package* I have on him." His voice dripping with hatred.

Tears start to fill my eyes. "Brody. Please stop."

Bella jumps up, yelling, "Who is that?"

I pull myself together and answer, "It's Daddy."

He then yells, "Fuck!" in my ear.

"I want to talk to Daddy." She beams and rushes over, so I bend down.

I tell him, "You need to talk to your daughter. I'm putting you on speaker."

Brody doesn't say anything, so I hit the speaker button.

Bella giggles, "Daddy?"

Silence. My heart speeds up praying he'll talk to her.

"My Bella Bug! Daddy misses you," he says into the phone, cheerful and bubbly, making her smile big.

"I miss you too. We come to see you," she says, twirling around excited.

They start chatting about her coming to visit and shit, but I tune them out as I try to hold it together. How can he sit here and fake being a dad? How can he go from vindictive to bubbly?

I hear the front door slam open, and I jump up startled. Bella screams, "Qwak's home. Yay. Qwak's home." Jumping up and down running out of her room, screaming Quick's name like she does every night when he comes home.

Oh shit.

I hear a string of cursing on the other end of the phone, as I take the phone off speaker, lifting it to my ear. I don't say anything, I just stand there and listen.

Brody is rambling noncoherent shit to himself. I don't think he's going to say anything else, so I say, "Well, I think I need to go now. I'll see you at the lawyer's office." I try to sound cheerful like he was just doing for Bella, but it's a bit shaky.

Within seconds, Quick rushes through the bedroom door with Gus following, both looking wind-blown and dangerous. Just the look in his eyes tells me he knows I'm on the phone with Brody. His hair's sticking out from under his bandana, and he looks like he's going to murder someone while holding Bella in his arms.

"Fuck you-you fucking bitch. I'll see you in a couple of days alright," he spits out before hanging up. Tears begin to fill my eyes again, but I fight them from falling as Quick grabs the phone from the side of my face.

Bella, not knowing what's going on, thinking the phone is still on speaker, keeps rambling, "Qwak, it's my daddy. Daddy?"

Quick lifts up the phone, looking to see if he hung up, as

Bella keeps jabbering. When she realizes he's not talking back, she says, "Daddy hung up, I didn't say goodbye." She looks sad, so Quick starts to tickle her, making her scream out in laughter.

He hugs her tight, giving her a kiss on the cheek, setting her down. "I need to talk to Momma, why don't you and Uncle Red play while Momma and I have an adult conversation," he says, grabbing my hand, pulling me into his enormous chest.

Gus picks Bella up, throwing her in the air. "What no love for Uncle Red?" Bella squeals in laughter as we leave them in her room, heading toward our room.

Our room?

When the bedroom door is closed, I say, "You got home fast."

I look into his wild eyes, and he answers, "I ran every light and broke a million traffic laws to get here. As soon as we headed out, my phone started vibrating. I pulled it out as soon as I got to a red light, when I saw the text from Dallas, letting me know he called you, we sped like demons to get here. Are you okay? What the fuck did the cunt have to say?"

I stand there willing the fire to ignite inside me to fuel my anger again, but all I feel is fear and dread. Like something bad is going to happen. The last time I felt like this Izzy was taken. I can't have anything happen to him – or Bella. It's me he wants.

"Ruby? Talk to me. You've got that look in your eyes again. What did he say?" Quick grabs my arms, giving me a slight shake.

God, he's gorgeous in a bad boy, fuck me 'til Tuesday kind of way. He's in worn-out blue jeans, a black hoodie under his black leather riding jacket and his cut, and a sexy as fuck bandana holding his hair back. I reach up to finger his hair that has curled up over his bandana from the wind.

Quick pulls me to him, gripping my chin forcing me to lock eyes with him and what I see is nothing but love and concern.

I smile. "Hi."

Quick's eyes soften as he leans down, placing a soft kiss on my lips before saying, "It's not your fault. You can tell me, whatever it is, it'll be okay. I'm here for you, Rube."

I close my eyes and take a deep breath. "He says he wants to meet with me alone at the lawyer's, that he has his own *package* on you for me to see. That he did what you said and looked into you before he came to get his girls."

Quick's body tenses never letting me go, hugging me tighter. I tell him about how I answered the phone thinking it was him, and what Brody said in return. How he knew Quick wasn't here, that's why he called. His reaction before Bella got on the phone and what he was saying when she took off yelling Quick because he came home. I tell him how worried I am that Brody heard Bella say his name, even though it sounds like she's saying quack like a duck. To my surprise, that makes him smile.

Just seeing him smile has me smiling. "What?" I ask wondering how he could be smiling right now. I thought he would be pissed off, ready to murder Brody, but here he is smiling.

"Nothing. Just that I love the fact she didn't give a shit about him and came running to me. I love her hellos each day," Quick says with a smile.

"She's pretty attached to you. I'm sure it's because you're in her life each and every day," I explain, knowing it's the truth. Bella has longed for a real male figure in her life. Brody's one month home and four gone isn't being a dad.

"Are you okay?" Quick asks again.

I nod my head. "It just took me off guard. When I yelled at him, it only fueled him to keep pushing."

"Come on. Let's go check on big Red and baby girl. I need to let him and everyone know what's going on. The guys are waiting to hear what happened," Quick says, letting me go to open the door.

Gus is lying on the floor in all his leathers with baby blankets covering half his body. Both Quick and I bust up laughing when we enter her room. "Look, Momma. Uncle Red is my baby." Bella's voice is filled with excitement.

Gus smiles with his hand resting behind his head. He just lies there completely content with her doing as she pleases. I know Gus needs to go and talk to Quick, so I say, "Bella let Uncle Red get up. He needs to talk to Quick and Momma real fast, and then I promise we'll play, okay?"

Bella pouts while taking the blankets off him, and he lies there waiting patiently for her to finish before picking her up, throwing her in the air. "I promise Auntie and I will take you for some ice cream soon too."

"Yay, ice cream," Bella says as he puts her down.

I tell Bella to stay in her room and play so we can have adult time in the kitchen. When I finally make it to the kitchen, Quick has taken his cut and leather jacket off while Gus takes a seat on a stool next to the island.

"Ya, alright?" Gus asks when I enter the kitchen.

I nod, grabbing three beers from the fridge. "It just surprised me."

"I wish I woulda known sooner. I just got word tonight he's been harassing ya," Gus says, sounding kind of hurt and mad.

I hand him a beer and try to explain, "No one knew until recently. I tried to handle it myself, and when Quick saw the texts, he kind of took over."

Gus laughs. "Ya I woulda too. The fuck face needs a good whoopin' sounds like."

Gus turns to Quick. "Look, I know there's more to all of this and when yer ready ye'll tell me. I know we've a lot goin' on dealing with Izzy's shite but don't think for one second I wouldn't be there for you if ya need me."

Quick nods his head, bringing his beer up for a drink.

"Where is Izzy? I haven't heard or seen her all day?" I asked, changing the subject.

Gus' face lights up. "She's been in the studio all day. I'm on me way up to Luc's now to get her." He stands up, slamming the rest of his beer. "Okay, so we'll see you tomorrow at the club."

Shocked, I asked, "Izzy is going to come out both nights?"

Gus smile, "I'ma make her. Big things this weekend, she's not missing it."

I laugh. Giving him a nod, I lift my beer taking a long pull from it thinking... *This should be interesting.*

15 | Engagement Pary
Quick

"It's about fucking time you two took the next step. I couldn't be happier for you, brother," I say, patting Shy on the back.

Shy smirks. "I wanted to ask her months ago, but with so much shit going on around here, there was never a good time."

"He should've asked her years ago, not months," Mac says, walking up, waving to the bartender, turning around to look at the girls dancing.

After Shy proposed, Ruby and the girls pulled Ginger to the dance floor where they've been most the night. The White Wolf Lounge is packed with friends and family here to celebrate the announcement.

"Quick, did you lose your bounce or your balls? You're not out there bouncing around like you usually are," Mac teases.

"I think he lost his balls. He's turned into a pussy since he started dating Firecracker," Dallas laughs, walking up.

I scoff. "Nah, I used to bounce around all the time picking up pussy – now… I'm happy just watching *one* pussy and counting down the minutes until *I'm in* that pussy." Pointing at my girl.

Ruby jumps around laughing, and I smile, feeling happy to see her enjoying herself. She's been so worried about going home and dealing with Brody. She must sense me staring at her because she turns around with a smile giving me a wink. I pucker my lips in a kiss, making her laugh.

"You've got it bad for my girl, don't cha?" Izzy giggles.

I don't take my eyes off of Ruby when I answer, "Damn straight I do. She's mine."

"Good. Can I talk to you?" Izzy's voice changes, sounding concerned, which draws my attention away from Ruby. I look over, seeing Shy and the guys moved down the bar chatting with other members. It's just Izzy and me standing here.

I smile. "Sure, what's up?"

Izzy leans back against the bar, looking off in the direction I was a few minutes ago. "I wanted to say thank you. Ruby just told me about Brody and how you've stood up to him." She pauses. Izzy tries to hide her emotions, but I can see through them. She's upset.

I grab my beer, taking a long swig. "Izzy, I'm in it for the long haul. I'm not letting her go. And that piece of shit will never hurt her again, verbally or any other way. She's mine, and I protect what's mine." My voice came out harsher than I wanted, but when her face relaxes, so does mine.

Izzy turns to look me in the eyes. "She's my life. I can't express how much I need her, and it makes me so happy she found you. Quick, you are a good man, and I just wanted to say thank you. Brody's a piece of shit and just be careful. He's got a lot of money, and he uses it to his advantage."

Hearing her say that, I know Ruby has kept my secret about my identity. Something pulls in my chest. Ruby needs Izzy just as much as Izzy needs her. It's probably killing Ruby not to be able to talk to her about everything that's going on.

"Iz, there is a lot you don't know about me. Things no one does, and soon it will all be clear, but I can promise you one thing. Nothing – and I mean nothing, will happen to her or that beautiful baby girl if I can help it. No amount of money will give him an advantage over me," I answer with a firm, determined voice.

She smiles, hugging me, and I give her a hug back.

"Brother, you'd better get your hands off *me one*," Gus growls from behind me.

Izzy laughs, releasing me. "Easy Red, I was thanking him for standing up to Brody."

Gus rounds me, pulling her into his arms. "I don't care. He doesn't need to have his hands on ya."

I laugh, taking a drink of my beer before lifting my hands in surrender.

A loud shriek sounds next to us, making us all turn. Storm, Ginger's aunt, and Mac's mom, hops off the stool, and yells, "Ah shit. This is my song." Shaking her ass as she makes her way to the dance floor.

Laughter erupts around the bar as all eyes are on Storm shaking her ass to "Rump Shaker" by Wreckx-N-Effect.

Izzy beams with excitement. "That's my cue." She follows Storm to the dance floor where Ginger's bent over, holding her stomach from laughing so hard, as she watches her aunt bust a move on the dance floor.

"Ma," Mac yells.

Another commotion sounds across the bar. "That's my girl. Get it, girl. Lish is coming."

All the men start whistling, making catcalls as Hawk's ol' lady comes barreling through the crowd, making her way to the dance floor too. Bear and Hawk stay seated at the bar laughing and shaking their heads at their ol' ladies.

I watch as the older ladies bust a move shaking their asses to the song with all the other girls cheering them on.

Absorbing all the goodness around me, I can't help but thank the gods that today everyone is here and happy. I couldn't be happier for my friends and their engagement. I don't know what tomorrow holds, but whatever it is, we'll deal with it.

All the boys are watching and laughing when I see Shy out of the corner of my eye. He answers his phone looking at me. I give him an understanding head nod. When he ends the call, he tilts his head to the back office area, and I nod again in acknowledgment. Shy nudges Mac and Dallas as he gets off his bar stool, not drawing too much attention. I finish my beer before getting up to follow, looking toward Tiny and Worm to fall in behind me as I make my way to the back of the lounge.

Along the way, we pick up Wolfe, Cash, Hawk, and Bear. Once we're all in the office, Shy says, "Just got the call from Whiz and everything's set up for us. They're keeping an eye on our little problem, and when we get there, we'll start to deal with our new business down there."

Shy looks at me. "You, Ruby, and Bella will fly out earlier than expected with Chain and Jammer." Shy looks over to Wolfe. "Then we'll go down a few days later."

"Does Giselle know we're all coming and what our plan is?" Wolfe asks.

"Whiz is the one who set all this up. None of us have been in contact with her. She knows we're coming to help but not the full extent," Shy explains.

I step forward and say, "I've never met her but have heard enough about her from Whiz and Ruby to know she's not one who's easily persuaded."

"Does your girl know anything?" Wolfe asks, folding his arms over his chest.

I shake my head. "Nothing. I don't want to add to her plate. I'll deal with that once I see how her aunt is toward me."

"Okay, well everything is set, so once Dallas sets up our flights, we'll let you know. That way one of the prospects can pick us up," Shy tells me.

"Alright, now let's get back to the party. Hopefully, Ma is done bumping and grinding on the dance floor," Mac says, grabbing his dad on the shoulder.

Bear chuckles. "Boy, leave your ma alone. She's just letting loose."

As we file out of the office, my phone vibrates.

Whiz: All good on my end. C U in 2.

Quick: Just met with Shy – all good on our end.

Sliding my phone back into my pocket, I hear "Feelin' Myself" by Mac Dre start to play and laugh to myself.

They want to see my old crazy ass. Well, here we go.

I start to nod my head to the beat and turn around, gripping my cut and I smile. Mac and Dallas bust up laughing as I turn for the dance floor, throwing my hands out – rapping the song. I grab my cock, dancing toward my girl. The guys start yelling my name as I get hyphy.

Izzy and Ginger see me first and both yell in excitement as I bounce around, rapping. When Ruby turns around, she starts laughing as I approach her, gripping myself. I lick my lips, grabbing her around the waist, thrusting my pelvis against hers.

Ruby's head falls back, laughing hard. I turn to see all my boys have followed me to the dance floor. All of them getting hyphy, throwing their hands in the air. We take over the dance floor as the guys form a circle with the girls surrounding them. I break away from Ruby, laughing and join in with my boys as we rap the words, acting out the song. The dance floor fills up, crowding around us as we all dance to the song.

The crowd gets loud, singing along. With an arm in the air, I move it up and down to the music as I grip Ruby around the waist, pulling her to me.

When the next song from "Get Ur Freak On" by Missy Elliot mixes in, the girls get loud, taking over moving against the men.

Firecracker is in full form now, grinding up against me as she shakes her ass. Smiling down at her, one of my hands grips her ass and the other slides down her leg, hiking it up against my hip. I nuzzle my face into her neck.

"We keep going like this, and I'm taking you to the back."

I pull my face back to see her reaction, and I'm met with glazed-over eyes filled with desire. She bites her lip with a smile. I smash my mouth against hers, demanding entrance. Our tongues dance as we thrust against each other on the dance floor. My cock is rock hard against my jeans, almost busting a seam.

Ruby moans, threading her fingers into my hair tugging hard. I break the kiss. "Fuck."

She giggles. "You okay, babe?"

I smile down at my girl. "Uh-huh. Better if I was filling this greedy little pussy with my cock." I lean down, giving her another passionate kiss.

"Just A Lil Bit," by 50 Cent begins to play, and we both break the kiss, laughing. Looking over at Mac, I think about when he danced to this song the first weekend she was here. Mac's dancing with some girl, and of course, he's singing to her. I turn back to Ruby, slipping both of my hands down, cupping her ass.

"This ass of yours has me hard as fuck. I could watch you all day and night." Pulling her closer, gripping her ass cheeks hard.

I give her a quick kiss. "I love seeing you this happy."

Ruby smiles. "I am happy. You make me happy."

I kiss her again, needing to be inside her, I start to move us off the dance floor.

Ruby moans into my mouth, gripping my neck with one hand, she slides her other hand down my chest over my stomach, slowly moving it over my hard cock, palming it.

A guttural moan erupts out of me.

I move us to the music as we exit the dance floor. My body ignites, feeling her soft body melt into mine.

Ruby breaks the kiss giggling. "What are you doing?"

I smile, giving her a soft kiss murmuring, "Just a little bit."

She drops her head back laughing at me, reciting the song. I suck her neck with a growl.

Just a little bit, my ass, I'm going to be balls deep in this pussy.

16 | Club DazZelle

Quick

"Where's your girl?" Whiz asks when I stroll through the clubhouse doors, followed by Chain and Jammer.

"Just dropped her at Club DazZelle," I answer, shaking his hand giving him a half hug.

"Are you fucking serious? We could have met there. Fuck, brother," Whiz exclaims excitedly.

I scoff, "Yeah but then we wouldn't have gotten any club business done. Let's get this over with so we can all go back there and hang out."

These past two days have been too easy. It has me on edge. We came a couple of days earlier than expected just in case Brody wanted to surprise us. Only five of us flew down here, while the rest of the club will be here in a few days. We got a hotel room, and I had the prospects scope out the area.

Once we knew all was good, Ruby contacted Brody's parents surprising them she was here early. They said they would meet her somewhere and pick up Bella, so we didn't have to see him. The exchange went good, and now we're kidless for a couple of days. When she goes to the lawyers, she'll get Bella back.

"Let's do this. Pussy is calling my name's brother," Whiz's voice booms loudly.

"We've picked up a few more bikes," Whiz's vice president, Cue, informs me.

"Good, I can' t stand being caged up in this beautiful fucking weather," I reply, itching to be on a bike to let off some steam.

I follow Whiz into his clubroom pulling out a chair, "So what did you find out about the store owner?" I ask Whiz. He's been looking into Ruby's Aunt's problem. She's been wanting to expand her club, making it half a nightclub and half a strip club.

But the owner next door has been hassling her trying to strong-arm her out of the area.

"Fucker's got money. He's the only one that wants her out of the area. Everyone else loves Giselle and the girls." Cue explains.

"Plus, George her co-partner of the club, is old as fuck and hasn't been bringing to the table what he used too," Whiz explains. Dallas already informed us about her partner that's why we were really here to talk to Giselle.

I nod my head letting him know I'm listening. "Well, we need to sit down with Giselle before we do anything. She's supposed to be there later so we can try to meet with her then. Ruby said she had some business elsewhere when I asked to meet her," I say, thinking about my talk with Ruby earlier.

I'm relieved that the conversation went as good as it did. I was worried Ruby wouldn't want us to get involved with her Aunt, but she said it would be good for her, that money has been tight with her partner not holding up his end of the business. Luckily for her, she's got the majority of her money running her high profile escort service.

Everyone nods their head. Whiz' SGT at Arms goes into details about the store owner next door. His daily routine, security and everything we need to know. Things we couldn't find out on a computer.

We go over what Dallas had told us and what intel they had and make a plan. An hour later ten of us are strolling through the front door of Club DazZelle.

The place is huge with a long bar on one side of the building facing the full stage. In the middle of the room, they have two small circular stages with poles. In the far back, there are enclosed booths, but the windows are closed with drapes. Probably for private parties or lap dances.

I make my way to the bar looking around for my girl. Whiz's men spread out heading for their choice of women. The two small stages have blonde bitches, and the big stage has a brunette flying around on the pole. I don't spend too much time looking at the dancers because my eyes are only looking for one bitch.

My bitch.

"So, I hear your girl can dance," Whiz says, handing me a beer.

I take the beer and smile. "Well growing up around here I'm sure it was hard not to learn a trick or two."

"You think she'll dance while she's here?"

Lowering my drink, I swallow and say, "Yeah, my girl loves to dance. I'm sure she'll dance one of these days."

Whiz turns toward me, "You don't freak the fuck out?"

I chuckle, "Fuck no! It makes me hard as fuck and knowing she's going home with me to ride my cock only fuels me more."

Whiz shakes his head taking a draw from his own beer. "I don't think I could handle it—"

I interrupt him, "It's not like she does it for a living. I don't think I would be able to handle her doing it when I wasn't around."

Whiz laughs. "Fuckin' A, exactly my point. I like looking and fucking them, but making one my bitch, not happening."

I laugh, turning to face the stage. I lean back against the bar. I watch as topless women walk about serving drinks, but I don't see my girl. Feeling uneasy I pull my phone out to text her.

Quick: Where ya at? I'm here at the bar.

Hitting send I scan the club again but still no sign of her. I'm about ready to text her again when my phone vibrates.

Ruby: I'm backstage with the girls and my auntie. Be out in a sec.

She ends her text with a kiss emoji. I relax knowing she's okay and texts back.

Quick: Take your time. I'm at the bar drinking with the boys.

I turn back to the bar downing my beer, flagging the cute

little bartender down for another. I'm surrounded by Whiz, and his boys and my prospects are to the side watching. That way no bitch can bug me. I see Whiz motion for someone, and when I turn around, I see a short, muscular girl with lots of curves saunter over. "Whiz, baby, how are you?"

Whiz leans back against the bar spreading his legs so the bitch can slip between them. She slides in rubbing her body up against his cock, as she racks her hands up his torso. He wraps his hands around her waist, "Dizzy, you're looking fine as usual?"

She gives him a kiss on the cheek resting her hands on his biceps smiling. He adds, "You working today?"

She's dressed in black pleather pants with a gold bikini top and matching gold heels. The bitch is fine as fuck. She glances over to me, catching me checking her out and smiles, "Who's your friend?"

Whiz laughs and is about ready to introduce me when I hear, "He's mine Dizzy."

My eyes shoot up from the girl to see my firecracker strolling my direction with a very attractive woman with her. It must be her aunt, but fuck me, she looks like she could be her sister.

Goddamn. Her Aunt is hot as fuck.

I smile spreading my legs so my girl can claim what's hers. Dizzy laughs, still watching me while caressing Whiz's arms, "Mmm–mmm he is one fine ass man. No wonder you left the dickhead."

Whiz and I both laugh, but my eyes are locked on my girl.

"Firecracker," I state.

"Quick." She replies in her sexy as fuck voice. My cock swells just hearing her call my name.

"Okay love birds," The woman says next to us.

Whiz clears his throat snapping us out of our heated stare. Ruby smiles, "Auntie, this is Quick. Quick, this is my Auntie, Giselle."

I turn to greet the lady, but goddamn she's even prettier up close. She radiates dominance and power. The bitch has me wanting to submit. Damn, no wonder why she's ranked one of the best Dominatrix around.

The guys are going to love this shit.

"It's nice to finally meet you," I say, reaching a hand out to greet her while sliding my other hand around Ruby's waist pulling her closer to me. Giselle watches my movement with caution. Raising an eyebrow, she shakes my hand and smiles. "The pleasures all mine. My niece speaks highly of you and your friends."

We release hands, and I nod my head, "As she does you. I think we're both lucky to have her in our lives."

She nods her head but then turns to the bartender and snaps her fingers. The bartender is there in seconds, "Yes Madam?"

"Set up number two for me and my guests. Open the view so we can see the show and get my friends whatever they want, it's on me," she says to the girl.

"Yes, Madam."

When Ruby's aunt looks back to us, she smiles an award-winning smile. "Here follow me to one of our booths where it's not so loud, so we can talk and still see the show.

Whiz nudges me. I nod my head, "Thank you. We'd love to."

I grip Ruby pulling her to me kissing her briefly before standing up. I nod my head letting my prospects know I'm on the move. They follow with wide eyes, and I know what they're thinking. Ruby's aunt is one fucking hot bitch.

Ruby is walking in front of me holding my hand, I tug her back and whisper into her ear. "Um... yeah didn't tell me your aunt was hot as fuck. Jesus Christ, she could be your sister."

She laughs, "My bad. I thought you'd seen pictures of her."

"Yeah, but I thought they were like old ones. She looked so young in them and damned they don't do her justice." I praise.

Ruby giggles.

I swat her ass moving her forward. This is going to be interesting, to say the least. My brothers are going to shit their pants when they see her.

"Now you know what I meant when I said the bitch could dominate me any fuckin' day." Whiz whispers, next to me.

I laugh. *No shit.*

Once we file into the room, I'm shocked at how big the circular room is, it would hold up to twenty people easily. A booth lines the walls with small circular tables and of course a stripper pole in the middle of the room. Three topless ladies come in opening the curtains letting us see out over the whole club. I just stand there looking out at all the people.

"Do you like it?" Ruby asks, next to me.

"Goddamn, don't show Lish and Storm this place. If they come out here and check this club out, they'll want to do a remodel once they see this shit." I laugh thinking about Hawk and the members, who all practically live at the strip club that Lish owns in West Virginia.

Looking out I see a group of twenty men all lining the main stage. Probably a bachelor party but what I don't see is any real security here. I look around more but only see two guys at the front door, and they look big but definitely wouldn't be able to handle it if a fight broke out. I say over my shoulder, "What kind of security do you have here besides those two fuckers?" I point to the front door.

Giselle walks over to stand next to us, looking out toward the club.

She answers, "We used to have more guys but with my partner not here as much, neither are his men. They stay with him, so we need to get more. That's what George was in charge of. I took care of the women, and he took care of security. Giselle turns to face me, "Whiz and his men have been helping out a lot these past few months."

I hear Whiz from somewhere behind me. "Anything for you, Mistress."

Fucking pussy.

I smile.

"Well, when my club arrives, we should sit down and talk," I say, turning toward her. I pull Ruby into my side giving her a squeeze. Giselle eyes my movement again, watching me with her niece and smiles.

"Madam…" a waitress calls out from the door.

Giselle turns and excuses herself from the room. Ruby just laughs slipping her hands around my waist. "See she needs you."

My phone vibrates as I kiss the top of her head. Pulling it from my pocket, I move us to the couch so we can face out toward the stage. I see the text is from Dallas, but it's a group text.

Dallas: Prospect says the aunt is hot as fuck.

I look over toward the door where the prospects are keeping watch. Chain looks over and smiles. *Fucker.*

I text back.

Quick: Bitch is hot…

Cash: How hot? Pictures were okay.

I laugh because the photos we saw she was more than okay. I text back.

Quick: Pictures don't do shit for her. She's hot as fuck and will make you drop to your knees and scream like a bitch.

I can see someone is texting, so I wait.

Mac: Goddamn it. I'm heading into a meeting now with a hard-on. She can make me scream.

Ruby hands me a whiskey, and I clink glasses with her before taking a drink. She sees me reading my texts and ask, "The boys talking shit?"

Looking up with a smirk, I say "Yeah, they're getting riled up over your aunt."

Ruby leans into my chest. "They'll have their work cut out for them if they think they can take her."

I chuckle but agree with her that Giselle is going to give them a run for their money. She isn't some small town slut who dances and fucks.

I look down to my phone and see Wolfe has chimed in.

Wolfe: No one touches the aunt. Mac, meetings in ten minutes. Pull your heads out of the pussy.

That's Wolfe for you – all business. I've seen him with bitches but never the same one twice. He's always on the down low too, never wanting Ginger to see him with another woman. I guess since Shy, and they all moved to New York, the West Virginia clubhouse has loosened up a bit, since all the kids are gone. Obviously, Storm has been letting loose now that Mac isn't around.

All the men reply with their goodbyes as I slip the phone into my cut.

"Is everything okay?" Ruby asks, lifting her drink to those perfect lips of hers.

I smile, keeping my eyes on her now wet lips and I nod my head.

"Whatcha looking at?" she purrs.

"Thinking about those beautiful wet lips of yours and how I want them around my cock," my voice thick with desire, has her eyes flashing with excitement.

"Hmm, that sounds fun!" she licks her lips biting her bottom lip with a moan.

My dick thickens beneath my jeans drawing her attention, as her eyes lower to my crotch. I'm about ready to haul her to the bathroom or a dark hallway when an amused voice says, "Going somewhere?"

Looking up I find Ruby's aunt smiling down at us with one eyebrow raised in amusement.

Fuck. Not now.

Ruby beams up at her aunt with pink cheeks from being caught drooling over my cock.

"Naw, we're not going anywhere, but I was thinking about taking this sweet, silky mouth of your niece's and putting my cock in it," I confess, getting a smack from Ruby and an almost shocked look from her aunt.

"Quick!" Ruby exclaims.

I chuckle, tugging my girl closer to me.

Giselle sits down next to me, which makes me feel weird, so I shift closer to my girl.

Giselle smiles, "I like you, Quick."

Facing her aunt, I smile and say, "Yeah, that's good seeing as I'm going to be in your niece's life from now on – meaning, for a very long time. So, it would make things hard if ya didn't."

Ruby takes a long drink, finishing it she places it on the table. Giselle just smiles at me. Those eyes of hers are always watching, and I don't take my eyes off hers, letting her know I'm watching her as well.

"I'm glad. She needs someone like you."

I interrupt her, "Someone like me? Care to explain?"

She chuckles, "If you wouldn't have interrupted me I would."

Ruby stiffens next to me as I raise my own eyebrow at her, not saying anything.

"As I was saying, I'm glad she has someone like you, to take care of her, cherish her and look at her like she's your whole world," her aunt leans back against the booth.

When I don't say anything, she continues, "I've been watching you since you've been in my club, you hold yourself well, you haven't touched or been touched by anyone. You surround yourself with men, not letting anyone including women near you. But most of all, you don't have wondering eyes. Instead, you only have eyes for my niece. You make sure everyone in the room knows you two are together by always holding her close. You make it clear neither of you is available. Very possessive of her and I like that." She smiles, breaking eye contact with me when a topless woman walks up with a drink for her.

I squeeze Ruby, not taking my attention off her aunt.

"Well, no offense but no one compares to your niece. Don't get me wrong I look, shit you have some fine ass women working here but anything I would say about a bitch, I'd tell my girl. I don't hide shit. I protect what's mine, and she's my only concern," I explain, letting her know no one has my dicks attention but her niece and that I'll protect her till I die.

Giselle smiles, "Good, now let's talk about what you can do for me? How can you help me?"

Jesus Christ this bitch don't fuck around.

I chuckle.

"Well, I think we should maybe wait for the others to join this conversation, don't you?"

"No. I trust you. If I make a deal, it will be with you. *Since you will be in my life, as you say for a very long time,*" her voice is serious with a hint of sarcasm.

For the first time, I look away from Giselle to look at my girl, who's smiling at both of us. She's quiet, which isn't like her, but I guess she's letting us get to know each other. I smile back, wondering if this is a test. Something seems off but searching Ruby's eyes, I don't see anything but happiness.

I turn back to her aunt, who I can't read for shit, so I ask, "what kind of deal are you looking to make with us?" I don't know what she's asking, we have a lot of business we could help her with, and I don't know what Ruby knows, so I play stupid.

She tilts her head back and laughs a full belly laugh. Goddamn, this bitch is stunning. Watching her, I see so much of Ruby in her. I wonder what her mom looks like. I take another sip of my drink, waiting for her to reply.

She laughs, "Seriously Rube. He's awesome. Your mom will change her mind and love him once she meets him."

What the fuck!

I pause, watching Giselle – watching me, analyzing, seeing how I'll react to every little comment.

This bitch is really testing me.

When I feel Ruby tense next to me, I snap my head toward my girl with questioning eyes. Ruby's smile vanishes giving her aunt a murderous look. Ruby doesn't talk about her mother. All I know is she's a roadie and dates some guy in a band.

I'm about to ask if she's okay, but Ruby turns her stunning golden eyes on me and smiles apologetically. "What my aunt means is my mom will love you. She just doesn't know anything about you. She wasn't happy about me leaving Brody, and we got into a fight. I haven't spoken with her since. She thinks I was making a huge mistake. So, in other words, she didn't want me to leave his fame and money."

Smiling, I lean in giving Ruby a quick kiss. When I pull back, I see a spark ignite in her eyes. *There's my firecracker.*

Hearing Giselle behind me say, "You have my approval, so again, let's talk protection and other things you can help me with."

I place another quick kiss on her lips and clear my throat, turning back to face her aunt. "No offense but I would need Shy, my president and brothers to be involved in these deals we make." I pause, looking at Ruby for a split second and then back to Giselle. "I'm here to help you in any way we can – some things my club will want to discuss in private. I'm here to move your niece and her daughter back to New York with me. I'm here to deal with all the problems we might have down here but know this – I have nothing but the best interest for you and your club. I trust my club and the Saints to do anything and everything in our power to help protect you. You have my word. You're family to my girl, and I protect what is mine and those they love," my voice's stern, letting her know I'm serious and for a split second her aunt drops her guard, letting me see something *is* wrong – scared or worried but whatever it is – it was a sign she does need our help. The woman just probably doesn't want to ask or let her guard down – just like her niece.

Damn these stubborn, independent, headstrong women.

"Thank you. That makes me feel good, and we do have a lot to discuss but no matter what or with who, I want my niece involved." Giselle looks to Ruby with love and respect. She says, to her niece, "I don't keep anything from her, and I won't start now."

Ruby reaches across me grabbing her aunts' hand within hers, while I look back and forth between the two beautiful women, vowing right then and there I wouldn't let anything happen to either of them.

Yeah, this is going to get interesting.

17 | Not Again
Quick

"Let's ride Rube," I whisper into her ear.

We've been hanging out here at Club DazZelle most the evening. I've met most of the girls and damn they're all fine and in all different shapes and sizes, but I need to feel the wind in my face and my bitch at my back. I've been itching to ride.

Ruby smiles, saying giddy, "Yes. God, yes."

I swat her ass to get up, "I'ma head out for a ride along the coast."

Whiz and the men all agree. We say our goodbyes and leave more than enough to cover all our drinks. Even though Giselle said it was on her when she left for a meeting a bit ago, I want to make sure she knew we aren't here for anything free. It's all business. We say our goodbyes and head out to the bikes.

I'm sitting on the bike when my phone vibrates.

Shy: 911 all members clubhouse.

My heart stops.

No fucking way. Not again.

I look over, and both prospects have the same look as me.

"Fuck." I roar.

Standing up, I dial Shy – no answer.

"Motherfucker," I yell. *Pick up.*

Ruby asks concerned, "What's wrong."

I dial Mac – no answer.

Next, I call Dallas – no answer.

"Christ, someone pick up the fucking phone," I say to myself as I pace in circles.

I dial Gus next – no answer.

When I dial Worm, he picks up on the third ring, and I hear

motors revving in the background. I yell, "What the fuck happened?"

Worm takes a deep breath, "I'm just pulling up to the clubhouse. Let me get the 411, and I'll call you back."

Before he can hang up I say, "No one is answering their phones. Call me back."

"I got you, brother."

I end the call as I turn to face several eyes locked on me.

Fuck!

I look to Whiz, standing close to Ruby with Chain and Jammer on her other side. I explain to everyone that we all got a 911 text, club-wide to meet at the clubhouse. Meaning something bad happened, and they need everyone there. Just like they did when Izzy was taken, and Gus was in the hospital.

Back when Dallas picked up right away telling me which flight to catch home and that it was bad. This time no one is answering. This is bad. I feel it in my bones. Club rules, you get a 911 text you drop anything and everything, the club has an emergency.

Chain and Jammer are pacing themselves texting other members trying to get ahold of someone, but they don't get any answer either.

My phone vibrates, and I almost drop the fucker.

Worm: We've been hit again – call from land.

Shit. My burners are at the hotel.

Rushing to my bike I announce, "I need a burner."

Whiz calls out, "Clubhouse. I've got plenty and more privacy."

We all nod in agreement. Ruby jumps on the back of my bike looking scared. We fly through the street in a matter of seconds.

Please God let them all be okay. Why the fuck does this happen when I leave? Fuck!

Whiz and Cue fly in front of me leading the fastest way to

the clubhouse. In a matter of minutes, we're walking into the main clubhouse, as I pull Ruby behind me.

Whiz yells at the prospect behind the bar to throw him a burner. When he does, Whiz hands it to me, telling me to use his office. Grabbing the phone, I motion for Chain to watch Ruby. Giving her a kiss, I tell her I'll be right back, before turning to follow Whiz.

I dial Worm.

"You good?" Worm answers roughly.

"What the fuck? When's my flight home?" panicked and worried about who it could be now.

"Don't think you are. Shy told me to hold everyone where they are until further notice."

"Who the fuck was hit?" I demand

"It's the girl again, but she's okay. One brother is gone. D was hit," Worm tries to explain without saying too much over the phone. It's loud in the background, like a bunch of people are talking.

D– for Dallas has been hit, meaning shot. Brother gone means dead. Who was dead? Fuck, please don't be Gus. Fuck and Izzy... Oh shit, Izzy was taken again.

"Goddamnit!" I yell, just as the door flies open with a furious Ruby and both prospects behind her.

"Please God tell me it wasn't G that's gone?" I say, holding my breath for him to reply. Feeling all the blood rush out of my face.

"Naw, N and D were with her." Worm answers. *Nick, Jesus Christ.*

"You said the girl's okay?" I ask, double checking.

"Yes. Shy will give you the details. He said to hold it down until he can explain. Try calling his burner in ten minutes. I gotta go." Worm hangs up.

I'm in shock as the call ends and I lower my phone.

159

Ruby is frantic, "The girl what? Is it Izzy? She's not answering. What the fuck's going on?"

Chain and Jammer both ask what happened.

I shake my head, "Something happened back home with Izzy. Nick's dead and Dallas' been hurt. I don't know where Gus is, but he said he wasn't with them. I have to call Shy's burner in ten minutes."

Ruby's eyes go wide, throwing a hand over her mouth as she starts to cry. I make my way to her, but she snaps out of it grabbing her phone, frantically dialing someone – who? I have no idea. When the call goes to voicemail, she dials again. Chain and Jammer are both in shock, probably trying to wrap their head around hearing our fellow brother, Nick, is gone.

Jammer snaps out of it first, asking, "Fuck, when are we flying back?"

Shaking my head, I answer, "I don't know. He said he didn't think we were, that Shy said for everyone to stay put until further notice and he would explain."

I turn and see Ruby dialing another number.

"Finally. It's Ruby. What happened?" Ruby blurts into the phone.

Silence. All eyes are glued to Ruby.

"Mia, please," Ruby begs as tears stream down her face. She stands there frozen, listening to whatever Mia is saying.

"Oh, my God," she whispers, placing her free hand over her mouth.

Everyone's hanging on to her every word.

"Okay. Please, tell her to call me. I'll text her right now. Thank you so much, Mia," Ruby says, before hanging up.

She's white as a ghost when she looks up, tears streaming down her face. "Miguel tricked Izzy into coming to her old place. The men were all in a meeting at the clubhouse when it happened. Dallas, Nick, and Trey went with her. Four dead bodies. Izzy's banged up pretty bad, but she's okay. Dallas is in surgery with multiple gunshot wounds. Everyone's at the hospital."

"We need to get home," I explain. She nods her head.

Fifteen minutes later I'm calling Shy, and he answers on the first ring sounding exhausted, "Brother."

My voice comes out thick with emotions, "Fuck. Talk to me."

Shy takes a deep breath. "You in a good place to talk?"

I nod my head, then realize he can't see me, and reply, "Yeah."

"Nick's down. Police and FBI are all over it since it happened at her old building. Fucker took out her old landlady. Dallas took multiple shots to his body protecting Izzy. He's still in surgery."

"We'll catch the first flight back," I say.

"No. The threat here is over. Miguel and his brother are dead. We need to handle that situation down there. Everyone is safe now. We just need to deal with Nick's stuff, but that won't be for a few weeks since it's all under investigation. Wolfe and everyone agreed to keep with our plans. This deal needs to be done, and your girl needs to deal with her shit, so you can move her back here. The faster we get the shit down there handled the faster we get home. Move forward with the neighbor and partner as we planned. See what you can get started before we get there, keep me informed, and I'll keep you posted once Dallas is out of surgery," Shy explains.

"How's Gus holding up? He's not answering his phone."

"He's in with Izzy being checked out. We have Wolfe and his men here, plus Luc and Beau's men. We got this end covered." Shy voice is stern, but you can hear the stress of today's event wearing on him.

"Okay. Keep me posted. Tell Gus to call me when he can.

Ruby's losing her shit over here." I explain, looking at Ruby pace around me.

"You got it, brother," Shy says before hanging up.

I relay what Shy told me to everyone.

Three hours later, we've talked to everyone including Izzy. Ruby was getting ready to book a flight home, but when I finally spoke with Gus, he was with Izzy, so he put her on the phone, so Ruby could hear her voice.

They both told us to stay here and deal with our shit so we can come home. Once Ruby heard Izzy's voice she felt better. We just got word Dallas made it out of surgery, but he's still in recovery. We're riding back to the hotel to get some sleep, with Chain and Jammer following us, in the SUV we rented.

Pulling into the parking lot, I see a sleek black Mercedes-Benz GLE similar to Ruby's parked outside our hotel. When Ruby's stiffens behind me, her grip tightening around my waist, I know it's Brody.

Motherfucker. This night keeps getting better and better.

Once I park and kill the engine, Ruby jumps off the bike pulling her helmet off.

"Quick, let me handle this, please." You can hear the panic in her voice, so I give her a nod because I want my girl to feel powerful enough to stand up to him. But, damn I could use a fight right about now, with everything that's happened tonight I'm so pissed off, that I could use someone to release my anger on.

Ruby turns around just as the driver door opens and our SUV pulls up. When the bastard gets out, he looks to the blacked-out windows, then to me and back to the SUV, realizing he's blocked in.

I smile. *The fucker is nervous. Good, he should be.*

"I don't want any trouble. I'm just here to talk," Brody says, loud enough for God himself to hear.

"Shut the fuck up Brody. You don't need everyone hearing

our business. What do you want? Where's Bella? You're supposed to be with her." Ruby yells not moving any closer to him.

Good girl. Stay close to me.

I size him up as I pull off my helmet placing it on the handlebars before I climb off my bike.

"Can we talk in private?" Brody asks, taking a step toward Ruby.

I take a step forward but stop when I hear her feisty as fuck mouth spout off to him. "Fuck, no. We have nothing to talk about Brody. It's over. Sign the damn divorce papers."

There's my firecracker. Goddamn, my dick gets hard hearing her talk like that.

I chuckle, crossing my arms over my massive chest and stare him down. He's close to my height, just not as built.

With a look of irritation, he glances over Ruby's shoulder, narrowing his eyes at me and says, "Well then I think it's time Quick and I have a little talk."

Cocksucker does know my road name. *Motherfucker.*

I take the two steps to reach Ruby and stand beside her, "So talk."

Brody runs his hand through his hair, "Look I know all about you and your club. I know it was you that had those men jump me. I got your demands, but I'm here to take my girls back."

"For fuck sake Brody, I'm not your girl anymore. You can still see your daughter, but it's over with us." Ruby fires back at him moving closer to me.

I put my arm around her shoulder moving her into my side. "Sounds like the lady just gave you an answer. We don't have a problem with you – if you just sign the divorce papers. Then we'll be on our way," I say, with an even voice not showing how pissed off I truly am.

But with my words, Brody's face turns from the boy next

door to one that is eerily disturbing. One I'm sure Ruby knows too well.

"You won't win custody of Bella. What I have on him will hurt you. Try to take me to court, and I'll bury you in attorney fees. You are nothing without me," Brody spits out, threatening Ruby.

This fucker.

Yep, this fucker just showed his true colors, and my patience just ran out. I release Ruby and take a couple of steps toward him, and he moves back.

That's right... keep moving back. You should be sacred, motherfucker.

"You think I'm scared of you or what you'll find? Think again, motherfucker. I *hope* you find out everything about me because when you do, mark my words. You'll freak the fuck out *and* back the fuck off. Because then… you'll know, *I can,* and *I will* ruin you. But, for the sake of Bella losing her dad. I'm telling you to back the fuck off, or else men way worse than I am, will come looking for *me* and crush *you* to get to me. So again, stop digging."

Brody's face tightens, and he grows a pair of balls because he takes the extra few steps between us, coming toe to toe with me, "I'm not scared of you or whoever it is that's after you. It only gives me more reason to protect my girls from you."

I laugh in his face, "Fucker, who do you think she feels safer with me or you? Does she look like she wants to go with you or even want you? Fuck no, she isn't your girl anymore. And…" I put my face within inches of his. "Tell your best friend to quit jerking off to videos and photos of my girl. We'll slap a restraining order on him if we need too – fucking pervert. And you shared her with him – fucking idiot."

The shocked look on his face tells me he didn't know his best friend has an obsession with Ruby either. I glare at him, "Yeah, check your boy's computer and check his ass or I will."

The back window to Brody's Mercedes-Benz starts to roll down. "What the fuck?" I mumble. Brody turns to look, and in a flash, I move, into action. I move so fast Brody doesn't know what hit him. I swing knocking him out with one punch, as Ruby screams for me. Chain jumps out of the SUV, gun raised at the car ready for whatever happens next. When I see small little fingers sticking out of the window, I realize who it is, and yell, "Bella!"

Instantly, everyone stops as I open the door to a sleepy Bella.

"Qwak, where's Momma and Daddy?" Bella rubs her eyes as I unbuckle her from her car seat and pick her up.

Knowing her daddy is knocked out on the pavement, I turn the opposite way heading toward the SUV. Ruby rushes forward crying, "Momma's here, Bug. Momma's here."

Handing a half-asleep Bella over to her mom, she snuggles her head into Ruby's shoulder. And within in seconds, she's fast asleep again. I turn to the guys, "Get him in his car."

I walk the girls up to our room. Ruby silently crying as she holds Bella tight against her.

Jesus, I'm enraged that this motherfucker brought his daughter here in the middle of the night. Who knows how long he's been waiting for us to come back. My mind keeps running through all the what-ifs that could have happened. I can't take it and need to deal with this shit. I can't sit still.

"I'll be back. Stay here and don't let anyone in but me or the guys."

"Where are you going?" Ruby asks still crying.

"Just downstairs to make sure everything's okay. I promise not to hurt him." I tell her trying to comfort her, but the worried look on her face tells me she doesn't believe me.

I kiss her forehead before heading downstairs.

I'm sitting in the passenger side waiting for Brody to wake up. Sitting here has given me some time to calm down, think straight and not do what every bone in my body wants me to do, which is to take him out. My hand clenches the gun that's laying on my thigh pointed at the son of a bitch. Both my guys are standing outside the car looking out.

His phone has been ringing off the hook. The only call I answered was his mom. I wanted to answer when Sam called. But thought it wouldn't be a good idea to threaten him while sitting in his best friend's car, holding a gun in my lap with Brody passed out in the front seat.

But I did answer his mom. I explained what he did and what I did. She said she was worried because he wasn't home with Bella. That he was in a mood earlier today and she was afraid he would flip out with Bella there. I told her Bella was safe with Ruby in the hotel and I was sitting here waiting for him to wake up. I told her the same thing I told Ruby, that I wouldn't hurt him but, we needed to have a talk. His mom was crying, upset he took Bella and brought her here tonight.

She sounded so tired. I told her I would take care of and protect Ruby and Bella, and I would have Ruby call her tomorrow.

When Brody starts to come around holding his head, I clear my throat. "It's about time you woke the fuck up," I growl.

Brody shakes his head before looking over at me and then my gun.

He freezes.

I smile.

We sit there for a few minutes, and I let him take it all in. I can see when he puts it all back together – Bella.

He looks over his shoulder, and I laugh, "Do you really think she would be back there? Do you really think *I* would be holding this gun toward you if she was in the fucking car?" My voice a deep sinister growl.

Brody's body relaxes slightly, turning his glare toward me. "Where the fuck is she?"

This fucker just doesn't get it.

166

Narrowing my eyes, I seethe through clenched teeth, "She's with her mom where she belongs. Not in the back seat of a fucking car in the middle of the night. Brody, you're making it really fucking hard for me *not to* want to hurt you really bad. But your Bella's dad. You need to get it together. You have a lot going for you. Don't lose everything over someone that doesn't want you anymore. Let her go. You still have your baby girl."

Brody's face hardens, and I know whatever is going to come out of his mouth isn't going to be good. His face says it all.

"I want Ruby. Having Bella ruined everything for me. For us." Brody's voice filled with so much resentment and hatred.

Hearing him say he didn't love that beautiful baby girl had my blood boiling and my finger itching to pull the trigger.

Mother-fucking-piece-of-shit-scum-bag-cunt.

The piece of shit doesn't stop either. He keeps going spouting his bullshit. "I don't care what anyone says. Ruby and I had it all. We were just starting out and having Bella ruined everything." Brody grips the steering wheel in frustration, and I needed to get the fuck out of this car before I beat him to death.

I take a deep breath in through my nose and out my mouth. *Keep it together.*

"Look I'm going to lay it all out there for you, and I pray to God for Bella's sake you listen and listen good." I throw a hefty size manila folder onto his dashboard. Brody's eyes dart from me to the thick folder back to me.

"We warned you, but since you don't seem to understand just how good we are, you might want to look at that." I pause. My jaw feels like it's going to shatter from gripping my teeth so hard as I'm trying to stay calm when I say, "I'm going to say this one time, and when I get out of this car, you'll have no more warnings. If the divorce papers aren't signed in two days when we go to the lawyer's office, I will throw *all* my money at you."

Brody's face goes from pissed off to confused. I just look at him and smile. He's still holding the stirring wheel, white-knuckled.

"Yes. I have money, and by the look on your face, you still haven't figured out who I really am. I have lots of money and I will, as you said, 'bury your ass in attorney fees.'" I grab the door handle, keeping my face locked with his and continue, "*And,* I will exploit you for what you really are – a piece of shit. If you want to talk to Ruby or Bella, you go through me – your mom has my number."

Chain moves around the car standing next to my door, drawing both of our attention to him. I know that means we have company, so I finish with, "If you don't heed my warning, I'm sorry for the wrath that will come down on you. Not just from me and my club, but the men looking for me. They will have no mercy." I start to get out of the car but stop, remembering I had his phone. I throw it on the dash and say over my shoulder as I get out, "Call your stalker friend, make sure you pass along my warning to him as well. Oh, and call your mom. I told her once you woke up, from me knocking you the fuck out, that you'd call her."

Slamming the door, I walk away not looking back. I pull my phone out and type in a number from memory that I haven't called in years.

A couple of seconds later I hear a car start and pull away. It wasn't until Chain said he was gone that I turned around just as the man I'm calling answers the phone.

"Good evening. The Walton residence, Malcolm speaking."

It's been well over two hours since Quick left me in the room to go deal with Brody. I've gone through all degrees of emotions. I've cried. I've screamed into a pillow. I've punched the pillow. I've panicked. I've even kicked the couch. Now I'm pacing the room worried sick. I can't believe Brody came here with our daughter in the car. He really doesn't have any care in the world for anyone but himself.

I texted Chain and Jammer, but they both said he was fine, and they had eyes on him. That they would have him call me as soon as he could, but he won't pick up his phone or reply to my texts. Which just threw me into another round of panic and irritation.

The call from Brody's mom threw me through a loop. She told me I have a good man and wanted to thank me for taking Bella. She cried to me, telling me she thinks Brody shouldn't be alone with Bella right now or until we figure shit out. He's too unstable. She's just looking out for the baby. I got off the phone in shock. She pretty much just told me she would be on my side in the custody battle. Which she said there probably wouldn't be one. That Brody was pretty much only fighting for me. He's lost his ever-loving mind if he thinks I'll ever be with him again.

It's been about an hour since I've spoken with anyone, I'm starting to lose my mind. I can't leave the room with Bella sleeping, so I've come to pace the room biting my nails. All the what-ifs are running through my head when I hear a key card click the lock open. I rush for the door and almost knock Quick over as he walks through the door.

"Whoa, Firecracker. Easy there, baby," lifting me up letting me wrap my legs around him. The minute I'm in his arms. I lose it and start to cry, burying my face into his neck, tightening my arms around him.

"Sshh, easy Rube. It's okay. He's alive and on his way home. I promise I didn't—"

I interrupt him, mumbling into his neck, "I know."

He walks me to the kitchen area, in our hotel suite, setting me on the counter. He rubs my back giving me a minute to collect myself, and once I do, I pull back to face him.

When I see him smile, I smile back as tears stream down my cheeks.

He pushes my wild hair away from my face tucking it behind my ears, but wild strands fall back into my face. "This hair..." he murmurs, running his hands through it, pushing it behind my shoulders. "This hair is what first caught my eye."

"Ruby Rube don't cry, baby. Everything's going to be okay. I promise," he says, in such a sincere, loving voice I want to believe him. I truly do, but I know Brody won't give me up.

I look down at my hands between us and twist them together, as my tears continue to fall.

Quick lifts my face up, so our eyes connect, but he keeps hold of my chin with his forefinger and thumb. "We need to get some rest. I've talked to Brody – he has until we meet with the lawyers to decide. I have things in play for either decision, but no matter what you'll get that divorce and, you and Bella will move back to New York with me. I promise. Now, tomorrow after I deal with some club stuff, we're going to get those movers and deal with all your stuff. Brody's the last thing we need to worry about." Quick says with a smile.

I mumble, "How?"

Quick leans closer, inches from my face and says, "I got you. I love you, Rube. Let me take care of you."

I'm shocked. My eyes search his and wait for him to panic or realize what he just said, but it doesn't come. He must read my mind because he says it again. "Yes, I said I love you."

Tears begin to roll down my face, again. Quick takes my mouth slowly, passionately kissing me. I moan into his mouth as he grips my ass closing the space between us, pressing his body up against mine. The kiss becomes needier as our tongues duel.

My body ignites, needing only one thing– him. I need him

inside me. I need him touching me. I need him devouring me. Fuck, all I need is him.

I become ravenous, grabbing hands full of hair, as he digs his fingers into my ass.

I slip my hands from his hair down his neck sliding my fingers under his cut, and slowly start to slip it off. But, he breaks the kiss removing it himself laying it over the counter, shedding his shirt next. I lick my lips watching all the muscle flex across his upper body as he moves. When he pulls his shirt over his head, I see it – the wolf tattoo across his chest. The wolf's eyes are staring back at me, looking at me like I'm its prey.

My insides tingle and I exhale – ready to be taken. When I look up from the wolf tattoo, Quick's smiling devilishly back at me. Jesus, he's beautiful. God really outdid himself the day he made Jacob Reeves Walton. My Quick. My protector.

"You like what you see, Rube." Quick's deep rumble has my legs vibrating and my pussy spasming.

I nod my head, gripping his jeans. I undo his belt as he tugs on my shirt. He looks over at the bedroom and says, "We should shut the bedroom door."

I nod again, still not able to use my voice. He leaves me on the kitchen counter rushing over to shut the bedroom door where Bella's sleeping in our bed. I have my shirt off and am shimming out of my jeans when he returns.

"Fuck I need to be inside you." Quick grips both breasts, engulfing one into his mouth. My head falls back, moaning his name.

Quick slips an arm around my waist lifting me up carrying me over to the table. Setting me down he pushes me back sprawling me out. He runs a hand down my neck, over each breast giving them a squeeze before continuing down my torso to the edge of my panties. With one swift yank, the panties are thrown to the ground.

Quick strips off the rest of his clothes, and kicks off his boots, pulling up a chair. When he sits down, he pulls me closer to the edge of the table, spreading my legs like he's a fucking Gynecologist inspecting my pussy. He begins to slowly run his hands up my inner thighs. Taking in deep breaths and exhaling through his mouth, just inches away from my entrance, sending goosebumps up my body.

He leans in, sucking my folds into his mouth, before slicing his tongue through my wetness. Quick groans before plunging his tongue into my pussy and begins to devour me.

I cry out, arching my back off the table. Quick increases his tongue, moving in and out, sucking my clit into his mouth, building the pressure making my nub hard and sensitive. I'm lost in the feeling, making erotic sounds, losing all consciousness. My breathing turns into panting as I chase after my rising orgasm.

I start to rock my hips when he inserts fingers. I can't take it. I'm close. "Yes. Fuck, yes."

I moan.

He withdrawals his fingers, spreading me wide, breathing heavily inches away from my pussy sending a wave of tingles up my body. With the tip of his tongue, he starts to flick it rapidly against my clit.

"Oh, fuck." My whole body begins to shake as my orgasms about to burst through me.

Quick enters two fingers again, and my orgasm explodes screaming out his name. Quick is lightning fast, covering my cries with his mouth, as he slams his cock inside me. My body's still humming from the first orgasm. So, when the second one rolls through me, my body becomes numb.

Quick leans back pounding into me, as my back scrapes against the tiled top, almost pulling me off the table. "Fuck!" he roars, pulling out of me. He pushes me further back onto the table to climb on with me, lifting one of my legs above his shoulder slamming back into me.

"Yes! Oh, fuck yeah," he cries out hammering into me faster and faster, chasing his own release.

Sweat glistens across our bodies as we both pant, "yes" with our climax at the brink.

I feel his balls tighten and his neck veins bulge. He lifts my other leg up to his shoulder, pushing both of them over my head as he slams his cock harder and deeper. Pounding into me, he mumbles incoherent shit as our bodies slap together. He's close, and his rhythm becomes erratic losing control. I hold my feet above my head and scream his name as my walls contract around his cock sending him over right along with me.

Quick leans down kissing me breathless while he continues to move in and out of me. I release my feet so he can lower my legs and when he shifts his body allowing them to lower, he hisses breaking the kiss. I look up at him with concern seeing he's in pain. "What's wrong?"

"Note to self, don't fuck on tiled tables. I think I fucked up my knees." He chuckles, pumping one more deep thrust holding it inside me for a few seconds before pulling out and backs up off the table.

I rise up off the table to look down at him, and sure enough, both his knees are scraped up from the tile table. Still laughing I say, "My back is a bit sore but nothing like that."

Quick looks up at me from inspecting his knees, and replies, "Well maybe that was because I had most of your body above your head off the table and my knees were under you pounding the shit into you."

We both laugh, I shuffle to the edge of the table watching Quick stand up and move back between my legs. I wrap my hands around his waist with his hands instantly going to my hair, pushing it out of my face. "You okay?" he asks, with a hoarse voice.

I take a deep breath glancing to his chest, where his wolf again stares back at me. I place my hands over his chest and begin petting his wolfs head and say in a humorous voice, "Yes, I am. I'm okay. Thank you."

He tugs my hair behind my head pulling my head back, so I have to look up at him.

"Are you telling me that or him that?" he says chuckling.

I smile, "Both, you both protect me."

"Always," he breathes.

Before he can say anything else, I blurt out, "I love you."

His eyes sparkle, and he smiles big hearing me say those words back to him.

"Rube, I love you, baby. Nothing and no one will hurt you. I promise. I love both of you girls more than my own life." My heart melts more for him, hearing those words from his lips.

In a shaky voice, I say it again. "I love you to Quick–Jake– Jacob Reeves Walton or whoever the fuck you want to be. I love all of you."

Quick smashes his mouth to mine for a deep passionate kiss. This time I break the kiss pushing him back so I can jump off the table, grabbing his hand I lead him to the couch nudging him to sit down. Once he's seated, I lean over placing my hands on his thighs. Quick licks his lower lip, eyes hungry watching my tits hang down. He reaches up cupping my breast, but I swat his hand away giggling, deciding to give him some of my sass. "You said you wanted this beautiful wet mouth on your cock didn't you?"

Quick's face lights up with a huge grin. I lean over placing a quick kiss on his lips before making my way down his neck, stopping to give the wolf a kiss before trailing kisses all the way down to his bobbing cock. I give a long torturously, mind-blowing, blow job. I blow him so good his head falls back, and his toes curl. When he cums down my throat, every muscle is tight as he clenches the couch, calling out my name.

After every drop is licked and swallowed, I'm being picked up and thrown to my back on the couch where he decides round three and four are in order.

Oh yeah. This day is ending on a good note. Tomorrow will work itself out as long as I have Quick by my side and in my bed.

18 | Surveillance

Quick

"What the fuck is wrong with you?" Whiz asks when Chain and I walk into the Sons of Saint's clubhouse. Chain busts up laughing. "Fucker has rug burns."

I snap back, "They're scratches, not rug burns."

Whiz's face goes from concerned to humorous as he outright busts up laughing. I tell them all to fuck off as I head to the bar, leaving them all laughing their asses off.

When I woke up this morning, I could barely move. My dick was raw from fucking until the wee hours of the morning. My legs and arms are sore as fuck from pounding that pussy all night. My tongue's even sore from working that clit multiple times.

Ruby wasn't in any better condition. I left her in bed, barely able to move. I told Bella, Mommy was tired and to let her sleep. When she finally got up, she was definitely walking like I left my dick up inside her. I fucked every hole that I could stick my dick in. I needed to claim my girl again, and she needed to feel claimed. I broke my own recorded coming five times. I mean I've gone more than five times but not without a break or nap. I couldn't get enough of her.

Fuck, my dick's hard just thinking about it. *Hell...no. Down boy down. I need a motherfucking break. Christ, I can't believe I just said that.*

I shake my head, putting a halt to my self-bickering that's going on in my head. I slowly sit on the bar stool, feeling every muscle scream at me, especially my knees, which got worse throughout the night by adding rug burns and couch burns to the tile scratches.

A prospect walks up asking me what I want when I tell him a beer Whiz slides in next to me.

"Don't fucking start," I grumble.

"Goddamn, she must be a firecracker to put you out of commission," Whiz teases.

I give him a sideways look warning him to shut the fuck up.

He puts his hand up in surrender. "Okay, okay. I won't give ya shit for being an old man."

I move to hit him, but I can barely throw a punch, my arms are like noodles from fucking Ruby up against the wall. My knees were so sore, but I couldn't stop. I had to have more of her. So I threw her legs over my shoulders pinning her against the wall so I could eat her pussy, before slamming back into her, fucking her hard against the wall. Sex last night was by far our wildest, most carnal fucking we've done.

It's not like we haven't fucked all night before, but I've never come five times, and I've never been this sore. We did some hardcore fucking. Thank fuck baby girl didn't wake up, with the TV on and the bedroom door shut she was out.

And I loved it. Fuck did I love it.

A smile creeps across my face as I take a long draw from my beer. I just wish I was still in bed with her relaxing with her soft silky body laying across mine.

"Well is your pussy ass going to be okay to ride and deal with this shit today or do you need to ride in the SUV?" Whiz says, teasing.

"Fuck off. I'll be fine. Just give me a few minutes to wake up and get some liquor in me," I explain.

An hour later, the whiskeys pumping through me and I'm feeling better than before – still sore but better. My dick's still wanting more of my bitch, but every time I go to adjust him, I remember he's injured and I probably couldn't even fuck if I wanted to, it's that sore. I chuckle to myself.

What the fuck. I'm talking like my dick's a person. Fuck, I need sleep.

"What the fuck are you laughing about now? Pussy that good you keep reliving it or something? Fuckin' A you've been acting like a bitch all day, all giddy and shit. Did you suck that pussy so good you became a vagina yourself or something?" Whiz says, next to me.

I punch him in the shoulder. "Fuck off. I'm just laughing. Why's it got to be about pussy?"

Whiz points to my dick and says, "Because the fucker rises each time you do. Now tell me it's not pussy you're thinking about?"

I look down to check my dick and Whiz busts up laughing, dropping his head onto his forearms that are resting on the bar.

"What?" I ask, laughing myself.

"Fuckin' A, I've missed you. You're so fucking gullible. Jesus, I need to get some pussy. Let's go," Whiz says, hitting me on the shoulder.

I text Ruby, letting her know I'll be riding, for her to text me if she needs anything, and I'll call her when I stop. I know she isn't going to do much today besides go over to her aunts. I left Jammer with her to drive her around and watch out for her and Bella.

Once we get a feel for Giselle's neighbor, depending on how this encounter goes, I can hopefully, head over to meet my girls and start loading the U-Haul.

We know the fucker has issues with Giselle. Regarding her patron's parking in front of his store and the noise. The owner's name is Raouf Assad, and he supposedly owns an insurance agency next door.

So, the plan today is to ruffle Raouf's feathers, parking in front of his store. We are hoping to interact with him before we head into the club. We want to piss him off for the next couple of days, so he'll complain to the building owner.

Whiz, Cue, myself, and about five other men pull up and stop right in front of the store. We wait for a spot, and when one opens, we swoop in as loud as we can. We sit there with our bikes still rumbling, taking our sweet ass time getting off. We all unbuckle our helmets while Cue's radio blaring overly loud, making us yell at each other.

No more than two minutes later, some fucker followed by four men come flying out the door. Yelling at us to lower the radio and turn off our bikes. I'm standing closest to the fuckers and say, "Eh?"

The frontman, who I know is Raouf, is furious, throwing his hands around yelling. I look to Cue, lifting my hand to my throat, making a motion to cut the music. When he does, I turn back around to face our furious neighbor and ask again, "What?"

The man moves to stand in front of me, flanked by his men. I'll give him this – he has some brass balls going toe to toe with a biker. I feel Whiz, and his men flank me with Cue and a couple of others still sitting on their bikes, ready to pull their guns if needed. Raouf is about a foot shorter than me but built, like he works out.

He demands, "I need you to move your bikes. This is my storefront, and you're making too much noise."

I look around like I'm looking for a sign before turning back to him with a fucked-up smirk and say, "I don't see no sign anywhere, saying this is your spot?"

Raouf's face turns red, balling his fists, his men moving in closer. I continue to eye his men with a smirk, as they close in around us.

"I do not want you parking in front of my store," he demands.

I step forward and his men tense, but they don't do anything. Raouf holds his head high, looking me in the eye. "As I said, there isn't a sign anywhere, and we will park here."

Just then the roar of more motorcycles sound in the distance, and within seconds five more bikes roll into our spot lining up behind us.

Raouf says something in his native language, who knows what the fuck he's saying, but his men start to move back. "I'll just call the cops for disturbing the peace."

I laugh. "The fuck you will. It's a free fucking country. We can do whatever the fuck we want. We aren't disturbing the peace – maybe you but not the peace."

Raouf spits to his side, and it takes everything in me not to lay the fucker out. "Men like you disgust me. I'll let the cops deal with your kind."

I step closer. "My kind?" I say, through gritted teeth.

One of his men speaks to him again, in their fucking language, and I look over Raouf's shoulder to the man. I smile. "Your boys calling you, best be on your way," I say, turning my back to him and winking at Cue, who smiles and turns his music back on.

Raouf and his men storm back inside, but Raouf moves to the window inside with his phone to his ear. Cue cuts the music, standing up he kicks his leg over to stand next to his bike with a shit-eating grin on his face. We all laugh, watching Raouf on the phone, as some of the men start talking shit, flipping him off as we walk over to the Club to have a drink.

Yeah, this is going to be fun, fucking with this cocksucker.

Twenty minutes later, two shields walk through the door of DazZelle, giving a nod to the bouncers making their way over to us. I look to Whiz and laugh, "You didn't tell me you're in good with the cops."

Whiz smiles. "I'm not, but you can say Giselle might be."

I laugh, as the shields walk up and we all swivel around to greet them with 'hello officers.'

One gives Whiz a nod. "Whiz, how are you doing?"

Whiz smiles again. "Officer Connor, I couldn't be better, shit, with titties in my face, a drink in my hand and a lap dance on the way, who wouldn't be – you?"

"Not as good as you it seems but at least the fucker next door called complaining again, so we get to take a break in here shooting the shit with you," Officer Connor says this, all the while staring at the blonde bitch dancing on the small circular pole next to us.

Whiz laughs. "So the fucker actually called and complained. He's getting ballsy that's for sure."

The officers laugh. The officer next to Connor winks at the topless waitress who brings over our fresh beers, placing them down. When she's done, she turns to the officer and exchanges words with him before walking away. Obviously, these fuckers are regulars.

Officer Connor looks around. "Mistress here today?"

Mistress? Oh fuck. Officer Connor is one of her men.

I take a drink of my beer hiding the amusement. "Naw, she'll be in later," Whiz says.

The officer nods his head as he continues to look around. When he stops to face me, he reads my cut, looking to Whiz, then back to me. "I guess you're the guy that had words with Mr. Assad."

I laugh glancing over at Whiz and say, "His last name is Ass-ad?" Whiz nods, laughing, but I turn my attention to the officer and reply to him, "Yes, he and his men got in our faces telling us to turn the music down."

The officer keeps eyeing my cut, with my road name on it, and I wonder if he knows Brody. I keep my eyes on his never looking away. The officer doesn't do anything but nod and say, "He's a fucking pain in my ass – is what he is. I can't wait till we can get something on him, so he's forced out of here."

I don't say anything but Whiz replies, "Well then you wouldn't get to come in here and hang out with us on a daily now would you."

We all laugh, and the officer says, "You got me there, Whiz. Okay, we've spent enough time here. We'll be on our way. Don't rile him up too much or we'll be back."

I look to Whiz and then back to the officers. When Connor sees the confusion on my face, he says, "You got something you need to say?"

I look to the officer and chuckle, "Naw, just shocked you ain't making us move our bikes."

The officer laughs. "It's not a metered parking spot. I could give you tickets for multiple bikes parked in one spot, but do you know how much paperwork that is and how many times I would be here ticketing your asses. Fuck that. We gave you a warning – right?" He looks at me, making sure I got what he is trying to say.

I nod, "I got it. Thanks."

He nods back before looking to Whiz. "Tell Mistress we stopped by."

Whiz lifts his beer acknowledging him as they turn and walk out of the place.

"Well fuck me," I say to no one, but myself.

This is good news. I look to Whiz. "You didn't tell us they were good with Giselle."

Whiz shrugs. "Depends on the cops on duty. They're not on her payroll, and we're good with them but nothing set in stone like I do over at the clubhouse. I have a few on the payroll, but again it depends where we're at. I've been getting in good with them here since I've been helping Giselle out, but like I said it's hit or miss on who gets called."

I keep staring at the door where the officers just exited.

We hang out for another thirty minutes before we head back out to the bikes. We hang around the bikes, taking our time getting set to leave, but the fuckers never came out. I guess we'll be back tomorrow to have some more fun.

I finally get to Ruby's aunt's place around two in the

afternoon. Jammer and I head up to the door and before I can knock the door flies open. "Qwak' here!" Bella screams, launching herself at me. Christ, this girl fills my heart with happiness.

I kiss her on the cheek. "Hi baby girl. How was your day?"

As I walk into the house, she answers, "Good. Mamma is still tired. An-tee is here with Momma."

I set Bella down, so she can take my hand and lead me down the hallway. Entering the kitchen, I see Chain sitting at the table eating food with Giselle and Ruby moving around the kitchen.

I give him a head nod, making my way over to my girl, wrapping my hands around her waist. Leaning in, I nuzzle my face into her neck, making her giggle. I whisper, into her ear, "How's my firecracker feel?"

Ruby turns in my arms, wrapping hers around my neck with a smile. I'm about to kiss her when I realize Bella is standing next to us staring. We haven't kissed in front of her yet. We've hugged and put our hands on each other, but we haven't kissed in front of her since that very first time.

I pull back, breaking our embrace, making Ruby's smile disappear. But when I turn toward Bella, recognition sparks in her eyes. Crouching down, I say, "What's to eat, baby girl?"

Bella's face goes from happy to sad. "Why didn't you kiss Momma?"

The room goes silent. Everyone stops what they're doing.

"You kiss me hello and goodbye. Why not kiss Momma?" she asks curiously.

Ruby places her hand on my shoulder, letting me know she's there if I need assistance, but Bella and I have become close, so I speak my mind.

I smile. "Well, I was going to but wanted to make sure it was okay with you?"

Ruby's hand stays on my shoulder when Bella smiles big and says, "It's okay. Momma needs kisses too."

I hear a few chuckles around the room and laugh myself when I reply, "I couldn't agree more with you. I'm glad you don't mind because I like kissing your Momma."

I stand up turning to Ruby, who's all smiles and pull her to me, placing a big kiss on her. Bella cheers and runs out of the kitchen, screaming, "I'ma get my babies. They need kisses too."

Chain and Jammer crack up laughing as I deepen my kiss, making Ruby moan.

When my phone vibrates, I break the embrace again, to grab my phone. When I unlock it, I see a text from Shy.

Shy: Call from land.

I look over at Chain. "Burner?"

Chain nods his head, reaching into his pocket, pulling out a burner phone, throwing it to me.

I look over to Giselle, giving her a smile. "Hello, Giselle." I turn back to my girl, giving her a brief kiss and say, "I'll be outside making a call, be right back."

Just as I'm headed to the front door, Bella runs toward me with her tiny little arms full of babies. "Qwak, kiss my babies goodbye."

I bend down to her level, raising a finger to my mouth to be quiet, I whisper, "Chain and Jammer love to give babies kisses. I have to make a call. I'll be right back. Have the boys start kissing them for me, okay?"

Bella's eyes light up. "Okay."

I stand back up, Bella running by me yelling Chin, Jam kiss my babies." I laugh, hearing her try to say their names, as I head out the front door.

Shy answers on the first ring, "Heard about last night. How's Bella?"

"She's good. Doesn't remember anything," I reply.

"Any word from fuckface?" Shy follows.

"Naw. Ruby talked to his mom, and it seems they laid into

him. He's going to sign, but we'll see," I say, sounding skeptical. "How Dallas? How's everything on your end?"

"Good. He's talking shit to everyone, so he seems to be back to normal." You can hear the smile in his voice.

"Good, glad he's okay."

"How did it go with the neighbor today?" Shy questions, back to boss mode.

"Fucker tried pushing today. Shields came into the club today after he called to complain. To my surprise, they were cool. They knew Mistress and was asking for her, so I think we need to talk to her about that as well," I inform him.

Shy's quiet for a beat before saying, "This bitch for real? What's your take on her? Is the risk and investment worth it?"

I answer right away. "Fuck yes – shits legit. The place is clean, and she runs a tight ship. I can tell she needs us but is too proud to ask. She wants Ruby involved."

"Is that going to be a problem for you?"

"Naw, my girls just like her aunt, all business," I answer truthfully. Ruby is a businesswoman and knows how to run shit.

"Alright, I'll pass on the information to Wolfe and the others. We'll be there by the end of the week. Blink's back. He'll be there before us," Shy says, sounding somewhat relieved. I'm shocked hearing our Enforcer is back.

"No shit?" I reply, sounding shocked.

Blink is a bounty hunter and the Enforcer for the West Virginia chapter. Wolfe sent him on a major hunt to find a couple of men on the run, that are worth a shit ton of money. Wolfe also wanted Blink to get information and some shit back from them before he turned them in.

He goes radio silent when he's hunting, so we haven't heard from him for months. Shy told me last month he checked in saying he was headed back but had to stop at the prison where his brother was, and nobody had heard from him since.

"Yeah, fucker's back. He'll be there soon," Shy says with amusement in his voice.

Blink looks like a lumberjack, tall, blonde, blue eyes, enormously large, clean cut, no tattoos beside the wolf insignia on his belly. The fucker looks like a model, laughs, makes jokes basically looks like a normal guy – not a killer. He might look like a god, but the fucker definitely has the devil in him, seeing as he hunts down men for fun – one scary mother fucker.

"Nice. It will be good to have him back finally," I push out, happy as fuck he'll be here to have my back dealing with all this bullshit.

"Hit me if you need anything. Otherwise, I'll text you our flight information so you can have the prospects pick us up."

I agree, and we end the call. I put the burner in my pocket and look around the neighborhood.

19 | Resurface

Ruby

"Wolfe will be here tomorrow, and we'll all sit down to make the final plans. The son of a bitch isn't going to budge," Quick says to Whiz about my aunts' neighbor. They've been fucking with him for the last two days.

Earlier I about shit my pants when I saw Officer Jeff Connor walk through the doors of DazZelle. I've known Jeff since high school. Quick went on defense mode, not letting me leave his side. He was pretty much claiming me, so Jeff would know who I was with. He wasn't a dick about either – he just made sure I stayed right by him. Luckily, for both of us, my aunt was here to pull his attention away from me.

We're in the booth, which I think Whiz and Quick have deemed theirs. The boys are chatting about club shit, while Dizzy and I watch Candy perform on the main stage. I'm relaxed, leaning against my man with his arm slung over my shoulder.

Wolfe and the guys will be here tomorrow afternoon, and my meeting with the attorneys and Brody is tomorrow morning. I've been worried since I haven't heard from Brody since the hotel incident. I talked to his mom and took Bella over to her earlier today to stay the night but nothing from Brody. We'll see how tomorrow goes.

"Holy fucking shit. Who the fuck?" Dizzy whispers next to me, I look toward the direction she's looking, and whisper, "Fuck me 'til Tuesday."

"Fuck, are they coming this way? Whiz, do you know those men? They don't look happy," Dizzy announces getting their attention. All of us look back out the window at the two men, who are easily over six-foot tall, with blonde hair, and so exotic looking I'm breathless. I can't seem to take my eyes off of them. It's like I'm in a trace.

The room is silent as everyone watches, but Quick jumps up first, "What the fuck?" followed by Whiz, as they walk to the windows of the booth to get a better look.

Quick is so fast. He's out the door leaving Dizzy and me here with our mouths open. I'm worried I should go with him. I try to get myself together, only managing to stand up and move to the glass. They look like twins but are so completely opposite, one seems to be fully tatted, and the other doesn't have a mark on him. I can see they are wearing cuts, but it's too dark to see their colors.

"Damn, I hope your man knows them because they're hot as fuck. Do you see every single woman in this place has stopped what they're doing to watch them?" Dizzy says, standing next to me.

I watch as Quick and Whiz approach the mammoth men, and they don't look happy. Words are exchanged, when one of the men reaches for Quick, I lose my shit, thinking they want to hurt him. I fly out of the room and yell, "Don't you fucking touch him."

The massive man has Quick up in the air as I'm screaming. When they hear me, the other man standing in front of Whiz goes to reach for me but Quick snaps. "Don't you fucking dare, Chiv. She's my ol' lady."

I stop cold. The men are all laughing. The one that's holding Quick in a bear hug sets him down, and Quick immediately pulls me to his side. "I don't see no cut on her back?" the guy that just set him down, says. I look up, cranking my neck back just so I can see these fuckers. Everyone is smiling down at me.

"Soon fuckers – soon," Quick returns.

For the love of God – they're gorgeous but not – if that makes any sense.

"Firecracker, this is Blink and Chiv, brothers of mine," Quick introduces me with laughter in his voice.

The guy that had Quick in a bearhug laughs. "Boy you found yourself a little spitfire, alright."

"Rube, that's Blink, he's the enforcer for our West Virginia chapter, and that ugly fucker is his twin brother Chiv, who just got out of the big house." Both men smile, giving me a head nod.

Okay these men and their fucking names, I can't hold back. "Blink, like in a blink of an eye and Chiv, like in you chivved someone in jail?"

Quick grips my waist as a warning. "Rube, what the fuck did I say about respect and not asking about road names."

I keep my stare on the two men, but it's Chiv's eyes that I lock onto, they captivate me. They're crystal blue, but the darkness behind them, tells me he isn't one to be fucked with, but I still don't look away. When I don't back down, he throws his head back with a roar. "Jesus, I go away for a few years, and you decide to get a bitch mouthier than you! Unfuckingbelievable," Chiv exclaims with amusement.

I don't know if I should take that as a compliment or insult, so I just keep staring at him, folding my arms across my chest. Quick laughs. "It was the hair and that feisty fucking mouth of hers that knocked me off my rocker all right. Now come on, let's get some drinks. Fuck, it's good to see you both. Why didn't you tell anyone Chiv was getting out early?"

Quick guides me back into our booth, followed by the men. Dizzy is beaming when we re-enter the room. Chain and Jammer are introduced to the men, guessing they've been gone since they became prospects.

For the next few hours, I sit and listen to them tells stories, no mention of club business or why Chiv was out early. Just funny stories of drunk nights at bars and shit these guys got into back in the day. Everyone is laughing and pretty fuckin' buzzed.

At some point, each of the men were hauled off separately by more than a few women eager to give them private dances. I love seeing my man happy. Hearing stories of him before I knew him, it was the highlight of my night.

When they mentioned Quick being the player and womanizer that he was, he would squeeze me tight giving me a kiss, making sure I was okay hearing about his playboy days. I would just laugh and give him reassurance I was good.

All the men are sitting with a woman on their laps while Candy dances around the pole in the middle of the room dancing to the song, "Sliding Down the Pole" by E-40 featuring Too Short. I get up for a refill while listening to everyone talk and laugh. As I'm standing there pouring our drinks, the room slowly quiets. Suddenly both Blink and Chiv heads snap to me, and the look of shock crosses their face.

"What the fuck?" Blink blurts out.

"Fuck me," Chiv pushes out.

I look at Quick and then back to the men. "What?"

Blink actually slow blinks a couple of times but doesn't say anything more. I'm about ready to yell at them but jump when my auntie says, "Are y'all having a good time? Do you need anything?"

"For fuck's sake, Auntie, you scared the shit out of me," I say, laughing.

Blink and Chiv stay frozen when Quick and Whiz chuckle.

My auntie puts her arm around my waist. "Sorry sweetie, thought you heard me."

Quick looks at his men and then back to us girls, but still, no one says anything.

"What the fuck is wrong with you two?" I ask the men, both with their mouths open in awe. Then it hits me – they're staring at my auntie. I turn to look at her, noticing she's wearing a black wig and a tight red dress with black stilettos – one of her Mistress Z outfits.

She looks hot as fuck. Okay, I see what they're stunned about.

I laugh. "Auntie, I think you have a couple of new admirers."

She smiles big but doesn't say anything.

Blink speaks first, but it's not to us – it's to Quick, "Has Wolfe seen her yet?"

I look to Quick.

Quick looks confused. "Naw, he'll be here tomorrow, Why?"

Chiv answers, "Have you seen his late wife, Foxy?"

Quick looks at both of us and then back to his boys but it's Whiz who pipes up. "Holy shit!"

I feel my auntie stiffen next to me and I lose my shit again. "Will someone fucking explain to me what the fuck is going on and stop fucking staring like you've seen a goddamn ghost."

Whiz laughs. "It's the wig, brothers. Her natural hair is light brown like Firecracker's."

Blink and Chiv look over at Quick. "Jesus Christ, she looks just like Wolfe's late wife Foxy right now. I almost shit myself."

Auntie steps forward making her dominance known. "Well, I'm glad you didn't do *that* in my club, but she must have been one hot bitch with great taste." She fills a shot glass of whiskey, slamming it.

I laugh as the men just stare at us. Auntie turns to me. "So your good. I'm headed out for the night. See you in the morning." I nod and give her a big hug. She turns to the men lifting a hand, giving them her sexy, sassy smile. "Night boys." And then she's gone, leaving all the men in awe.

Quick finally speaks up, "Fuck, I never noticed, but that's the first time I've seen her in a wig."

I grab the bottle and pour myself a shot, slamming it. "She has a client. That's why she's dressed like that." Slamming another shot, I move to sit next to Quick.

Everyone is looking at me. "For fuck's sake, what?"

Everyone now starts laughing, except me.

Blink shakes his head. "Wolfe's in for a big motherfucking surprise if she wears *that* in front of our prez because that bitch seriously could have been Foxy's twin sister."

"Maybe we shouldn't say anything. She wouldn't wear the same outfit tomorrow, would she?" Whiz asks, looking over at Quick.

The realization hits me. "Wait, do you mean Ginger's mom?"

Everyone looks over at me, nodding their heads.

Well, fuck me.

20 | Let Me Go
Ruby

"It's going to be fine, sweetie," my aunt says, trying to calm me down.

I left the hotel early this morning with Chain, so I could run by and pick up my aunt. Quick asked me if I wanted him there, and I said yes. I didn't know how it was going to go or if Bella would be with us. I didn't care if it hurt my case or not, I needed him there.

Quick told me he would meet me at the courthouse, where we're meeting with the attorneys and mediator. But, he had some errands to run first.

"Ruby?"

I snap out of my daze and look to my aunt, whose face is filled with concern. "Sorry. Yes, I know. I'm just nervous," I try to explain.

Chain clears his throat at the door where he's standing there waiting. It's time to go, but I haven't gotten off the couch to go. Nerves and panic have me rooted to this spot.

I need Quick. I need his strength.

Panic starts to build in my chest, and what-ifs run wild.

Chain stalks over shoving a phone in my face. A phone I hadn't realized rang. I look up to Chain, the badass biker who looks sympathetic and sweet.

I smile, reaching for the phone, when I put it to my ear, a loud, but soothing scream barrels through it. "Put her on the fucking phone. Shove the damn thing next to her ear if you have to."

Izzy.

The panic subsides just a bit hearing my best friend yell at the badass biker, making me giggle. When she hears me giggle, she says, "Ruby Rue, how are you?"

With a shaky voice, I reply, "Panicked, scared, pissed, fuck, you name it, I'm feeling it. What if—"

Izzy cuts me off, "Fuck that! No what-ifs. You got this. I promise. It'll be okay."

I whisper in the phone, "But, what if it's not? I can't lose my Bella Bug. He isn't going to let me go." Tears fill my eyes as I take a deep breath.

Izzy's voice gets low and calm. "I just got you back. There is no way you're going to lose, Bug or the divorce. You deserve this. It'll be okay. Pull it together and get your ass over there. Be that badass bitch you were born to be. We have your back, I promise. You're going to be late, now get up and do this."

I look up to see Chain and my aunt both smiling at me. I shove my shoulders back, shake my head clearing away all the bad thoughts. I say with confidence, "Okay, I can do this. I got this."

I stand up, straightening my pencil skirt and matching blazer. "I love you. Thank you for always knowing when I need you." My voice is full of love, hoping she truly understands how much she means to me.

"I love you too, Ruby-Rue. Call me when it's over," Izzy replies softly.

Thirty minutes later, I'm back to being frantic because the traffic was beyond horrible, making us even later than we already were. I knew Brody, his parents, their attorney, Bella, my attorney, my aunt, the mediator and maybe Quick would be here for the meeting. What I didn't expect to walk into was a room full of people.

Walking into the court office, I stopped dead in my tracks. On one side of the room was Brody, his parents, and their attorney. On the other side of the room was, three suited men that I didn't know, standing next to my attorney. When my eyes landed on Quick, my knees went weak, and I exhaled, "Holy shit." My badass biker, always in jeans and a cut was standing before me in a three-piece suit, looking so GQ my pussy spasmed.

When my aunt exhales, "Holy shit." I look beyond my man, to the people behind Quick. My eyes fill with tears to see Luc and Mia, holding a very excited Bella and Blink. I'm a little shocked to see him, since I just met him the night before, but boy does he look good in a suit.

Quick must sense my distress and confusion because he's to me in seconds pulling me into his arms. "Shh, Rube, I got you."

Tears falling from my eyes, I stutter, "How...why..."

"Mrs. Malone?" someone calls from the front of the room.

I wipe my face, taking a deep breath, pulling away from Quick. He moves to my side when he sees I'm ok, putting the room into full view, with everyone staring at me.

I've got this. Be the bitch I was born to be.

Izzy's voice repeats over and over in my head. I smile, straightening my skirt. "Sorry for being late." Moving to my side of the room.

"Mrs. Malone, your attorney has started on your behalf. Please take a seat so we can continue." The woman mediator states, not looking too happy.

Mia and Luc walk toward me with Bella, as soon as I'm close she throws her arms out wanting me. Smiling, I grabbed her, pulling her into a hug. "Love you, Bug."

"Love you too, Momma. Mia's taking me for ice cream," she whispers with a giggle.

I smile, nodding my head with excitement. Mia puts an arm around my waist, giving me her silent support, and I turn to her, giving her a half hug, as I hand Bella back to her.

Luc leans forward giving me a hug. "You got this," he whispers, following Mia and Blink out of the office. and I return a smile.

Quick's hand is at the small of my back guiding me to my attorney and the three men in suits.

"Mrs. Malone, are you ready?" the mediator asks, sounding irritated.

My attorney stands up as I sit down next to him and we both say, "Yes," at the same time.

"Mrs. Malone, you should be very proud of your daughter. I'm glad I was able to see and speak with her before she left. Your daughter is a very happy, sweet, intelligent beyond her age, well-loved little girl."

I glance over to Brody who is looking down at his hands, but I can see the look on his face, and it isn't good. Looking back to the mediator, I say, "Thank you. She is the light of my life."

The mediator smiles for the first time.

"Okay, since we lost some time and I have another meeting to attend we'll start with the custody issues, I've done all the interviews with the character witnesses, and I'll leave the divorce proceedings to be handled by the attorneys."

My attorney, who is still standing, grabs some papers and is about ready to say something when the Malone family attorney blurts out, "We would like to file for full custody."

Mrs. Malone's face mimics mine in horror. I cry out, "What? Are you kidding me? And what, take her on the road with you when you tour?"

"Mrs. Malone."

Tears fill my eyes.

This can't be happening.

"Mr. Malone? Are you seriously considering trying to fight

for full custody when you're hardly home? I know this because I'm a fan and actually looked up your schedule. Now can you explain to me how you would be able to raise a toddler and be on tour?"

Mrs. Malone's face is red and only getting redder as Mr. Malone stares daggers at me. I know Mr. Malone backs and encourages Brody in anything he does, even beating women it seems.

Brody's face says it all. He's in one of his – I am God, and I deserve it all – kind of moods.

"Ma'am, in all honesty, I want *both* my daughter and wife back. I don't want this divorce."

Quick, who's been silent next to me, grips my hand under the table. For support or to hold himself together, I don't know, but I squeeze back. My attorney completely irritated with Brody's drama turns into the pit bull, I was told he was.

"Mr. Malone, we have sent you several offers in the mail. You know Mrs. Malone does not want to be with you. The sooner you realize that, the sooner we can quit wasting everyone's time. Isabella and Ruby have started a wonderful new life in New York. Ruby has a well-paying job with the support group to back her in raising Isabella. My client is not asking anything from you, no alimony, no child support, nothing. All she wants is a divorce and full custody of her daughter. You will have visitation rights, as will your parents. She is willing to work around your touring schedule. My client's not being unreasonable. If you push us to take this to court, you will lose, and you do know what I'm talking about."

Meaning all the shit we have on him. Brody's face turns beet red. "You might have dirt on me, but I have dirt on him." Brody points to Quick. "He isn't fit to take care of my girls," he seethes, clenching his fist on the table. Which I know the mediator can see just as I can.

God, Brody, just stop. Please. Let me go.

The youngest of the suited men I don't know stands up buttoning his suit jacket, clearing his throat. "The man you state is not fit to take care of your girls is none other than Jacob Reeves Walton."

I gasp, snapping my head to face Quick.

Oh, God. He's outing himself – for me. No. No. No.

I mouth, 'no' to him and he just smiles back at me lovingly.

Tears fill my eyes.

"Is that name supposed to mean something to me? I know who Jake Reeves aka Quick of the Wolfeman MC is," Brody snaps back, but this time his attorney and father both lean in to shut him up, but he keeps making things worse for himself. "What? Don't tell me to shut up."

When Mrs. Malone smiles at me, I smile sympathetically back. She has always had to deal with the aftermath. She and I were always picking up after the Malone men. Where she gets her courage, I have no idea, but throughout all these years of putting up with them, she has never stood up to her boys – that is until today. Mrs. Malone stands up, clearing her throat.

"Mrs. Malone," she stops and giggles. "Funny saying that seeing as I'm Mrs. Malone too." She pauses.

"Margret, sit down. Now," Mr. Malone barks his order pushing his shoulders back, never looking at his wife.

But she doesn't sit down, she keeps going.

"Ruby Malone, you are the best daughter-in-law I could have ever asked for, and you are beyond a wonderful mother. I'm sorry."

Mr. Malone glaring at me, snaps again, "Margret, sit down now."

"Mr. Malone, I think it's best if you remain quiet until your wife is finished, or I'll have security remove you. Please continue, Mrs. Malone."

Margret pushes her shoulders back, giving herself the

reassurance she needs, and I smile back at her trying to give her the support she needs.

"As I was saying, I'm sorry for all of this back and forth. I'm sorry I wasn't there for you during the marriage. But enough is enough, I will not sit back and not say a word. What matters right now is that baby girl. I will back you in the request for full custody. I do not think my son is capable of caring for our sweet Bella."

Mr. Malone's face turns fire engine red, and Brody looks irate but devastated as he stares daggers at me, or maybe it's Quick sitting next to me but either way, he's pissed. Mrs. Malone turns to look at her boys and addresses her husband first. "I will not sit by and let you or your son hurt my granddaughter. Harold, this is not a contest or something you can win, and…" She looks over at her son. "Brody just let her go, son. You don't deserve her, and you definitely can't buy your way out of this."

Mr. Malone kicks his chair out from under him, standing abruptly, seething. He looks to his wife, giving her a murderous glare. Margret squares her shoulders and smiles at him before he charges out of the office. Fixing her suit blazer, she squares her shoulders to address their attorney, who is standing there with his mouth open in shock. With her voice even more confident she demands, "Stan, I pay you. You know I handle everything, so if you still want to keep your job and get that hefty bonus, we pay you. You will finish this deal – today. I have read their offer, and I want you to add a very generous amount of child support to the offer." She clasps her hands in front of her, glaring at her son. "God knows my son makes enough money, and he can help in supporting his only daughter."

The room goes silent. I think everyone is in shock at this outcome. It isn't until the mediator starts laughing that the room snaps out of it.

"Well, that was definitely not the way I thought this was going to go, but I am very pleased and hope with your support,

Mrs. Malone that it will be upheld," the mediator says, getting up from her desk. "Attorneys prepare your final documents, and I will review them before they sign."

Brody kicks his chair out just as his father did and storms out, not even looking at his mom. Like the spoiled little brat, he is, running off to his daddy. I push my chair out and immediately cross the room to embrace my mother-in-law. "Thank you! Thank you so much!" I rush out, my voice raw with emotions.

"Ruby, I should have done that a long time ago. When he took her to the hotel, that's what woke me up and snapped me out of my stupidity. I just really hope I will have my own visitation set up because that girl of ours is one amazing little girl." Margret's eyes filling with tears, matching mine as we embrace once more.

"Momma! Gma! Guess what Mia got me?"

We both turn to see our Bella Bug rushing in with a big bear stuff animal. Margret squats down, picking her up in her arms. I turn to see all the men in my life standing around waiting patiently for me. Quick is talking to the attorney and the men in suits. Blink, Luc and now Chain are chatting behind them. Chain told me when he dropped me off earlier, he was ordered to wait outside with whoever had Bella to keep an eye on them. But I wonder if it was because they were going to bring up Quick's real name.

"You got a good one there. Did you know?" my auntie says from behind me, giving me a startle.

Not taking my eyes off my beautiful, badass, biker-slash-millionaire, I say, "Not until after I fell in love."

"That's good, sweetie. I like him a lot, and you deserve the best. I'm gonna take Bella home so you can wrap things up here. Do you need a babysitter for tonight?"

Without turning to her, I smile. "Yes. Tonight, let's dance and party."

Quick glances up from the men scanning the room and when

our eyes lock, the love that is exchanged between us is undeniable. I bite my lip and head toward my man.

Quick turns, reaching an arm out, pulling me to his side, giving me a kiss on the temple before introducing me to the three men I don't know. "Ruby, this is Malcolm Mc Cullen, the head of my household." I try to hold in my shocked, what the fuck look, but I know he saw it flash across my face, before I smile, extending my hand to him.

Quick continues, "This is my godfather, Sebastian Wright. He co-owns and runs my family business."

Co-owns. Family business. What. The. Ever. Loving. Fuck.

Sebastian smiles, taking me by surprise when he pulls me out of Quick's side, giving me a full embrace.

"Oh! Hello," I laugh, hugging him back.

"Easy there, Sebs," Quick laughs.

Sebs?

Sebastian breaks the embrace pulling away but doesn't let me go. Instead, he looks down at me with an ear to ear grin. "Thank you."

"Okay. Okay." Quick breaks us apart turning me to the last man. "Luis Wright, this is my Ruby. Ruby, this is Sebastian's son, and lifetime best friend, slash attorney."

What! Best friend. Holy Shit!

I smile, extending my hand. I'm freaking out right now. This is a whole other life I don't know about. I have a lot of questions running through my head. Quick and I seriously need to sit down and talk about this shit and soon.

"It's nice to meet you all. Thank you so much for coming. I wish it was under different circumstances, but none the less I'm truly grateful you're all here."

"Not as grateful as we are, I'm sure," Sebastian speaks, and all the men nod their heads in agreement.

I look up at Quick and then back to the men confused.

The older gentleman, Malcolm, smiles. "See my dear, Jacob

hasn't called for our help in a very long time. So, you have, to understand when he called, we were all very interested in who won our boy over."

I look to all three men who are over the moon happy right now. All the links to his past life.

"Ruby?"

I turn when my attorney motions for me to come over. I excuse myself from the men and try to pull myself from holy fucking shit land back to my reality.

It takes us another hour to go through everything, but when it's all said and done, I feel good. The two attorneys, Margret and I finalize everything. The attorneys went and came back from having the mediator sign off, and now we're waiting on Brody. Brody was called back and should be here any minute. Luc, Mia, Blink, and Chain all took off, leaving me with Quick and his friends or family.

Shit, I don't really know what to call them.

I was in the middle of finishing up with the attorneys, so I didn't get to eavesdrop on Quick and his people's conversations, but I could feel them watching me.

I'm standing with Margret when Brody walks back into the office, along with Sam.

Oh shit.

Quick and his family stand, watching Brody, from a few feet away.

Brody stalks toward his mother, and I take a few steps back seeing the wrath he's about ready to leash.

"*Mother.* Did you and *my girl* finalize *my* divorce?" Brody clips, sounding like a spoiled little brat.

Margret, not skipping a beat, replies, "Yes, *son.* You need to sign your divorce."

Brody scoffs, folding his arms across his chest like a little kid about ready to have a tantrum. "We'll see," he spits back.

I've had about enough of him being a dick, I take a step

toward Brody, but stop when Margret shoots an arm out to stop me. "Don't you move, Ruby. My son needs to be taught a lesson." She pauses moving in front of me, squaring off with her son who towers over her. "You better listen and listen good, son. You will sign these papers right now. If you do not leave Ruby alone, I will exploit you myself. Your spoiled ass needs to grow the fuck up."

I gasp, hearing her curse. Brody and Sam's faces morph into shock hearing her curse.

"I'm your momma, not your mother. Don't act like I haven't been taking care of you all your life. So, pull your head out of your ass. You are going to be something huge if you only get it together. Think about your career. Now sign the papers before I cut off every bit of your inheritance and give it to your daughter."

Everyone in the room is silent. Sam and Brody both still look shocked, probably from never seeing this side of her before. Brody goes to look over her shoulder at me, but Margret lifts her hand with a pen. "Don't you worry or look at her, sign the papers."

Brody huffs, grabbing the pen moving to sign the papers. Sam, on the other hand, has no problem staring at me. Margret turns her fury onto him "Samuel, you are like a son to me but so help me God if you don't delete those files of Ruby and quit stalking her, I will put a restraining order on you myself. You two boys need to pull your heads out of your ass and focus on your careers ahead of you. NOT this poor girl behind me that doesn't want either of you. Now…"

Brody straightens from signing where his attorney motioned.

"Let's go boys. Stan call me with the details and bill."

Margret grabs both boys' arms and hauls them out of the office like they're fucking teenagers.

I just stand there in utter shock.

What the fuck just happened?

21 | Explanation
Quick

After the shit show was done and they left the court office, we all stood there in silence. That is until Ruby bends over laughing hysterically. My girl was crying so hard I had to grab her around the waist. The guys just looked at me worried and amused at the same time.

"Ruby?" I say, trying to get her to calm down.

But she just keeps holding her stomach bent over laughing.

When the two attorneys walk up with their briefcases in hand, I give Ruby a shake. "Ruby, stand up."

It isn't until the Malone's attorney, Stan speaks up. "Mrs. Malone, are you alright?"

Ruby stands up face red with tears rolling down her face. Wiping her cheeks, she clears her throat. "Yes, I'm fine."

Ruby's attorney speaks up, "We'll file these papers today. I'll be in touch with you soon."

Ruby takes her attorney off guard by grabbing him and hugging him. "Thank you."

He looks to me and with one hand taps her back, "Your welcome."

When Ruby turns to me and the guys her face goes from relieved to blank. I know she has questions so before anyone can say anything I turn to my guys and say, "Okay, since we're all at the same hotel let's all head back, get changed and meet in my suite to discuss our other business."

Ruby's head snaps to me. "Other business?"

I keep looking at the men and when they all nod and start to leave, I turn to Ruby, pulling her into my chest, hugging her tight. "Rube, I think it's time we have that talk about my past.

All of it. You need to know everything about me and I'm trusting you to keep what I say between you and me."

Ruby's body relaxes into mine as she exhales a long breath.

Once we're settled into the SUV and I pull out into traffic, I start, "I know you have a bunch of questions but if you can hold off on asking them until I get through my story, I promise to answer all of your questions." I look over at her to see her turned in her seat, giving me her full attention. I smile, give her a wink before turning my attention back to the road and continue, "My parents were high school sweethearts, both came from good families. They got married a few years after they were out of high school and then I came little over a year later. My parents wanted a big family as they both were only children. But when my mom almost died from complications, during the delivery, the doctors told her the risk was too high, so they decided one was all they would have. They thought of adopting, but I guess you could say I was a little hellion and ended up being enough." I pause, slipping a glance over to see Ruby smiling.

I chuckle. "My father was over the moon and content having a boy to carry on the family name. They named me Jacob after my grandfather, on my dad's side, who died of a heart attack at a young age, before I was born. Reeves is my mother's maiden name. I had a great upbringing, spoiled but it was good, I was a little brat." I pause, thinking of today when Margret scolded those boys because my momma used to do that to me but at a younger age when a momma is supposed to teach her boys right from wrong.

"My parents loved me. I loved them. I had friends. I had girlfriends, but never for long, I was too wild and loved to party. When my parents died in a sudden car crash, my whole world ended. I was young when I was thrown into the family business, just like my father when his dad died. I didn't want to be a corporate guru. That was the only thing my father and I fought about, and he always thought I would come around when it was time. Since I never really knew what I wanted to be, we never dealt with it. I was just out of high school and in college when they died. Sebastian, my father's best friend, had worked with him since high school. He knew the business. He was my Godfather. Luis and I both talked about how we wanted to do something different than what our fathers did. Luis did what he wanted and became an attorney. Me – I spiraled out of control, dropping out of college." I pause again, needing a minute. Talking about my past has my chest hurting. The pain I feel to this day is sometimes overbearing.

Ruby reaches out, putting a hand on my thigh. I look down at her hand, then up to both of mine gripping the steering wheel, white-knuckled. I release one hand lowering it down to entwine it with hers before I look over to see her still smiling, with concern etched across her face.

I take a deep breath, looking back to the road glad I have a reason to look away. "Malcolm was the head of our household, like a butler of sorts, but so much more. I've known him all my life, and after my parents died, he took care of me. Between Malcolm and Sebastian, they were my legal guardians. I was fighting, drinking and just losing myself in sorrow, which turned to hatred. I needed to get away from it all. When I told them both my plan, they each said hell no, but once I brought in Luis with a detailed plan, they couldn't say no."

"Plan?" Ruby whispers more to herself, probably not realizing she said it aloud. I look over at her and smile.

"Yes, Luis and I came up with the ultimate plan. Sebastian at the time was vice president, and my father was president so when he died, Sebastian became acting president. I didn't want to work for my family's company, but I didn't want to lose it either. I knew Sebastian would be in my life no matter what. So, I made him co-partners giving him forty percent of the shares. I gave ten percent of the shares to Malcolm. Sebastian would have full run of the business and could do as he pleased, making me a silent partner. My plan was to see the world for a few years, get my head on straight and when I figured out what I wanted to do with my life, deal with it then. Malcolm would live and run the household like he had all my life. It was a perfect plan." I stop talking and release her hand.

Needing to pull over for this part of the story, I signal to get off the highway. When I pull onto the side of the road, I put it in park, turning to face Ruby, who looks freaked out.

"Oh, God. This is the bad part," Ruby whispers.

I give her a small smile, but she doesn't move. "It was a great plan. I moved around for a few years. Like I said to you before, I changed my name. We thought it would be good just in case I got out of hand, or something happened it wouldn't be traced back to my family name. Unless I was jailed, that is. I met Whiz and his club, hung out with them a lot. Loved being on a bike. Even went on a few rides after getting to know them. They called me a hang around, hoping one day I would prospect for them, but I kept moving around. I was and have always been in contact with Sebastian, Luis, and Malcolm but less and less because the more freedom I had, the more I loved my independence. I missed them, but the longer I was gone, the more I couldn't see myself going back to that life. Luis came out to see me a couple of times, but that was it."

"But..." Ruby drags out.

"But, when the incident with Shy happened, I had to cut all ties," I say in a low voice.

"What happened? Please tell me," Ruby begs.

My heart starts beating, and panic washes over me as what-ifs start firing off in my head.

What if she hates you? What if she leaves you? What if she doesn't understand?

"You're scaring me, Quick. You can tell me anything, and it won't change the fact I love you," she declares.

I rasp out, "I hope so."

Ruby unbuckles her seat belt and leans over grabbing my face with both hands, kissing me hard. Pulling back a fraction, she says, "Nothing. I mean nothing will take me away from you." She sits back in her seat with a worried look on her face, "Unless it has to do with hurting women, and children or molestation, shit like that is a hard hell fucking no.

I bust up laughing. *Christ, only my firecracker.*

"Fuck no, it's nothing like that," I clip out.

Her face lightens, and a huge smile spreads across it. "Okay, then you're good. Keep going."

"I killed two people," I blurt out.

Shock flashes across her face, but she recovers quickly by asking, "Men from that bad club?"

I nod my head. "I did it. I can't tell you details, but they came after me and hurt me really bad. Shy came and got me. When I was healed up, I contacted Luis first. Sebastian and Luis flew to New York to see me. Wolfe and Shy were both with me, and we all decided it was time I cut ties, or at least until things cooled down. They set me up in a hotel and Dallas set me up with an untraceable account so monthly money could be deposited into my account. I would send an email to all three of them from an untraceable email every month saying I was okay and that things were okay. But otherwise, I wouldn't contact them. I didn't want my shit to be traced to them. So, I cut all physical ties until recent."

"Because of me?" she murmurs.

"Yes, and no." I run my hands through my hair. "I miss my family. Seeing Whiz and talking with all my brothers had me thinking. Why am I leaving and in hiding when we don't even know if they are looking for me. It's why I've never stayed with a woman. I've been living in fear but when Shy asked me why, I couldn't answer. I can handle myself. I'm not the same young kid anymore. Having you and Bella in my life has changed everything."

"How? Do you want your old life back?" she asks.

"Fuck no!" I exclaim with a laugh.

"I love being a Wolfeman. I love my life, but I miss my family. I should be able to see them when I want. We're all older now and can handle it. I will never go by my birth name again just because I don't want anything to come back on my family if I fuck up." I pause, reaching for her hands. "But if I start a life with you, I'll be giving you my real name along with any children we might have."

Ruby has tears in her eyes when I pull her to kiss me, but she pulls back, questioning, "But you told Brody and them your full name today. Isn't that putting your family in your shit?"

"Rube, that was me staking my claim on your ass. If I must throw my name around to help you in any way, I'm going to do it. Today had nothing to do with the club. It has to do with you and me," I explain.

"So what other business do you need to talk to them about?" Ruby inquires, sitting back down in her seat.

"Before we get into that, do you have any other questions about my past? I want to close this subject and move on."

"Of course, I want to hear more about your family, but you explained everything I need to know. I know I can't ask about what happened with Shy, so no, I don't have any questions – that I can ask," Ruby replies.

"Rube, only four people know what really happened, and two of them are dead, so yeah, you need to let that go," I grunt.

"Have you killed anyone else?" she says, shocking me. I wasn't expecting that question from her, so I pause to answer.

"I guess that pause answers my question," Ruby says, her voice a whisper.

Snapping out of being shocked I fire back, "No one that didn't deserve it. All these men were very bad men, rapist, murderers and so, forth. I will protect my life, the life of my brothers and anyone else I care about. I don't regret my choices," I confess to her, hoping she understands.

When she nods her head not saying anything, I know she's mulling it over, so I let her be, turning in my seat, starting up the ignition. Pulling out into traffic, I glance over and say, "We need to get to the hotel, everyone will be waiting for us."

I'll leave it at that for right now, giving both of us time to get our heads right. Especially her with everything I've just told her, she has a lot to absorb before we throw her more shit.

I hope my firecracker can take it.

Ruby

Holy shit! He's killed more than one time.

I sit in the truck thinking about all the shit he just laid out for me to hear. I needed to hear it, and it doesn't alter my love for him. I look over at him, and my heart melts seeing my badass biker, all dressed up in a three-piece suit. *Fuck me.*

"Rube, you keep looking at me like that, and I'll be pulling over again, but this time it won't be to talk." Quick's husky voice has my woman parts tingling.

I smile. Yeah, my badass biker. *But he murdered people...* A little voice in my head says. He would never hurt me though, and I know that down to my soul. I feel more protected and safe with Quick than I ever did with Brody. Plus, he loves Bella. That little voice starts to fuck with me questioning my relationship but the good out weights the bad. By the time we get back to the hotel, I've processed what he's told me, how Margret came through for me and how I don't need to worry and just go with the flow.

Quick kills the engine, turning to me with concern. "You good?"

I nod my head with a smile. Looking at him.

"Rube, I need your words, baby. I need to know everything I just told you isn't going to come bite me in the ass. That you still love me." The vulnerability in his voice has my heart-aching. He's worried I'll leave him for what he just told me.

I lean toward him across the seat, wrapping my arms around his neck, I press a soft kiss on his lips before telling him, "I love you, Jake Reeves Walton. I know you would never hurt Bella or me. I've never felt more loved and safe than I do with you. So, you have nothing to worry about."

Quick lets out a breath, smashing our lips together for a deep kiss.

"Now, let's go in so we can get this other business done. I really want to get to know your family, but I really can't wait to show you how much I like this suit on you. And the only way I can properly do that is while I'm stripping it off you, yeah?" I say to him breathlessly.

Quick must like this because we're out of the SUV within minutes, as he hauls us through the lobby to the elevators. To my surprise we run into Luc and a man named Rick, that I've never met, heading up to our room.

On our way up to the room, Luc congratulates me on the divorce and how happy he is for me. I thanked him for coming to support me and asked where Mia was. He told me she was shopping but would be back soon. I didn't ask the big question of who the fuck Rick was or why they were coming to meet in our suite. I guess I'll find out eventually.

I also didn't know the brothers were meeting us either when Blink – now back in his jeans and cut, Chiv, Chain, and Jammer knocked on the door with arms full of drinks followed by Malcolm, Sebastian and his son Luis.

Quick kept his suit on but took the suit jacket off. I gave him a look that I wasn't happy he removed clothing. He smiled, giving me a wink but kept talking to Malcolm and Sebastian. I helped the boys put the drinks in the kitchen and made drinks for everyone.

When I handed Quick his beer, I asked what was going on, he just said that everything would be explained in a few minutes. So, the next few minutes I watched everyone be introduced that wasn't at the courthouse today. I felt his family members' eyes on me, watching me move around the suite. When I caught his Godfather watching me, I smiled but turned away nervously.

Now I'm really confused as I sit next to Quick at our kitchen table, along with Luc, his friend Rick, Luis, and Sebastian. While Malcolm, Blink, Chain, and Jammer all stand around us in the kitchen with drinks in their hands.

I'm trying to hold it together, but everyone is just chatting about nothing, and all I want to do is ask what the fuck is going on.

Quick is first to speak, bringing everyone's attention to us at the head of the table. "Okay, I think I need to explain to Ruby why we're all here today. Plus, I think it will get Chiv and Blink up to date on what's going on. I know Shy gave you the rundown but not the full extent of what we're going to offer Giselle."

I sit up straighter hearing my aunt's name as my head snaps to Quick. He turns to me with a smile. "Rube, you know Whiz's been helping your aunt out these past few months, well what you don't know is we've been looking into all her problems."

"What do you mean all her problems? You mean security?" I ask, sounding a little bit irritated and defensive of my aunt. Everyone looks toward me, but I don't give a fuck. Them "looking" into my aunt isn't cool.

"Rube, you know she's been having some issues with her neighbor as well," Quick says softly giving me a look to trust him. I nod. He continues, "Well, what we know is your aunt wants to push the neighbor out so she can expand, having a night club next to her strip club. She wants to revamp the club, making it into a more upscale gentleman's club." I know all of this, so I keep nodding. "Well, what you don't know is we've been working behind the scenes to buy the building."

My head glances around the table to see all the men still watching me. I look back to Quick. "You're taking my aunt's club away from her?" I say through gritted teeth.

Quick fires back, "No! God no, we're going to offer her the opportunity to become partners with us. We'll buy the building, push her neighbor out legally and back her as a silent partner in the next club. This will give her the security and money to help her achieve all that she wants." Quick finishes his sentence with a smile.

What the fuck? I know my face says it all because he leans in to say, "We're here to help your aunt. She's going under and the only thing saving her is her escort service. Her partner is a piece of shit. We're offering her an out, to keep her club plus give her the dream she's always wanted."

They don't know my aunt. I shake my head. "Um, have you told my aunt about this?"

There's a knock at the door, and I'm about ready to lose my shit. "Now who the fuck is here?" I blurt out not even thinking of who's around the table.

I hear a few chuckles, but don't bother trying to see who thinks this shit is funny. My eyes are too busy watching the entryway. Blink opens the door and in strolls Shy, Tiny, Worm, Cash, Wolfe, Bear and Hawk from our club and Whiz, along with two of his men.

Blink hugs his brothers that he hasn't seen in months, but when the brothers see Chiv, they all get loud and excited to see the brother that has been in jail and didn't know was released early.

For fuck's sake. The room just got real cramped with all these men. I look over at Quick's family, and they don't even look fazed at all with the bikers getting rowdy.

Quick grabs my hand and says in a low calming voice,

"Rube, we have a meeting set up tonight to go over all of this with your aunt. What we're discussing right now is what my guys and Luc's guys have come up with on the sale of the building."

"She is going to flip the fuck out. She'll think you're taking over," I rasp out.

"No, she'll have full reign on everything. She will continue to run it just as she is, but obviously, Whiz's crew will be security. We're only going to be her silent partner, pretty much just like her old partner was, but we won't be in her way. We'll get a cut, but we won't be involved in the decision making unless things get bad."

I sit there staring at him and before I can say anything, the men make their way to the table saying their hellos. When Quick gets up, the brothers that just arrived make cracks about him being in a suit. He talks shit back at them, laughing as he finishes the introductions.

I'm still in shock when Cash nudges my shoulder. When I look up to see Cash's beautiful gaze on me. "You good, shorty? Thought I would be walking in here seeing Firecracker in full force hearing your divorce was handled today."

I stand up giving him a hug. "Thanks Cash."

Cash pulls back slightly to look me in the face. "What's up?"

Quick moves behind me. "I was just telling her the plan and stuff."

Wolfe and Shy move up behind Cash when he asks, "You don't approve of us helping her out?"

I look around the room before answering truthfully, "I know my aunt is like me, we don't like to ask for help. It will be a shock, just like it is to me. She'll probably get defensive like I just did. Maybe, if you word it better than Quick did, she will hear what you're trying to tell her, instead of freaking out.

Sebastian and Luc both bust up laughing but Luc speaks up, "This is why I love her working for me."

Sebastian looks over to Luc. "Yes, I'm starting to like her more and more."

Quick pulls me from Cash's arms. "Fuck all of you. Now can we sit down and go over all of this and y'all explain it to *my girl* the *right* fucking way. Christ, where's Dallas when you need him. Fuck, I need a drink."

Once all the brothers get a drink and are settled, Luc takes over and explains in detail the sale of the building, the contracts that all the tenants have and more shit. I lost my concentration after he mentioned that Quick and Luc would be buying the building together – giving Giselle the opportunity to be a part of the sale. I was fighting back the tears.

Quick and Luc were buying the building to help my aunt out.

He explains all the different offers they will give to my aunt, with them being co-partners, silent partner. Depending on what she says or decides, they have all options covered. The biggest one being they're buying the building regardless if my aunt buys-in or not. If she doesn't want any help after moving out the tenants, so she can expand – it's okay because they're making money on the purchase of the building.

But I know my aunt, and she needs help. All the men ask their questions and give their advice. I just sit there listening to them. My irritation is gone by the time they're finishing up. I'm nothing but thankful for these men.

They haven't only come to my rescue but my aunts as well. When there is another knock at the door, I ask, "Is that my aunt? Seeing as she's the only one not here."

Luc smiles, getting up with Rick, who I now know is his attorney and says, "No, that would be Mia. I've got to go with her, but we'll meet you all at Club DazZelle tonight."

Mia walks into the room full of smiles and when she sees all the men, fans herself, "Aye Papi, so many hot men in here." She giggles.

Luc laughs, pulling her to his side, giving her a kiss.

Everyone says goodbye to them. Malcolm, Sebastian, and Luis stand up next. "We're going to hit our room, shower, change and meet up with you before heading to the club."

I look to Sebastian. "You're coming tonight too?"

Sebastian laughs. "Honey, you couldn't keep us away even if you tried. Our boy has finally called on us. We're here for a while."

Luis cuts in, "Strippers, plus my best friend and did I say strippers?"

Everyone laughs in agreement.

They leave setting a time to meet up, and then it's just the Wolfemen and me. Shy updates us on Dallas, Izzy and everyone back home. I notice Wolfe watching me, and when I glance his way, I smile. He returns my smile but asks, "So, now that everyone is pretty much gone, and you've heard everything, how are you really feeling about this? You know your aunt the best. What do you think she'll do? Will she be upset with us stepping in to help?"

He folds his arms over his impressive chest. Wolfe is a very attractive man for his age. I've always thought of my aunt when I see him. That she should meet him but now that I know about his late wife, I'm hesitant about their meeting.

"Honestly, I don't know. Depends on how you all approach her and who explains it to her. I think she needs help and won't ask for it, but it's also getting really bad—"

Wolfe cuts me off, "But, what do you think of all of this? Do you want us to help her and step in?" The room becomes quiet as Wolfe's voice isn't soft and calming. He seems aggressive and irritated.

I tilt my head and analysis him a second before answering. "What I do know is you and your brothers are good men. You've done nothing but been supportive of my situation and helping my daughter and me during this rough time. I think my aunt would be lucky to have all of you behind her, helping her finally get her dream."

Wolfe, whose face is stone, but after a few seconds of us staring each other down, it breaks when he cracks a smile. "Good." He moves toward the kitchen to grab another beer but stops, "Glad to hear today went well for you. Hopefully, by the end of tonight, we'll all have something to celebrate."

Everyone lifts their drinks congratulating me on my divorce. Tears fill my eyes, lifting my drink too, I mouth thank you because my throat is clogged with all this biker love.

Quick slides his arms around my waist from behind, murmuring into my ear, "You ready to strip me of this monkey suit." My smile widens as I nod my head.

"We need to get ready. I need to get out of this monkey suit and shower. Help yourself to whatever," Quick says, grabbing my hand.

The men heckle him about the monkey suit as Quick pulls me into the bedroom, shutting and locking the door.

Oh yeah, I'm so ready to pounce on my man.

22 | Time To Celebrate

Quick

"Christ, we're in trouble if my ol' lady sees this fucking place," Hawk says to all the brothers sitting at the bar.

We've just gotten to Club DazZelle, which is packed tonight. Our usual private room isn't available yet, so we've taken over a good part of the bar with Shy, Wolfe, Hawk, Bear and me, sitting on stools, with our backs to the bar looking out toward the club. Tiny, Worm, Cash, Bear, Blink, and Chiv are standing around us, as we all take in the club.

We decided to come straight here instead of hitting up the Sons of Saint's clubhouse first. Wolfe wanted to check the place out before the madness of the night got started. He wanted to handle business first. He knew if we stopped there first, everyone would start drinking and get fucked up. We'll probably end up at the clubhouse later tonight after we're done here.

Ruby went to the back area to check in with the girls and see if her aunt was here. Ruby contacted her aunt asking about Bella, but Giselle told her that Margret, Brody's mom wanted to spend more time with her. Since we were planning on getting a babysitter anyway, it worked out perfect. So her aunt came in early to prepare for all of us being here since we're going to have a big group tonight with Whiz's whole chapter, all the Wolfemen, plus Luc and my family.

Luis texted earlier letting me know they would meet us here. He was going to dinner with Luc, Mia, and Rick to discuss some other business, which was fine with me, it gave me a little more time with Ruby. After she sucked my cock dry, showing me just how much she liked me in a three-piece suit, I returned the favor, three more times. I was fucking her in the shower, one last time before we needed to leave, showing her how happy I was her divorce was done. My dick didn't want to stop, but then again, it never does. I could fuck her all day and night and still want more.

"Firecracker going to dance tonight?" Cash asks, looking around the club.

"I don't think so, but you never know with her," I begin to say but remember how tired she was after I fucked her senseless. "But seeing as I just gave her a really long workout, she might be too tired," I declare with a laugh taking a swig of my beer.

"Goddamn, there are some hot fucking bitches here," Worm says, practically drooling at the mouth.

"Easy, Worm. We got club business first before you start Worming your way through the bitches one at a time," Tiny teases.

"Why are there so many more hot women here?" Hawk questions.

"Because Lish hasn't recruited new pussy in years. And you fuckers in New York just go to night clubs to get good pussy instead of getting new club girls," Wolfe explains.

"Well, Lish needs to do some new hiring. Because fuck me, these bitches can dance *and* they're hot as fuck," Cash replies.

Hawk laughs. "You gonna be the one to tell her she needs better pussy at the club? Be my guest but don't get me involved."

"Fuck just let our ol' ladies come here, and shit will change real quick." Bear shakes his head. Then adds, "Y'all know them ladies want to be the best. Show them this, and it will be all about a remodel."

I just sit there amused, listening to my brothers laugh. All of today's activity's start to filter through my head as I let it all sink in, my heart feels like it's going to burst with so much goodness filling it right now. Seeing Malcolm, Sebastian and Luis made me realize how much I've missed their crazy asses. Sebastian and Luis didn't change too much. Malcolm definitely has aged these past few years, but he's still feisty as fuck.

"You good, brother?" Shy asks next to me.

I turn to him with a huge smile. "Fuck yeah, couldn't be better. Just thinking about everything that went down today."

Shy smiles. "Good, glad it worked out having your family here and involved."

I take a swig of beer before replying to him. "It was the talk you gave me before I came to get my girl. Then the talk I had with Whiz about the past, and I just said, fuck it. I've been floating through life worried about what the Crows would do if they find me again, but really what do they have on me? Nothing. They beat my ass because I wouldn't tell them who did it. They fought with you because they hate our club. If they find me – oh, fucking well. Like you said we'd deal with it, but overall no one knows anything but the two of us. So, I'm living my life."

Shy turns in his stool to face me with a huge grin on his face. "Fuck! Finally, you get it. Brother, we've been telling you to live your life. Fuck them motherfuckers. Yes, it would be a bitch if they flipped out, but we would handle it. You're not the only reason we don't want to deal with the Crows. It's been years and years of beef with them."

I lift my beer. "Wolfeman for life, brother." He tips his to mine. "Wolfeman for life." Slamming the remainder of our beers.

Blink and Chiv have moved further into the club toward the back where our private room is, as they watch two brunettes dancing on a single pole together.

Chain standing at the end of the bar, while Jammer is at the front door watching our surroundings.

The main stage lights dim to almost nothing, blacking out the stage when a seductive voice announces, "Please make some noise for our girl, Destiny." The crowd starts to whistle with catcalls throughout the building. "The Hills" by The Weeknd blasts through the speakers as a spotlight clicks on shining down on a bitch sitting backward on a chair with her back to us. Her long, jet black hair cascading down her back, making it look as though she is topless.

When the beat drops, she snaps her head back and slowly lowers herself into a backbend off the chair, exposing her huge tits that are practically spilling out of a very tiny black bikini. She runs her fingers from her pussy up over her stomach, gripping her breasts. I look around to see every damn man is transfixed on her, probably hoping that fucking bikini snaps off.

I look back to the stage, and the bitch has one handful of her hair pulling it, the other one around her neck in a choking like grip, all the while grinding the chair.

"Jesus Christ. My dick's in love," Worm announces.

"The bitch can move. Fuck, she can bend over me any day," Cash returns.

Watching the girl, no one really notices the group of men next to the stage. A bachelor party that I can tell by the looks of them have been here for a while. When the girl gets closer to the edge, the men stand up crowding the stage as they throw money at her.

I stand up, along with my brothers, already knowing how this is going to go. Hawk being the first to move closer. The songs almost to the end when one of the cocksuckers reaches out, grabbing the bitches foot making her trip. We're on the move pushing men out of the way trying to get to the crowded stage, where the fucking guy is trying to pull the girl off stage.

We're almost to them when a loud crack soars through the air, followed by a man screaming. I stop instantly – another crack. The stage lights up, and everyone freezes seeing Giselle or by the look of it Mistress Z, walk out with a bullwhip in hand ready to strike again. When she does, I shit you not every mother fucker in the room looks like he's ready to either bow down or blow their wad. The bitch is stunning in a black full body leather jumpsuit and her black fucking wig.

Sonofabitch.

I swing around to see Bear, Hawk, and Wolfe standing there in complete shock. "Holy. Fucking. Shit," Cash breathes out next to me.

Giselle points out which men need to go when security starts pulling the men from the ground holding their injuries. Wrapping the bullwhip across her chest, Giselle bends down to help the girl up and escort her backstage.

The seductive voice from before comes over the speaker, this time mad as hell, "Motherfuckers if you don't keep your hands to yourself, Mistress Z will hurt you really fucking bad. You cocksuckers know the rules. Do. Not. Touch. The. Dancers! You've all been warned. Don't fuck around." The voice pauses, and when she speaks again, the sweet seductive voice says, "Now, next up is our sweet Candy girl."

I move toward Wolfe, but Blink is there before me. "It's not her. It's the aunt with a wig on. It's not her, Prez." Wolfe turns on his heels and heads out the front door followed by all the brothers.

Jesus Christ.

Once everyone's outside, I see Wolfe taking a couple of deep breaths with his hands in his hair. Bear, Cash, and Hawk look just as shook up.

Blink keeps talking. "Brother, I saw her dressed in something like that last night when I was here, and I almost shit myself. Quick said it's the wig, but damn she looks just like Foxy. I saw her again today, but she doesn't look like Foxy without the wig."

Bear yells, "Shut the fuck up and give him a minute," walking over putting himself in front of Wolfe like a wall giving him some privacy to get his shit together.

When the door swings open, Ruby runs out of the club, in a panic, hair flying wildly around her. My dick instantly hardens. I whistle, letting her know where we are and make my way over to her. The group of us are all hanging out in front of the

225

asshole neighbor's storefront, but it looks like his store is closed.

"Fuck, is Wolfe alright? When I saw what my aunt was wearing when she helped Destiny back, I freaked out on her." Ruby turns to Wolfe. "Are you okay? I'm sorry my aunt wore the black wig again. It's her favorite."

Wolfe turns to Ruby. "I'm good. Just took me by surprise."

"Fuck, took us all by surprise, brother," Hawk announced.

The sound of rumbling cuts through the night and when a big group of motorcycles pulls up, I notice it's Whiz and his club. When Whiz sees all of us outside in front of the dickhead's shop, they all stop in the middle of the street, some pulling to the side. Whiz yelling, "You all good?"

I nod my head replying, "Just getting some air. See you inside."

Whiz looks from me to Shy, to Wolfe, then back to me. He isn't stupid and knows something's up but just gives us a nod back and takes off to park.

Wolfe announces, "I'm good. Let's head back in."

Everyone follows Wolfe back inside, taking up our spot we had before we all jumped up to protect the stripper. Everyone tries to relax as Whiz, and his men file into the club. Ruby moves all of us into our private enclosed booth, where we can have some privacy. Three women file into the room one going to the pole while the others work the room getting drink orders.

Ruby tucks herself into my side, as we fall onto the couch she says, "Babe, I feel bad we should have warned him. I didn't see her until after the commotion."

I kiss the top of her head. "It's all good but goddamn, Rube I think almost every man came in their pants hearing and seeing her wield that bullwhip. Fuck, you might need to get an outfit like that, but I'm doing the whipping and tying up. You just wear the outfit." I laugh, seeing her face light up.

Mental note… my bitch likes kink.

Fuck my dicks hard again. "Firecracker you liking kink has my dick rock solid. Might need to have a quickie out back if you don't stop looking at me like that," I declare, swatting her ass.

Yeah, my little firecracker likes it kinky alright.

An hour later, we cleared out the private room to have this meeting before it got too late, or we got too drunk. The presidents, Shy, Wolfe and Whiz, along with their vice presidents, Cash, and Cue are sitting on one half of the booth. Luc, Mia, Rick, Sebastian, Luis and I are along the other half of the booth. Ruby left to tell her aunt we were ready for the meeting and to make sure she didn't wear her black wig.

When the door opened, Wolfe was tense sitting next to me, fully alert and ready for her to walk in with her black wig looking identical to the love of his life Foxy. But when Giselle walked through the door, she looked completely different. She changed her clothes into a form-fitting black cocktail dress, and her dark blondish brown hair that is usually wild with curls is now bone straight. She's still fucking gorgeous, but she didn't look like Foxy.

Ruby introduces her aunt to everyone, leaving Wolfe to be the last introduction. Once introduced Giselle instantly apologizes, "I'm sorry about earlier. I had just got here from a session and was going to change, but when I saw that fucker grab Destiny, I lost it. I'm sorry for shocking you." Smiling down at him sweetly waiting for him to reply, but Wolfe's face is stone blank, nothing in return.

When he doesn't reply she starts to turn to walk over to me, but he growls, "You have a lot of her facial features too, but the black wig makes you almost identical." Everyone is quiet, hearing his voice rough and filled with so much pain.

More Silence.

Giselle turns back to him with another sweet smile, saying softly, "She must have been beautiful. I'm sorry for your loss. Once the meeting is over, I'll leave."

Wolfe shakes his head snapping out of this daze, snapping, "No, I'm fine." Hearing his own voice come off so harshly, he takes a deep breath and with a slight grin says to her, "Sorry. Yes, she was beautiful, and you are as well. You definitely were a shock to my system, but you're a breath of fresh air. Please stay and have a drink."

She nods her head in appreciation before moving to sit next to Ruby on the other side of me.

Everyone sits back, taking in everything that just happened. Wolfe speaks again, "Okay, so Madam—"

She interrupts him, "Please, just call me Giselle."

Wolfe pauses, giving her another long look before continuing. "Okay, Giselle. We've all put together some really great ideas and plans for you, but I believe, as does everyone here, that Ruby should present this to you."

All eyes turn toward Ruby and me. I'm just as shocked as Ruby looking around the room.

I say, "When did this get talked about?"

"When you two were *getting ready.* After talking to Ruby about how she felt, I called Luc and Luis, and we all agreed. Ruby knows us, knows her aunt, we've told her our ideas. I think she will know best and will present it to Giselle in the best way possible."

Ruby and her aunt look at each other.

Ruby lets go of me, standing up walking over to Luc who hands her the stack of information to give to Giselle and herself. I sit back and watch my girl present our ideas to her aunt. Instantly you can see the businesswoman snap into action, taking charge of the situation. She does it in a way her aunt doesn't even flinch. Instead, she asks questions and tells us her arrangements with her current co-partner. The meeting begins, opening up for Luc to talk, along with Whiz and Wolfe to put in their advice and opinions.

An hour later, we have a plan. We've all agreed upon things, but we will still need to finalize everything once the paperwork is completed. I was right, Giselle doesn't have money to spare to buy the building, so Luc and I will go in halves and buy the building. Giselle will hire Whiz's clubhouse for security and help her remove some tenants. Along with helping her tell her co-partner, he's out, and a silent partner will be stepping in which will be the Wolfeman. The Sons of Saints will get a cut of the profits, seeing as they will be helping Giselle run things, but they will not have their name on the business or the building. My club and I will be fronting most of the money for the remodel.

Everyone is chatting and excited with the new business endeavors when Cash demands, "Firecracker this calls for a dance. You need to dance for us."

Now, this gets Sebastian and Luis' attention since they didn't know Ruby danced. Ruby, who's somewhat buzzed now replies, "Yes, Cash, I'm going to dance tonight." She pauses seeing his face light up, then giggles, adding, "But I'm sorry tonight will only be a private dance for my man." falling onto my lap with a squeal. My chest constricts because I would never tell my girl she couldn't dance for my brothers because I know damn well no one would overstep but for her to deny them for me, makes me overly happy.

Damn straight. My firecracker.

Giselle laughs. "Sweetie if you're going to do that, you best get on it because the rooms are booked the last three hours of the night."

Ruby wiggles her ass over my rock-hard cock. I grunt, "You heard her, lead the way." Swatting her ass to get up.

I watch as my ol' lady guides us to the door, swaying that fine ass of hers. I laugh hearing my brothers complaining how fucked up it was, while my family just watches me walk away in what I can only describe as envy across their face.

Yep, I found my ol' lady. The one person I can't live without. That's my firecracker all right.

Ruby leads us into a much smaller, darker room where there's just one wall with a bench seat, a round platform with a pole in the middle, with a couple of single chairs that you can move closer to the pole or just have in the room so the stripper can do a solo chair dance.

Ruby nudges me to sit down on a chair, when she locks eyes with me, I see the fire blazing behind them.

Oh, yeah. My feisty little Firecracker is here to play.

I bite my lower lip, making a low growl.

She smiles. "Sit down."

I don't say anything, as I watch her move to the corner of the room. When she pushes against the wall, part of it pops open, revealing a hidden compartment. In there is a stereo, buttons and a couple of bottles of whiskey.

Well damn. You'd never have to leave.

Ruby returns with two glasses of whiskey, handing me one, she lifts hers. "To us and our future."

I clink glasses with her, as I gaze up at her. I nod my head shooting the whole drink back. Handing her the empty glass, "Is there videos in here? Because I'm thinking I'm not gonna be able to not fuck you."

Ruby takes my drink, turning to head back to the corner and says over her shoulder, "This room is a 'full service' room." Placing the empty glasses in the cubie she continues, "The dancer has the option of turning the video off..." She flips a switch and smiles. "Which I just did."

Ruby's hair is wild all around her face making my hands twitch to run them through it, even pull it a bit. She's wearing a tight little lacey see-through top, giving everyone around her a glimpse of her mouthwatering tits with just enough cleavage pushing up from her bra to make you want to see more.

I groan shifting in my seat to adjust my cock. It's been painfully hard most the night and, definitely needs a release.

Ruby turns to the stereo shaking that fine ass of hers, bending slightly, showing me her silky-smooth legs sticking out from under her very short jean skirt. I know she isn't wearing any underwear because I ordered her not too. I knew I would need easy access tonight and right about now I need to be bone deep in that pussy of mine.

The lights dim even more, and Ruby turns from the corner. Just as "Please Me" by Cardi B and Bruno Mars starts to play.

I smile.

Oh, she is, definitely going to please me. Yeah, baby.

Ruby moves toward me lip-syncing the song about no panties being in the way or some shit. *Fuck she's beautiful.* Ruby keeps singing while seductively moving her body. I don't take my eyes off hers though. She slowly lifts her shirt as she moves around me and when she's done a full circle, her shirt is gone. I lick my lips. *Oh, baby. Fuck yeah.*

"Mine," I growl.

Ruby smiles hearing me claiming her. She keeps dancing seductively moving to unbutton her jean skirt turning her back to me she teases me slipping the skirt lower and lower before dropping it while bending over exposing all that is mine for the taking and that I'm about ready to pounce on again.

Slowly unfolding herself, she stands up straight, turning toward me. She prowls over to me, gripping my knees, spreading them dipping down doing some fuck me dance before popping back up.

"I'm about ready to lose my shit so this dance better hurry up." My voice is demanding, but you can hear the pleading in it.

When Ruby's standing in front of me with just a bra on, she

moves to straddle me, wrapping her arms around my neck. My hands that were resting between my legs now cup her saturated pussy.

Oh yeah. She's ready.

"Please me, baby," she says breathlessly against my neck.

I snap, feeling her warm pussy against me I grip her ass cheeks. "Bend backward," I say in a husky growl.

Ruby lets go of my neck to lean back. I spread my legs just a bit so she can do a backbend between them as I hold her hips against me. I watch her through the mirror and when our eyes meet, I tell her, "Reach for the ground, Rube. I'm gonna eat this pussy of mine." I move her legs straight up against my chest. When Ruby's hands are secure against the ground, she smiles when I motion for her to spread her legs into the splits.

Absolutely stunning. Fuck I'm one lucky bastard.

In one motion, I grip her hips and lift her pussy up to my face lifting her whole body up off the ground, hooking her legs over my shoulders. I stand up with her body hanging from my shoulders with an arm around her lower pelvis, securing her to my body as I devour her pussy. Sucking, fucking, nipping like I'm a crazed man. I reach over with my other hand slipping it down her torso, gripping her breast, twisting and teasing her nipple.

My eyes are focused on us in the mirror, watching my firecracker lose her mind.

She moans, "Oh. Oh, yeah. Fuck yes." Her thighs clench around my head, locking it to her pussy as she starts moaning guttural cries of pleasure.

"Come on, baby. Fuck me, baby," Ruby begs.

I slide my tongue out and rapidly flick her clit, making her legs start to shake. I move us toward the bench laying her down. The next song "Touch Me Tease Me" by Case, Foxy Brown, and Mary J. Blige begins to play.

Keeping my mouth on her pussy and clit the whole time, I

insert two fingers moving them in and out fast. Hitting the right spot, I send her over screaming my name. I stand up, taking my cut off, putting it on the bench. I'm about ready to explode, and I'm crazed with need to be inside her. I command, "Stand up, face the pole and bend over. I want that ass in the air."

Ruby starts to move, but I can see she's still coming down from her climax I just gave her, so I pick her up moving her to the small platform with the pole, taking her bra off and throw it. I grab her arms, extending them out toward the pole. My voice is more urgent sounding this time. "Grab on to it and don't let go."

Moving my hands to my own jeans, I feel my chest start to rise and fall faster and faster, as I take shorter breaths. I feel like one of those kids that, has to pee so bad, he has to do the pee-pee dance while trying to get his clothes off in time, so he doesn't piss himself.

"Fuck!" I growl trying to calm myself. I can't breathe. I'm about ready to lose control.

I grab my steel cock, gliding it to her entrance, swiping it a couple of times using her cum to slicken my cock before ramming it into her sated pussy. Ruby cries out, "Yes. Quick, yes."

I pump into her rapidly with both hands on her hips, but I need more. "Lift your arms higher above your head but don't let go of that pole," I command moving us a couple of steps away from the platform that the pole is on, making her bend forward more, as I kick her legs out further moving in between them so I can thrust up deep into her. I ram her hard a couple of times making her cry out in pleasure, screaming for more, so I lean over slightly reaching an arm around gripping a tit before moving up to her neck holding her in place, lightly grabbing it. The song ends halting the room into silence, leaving only the sound of our sexual exertion and bodies slapping.

Ruby moans, "Fuck yes. Harder baby, fuck me."

Hearing her want me to fuck her harder has me grunting my approval just as "Anywhere" by 112 blares through the speakers.

I use all my force and start jacking my rock-hard cock up hard and deep. I feel her walls contracting around my dick. Once I get the rhythm right, I pick up the pace. I'm pounding her so hard and fast that it's making her body thrust forward practically lifting her almost off her feet. All you hear is her tits slapping in unison with her ass hitting against me.

She's close, hearing her purr as she chases her orgasm. I grip her windpipe tighter, sliding my other hand from her hip down to her clit. "That's it, my little firecracker. Come baby come hard for me." I tighten my grip on her throat, even more, applying just the right amount of pressure, sending her over for the second time with her release crashing through her. I feel her pussy spasming all over my pulsing cock.

I move both hands back down to her hips holding her up as the wave of ecstasy continues to wash through her.

"One more...Hold on, Firecracker I'm about to explode baby. Wait for me, Rube."

Ruby starts to chat, over and over again, "Yes. Yes. Yes."

Fuck I want more...

I feel like a caged animal, chasing its prey, needing more, wanting more. Reaching over her I slide her hands down the pole, which puts her head down lower pushing her ass out at me more.

"Goddamn beautiful. My Ruby-Rue. All mine." My voice is breathy.

Sweat drips from my face. I lift one of her legs, hiking her heel on the platform I'm all about fucking hard and dirty. I smooth my hands over the swell of her ass as I rock into her with deep, long thrust as I praise her body bent over in front of me. I use her cum dripping between us to lubricate my thumb. I grip her ass high sliding my thumb down between her cheeks slipping the tip in, pulling it out and slipping it back in, milking her asshole.

"Fuck me, baby. Hurry, fuck me hard. I'm close," Ruby begs as she thrusts her ass back, meeting my thrust in both holes. My free hand grips her leg, lifting it higher, holding it as I hammer into her simultaneously while milking her ass.

Ruby's words are so slurred, I can't understand her, I'm too focused on my own release.

Fuck yes. Ah. Yeah.

My thrusts are becoming erratic and more carnal, digging my nails into her thigh pounding into her.

Shit, yeah. Ah. Fuck, yes. "Fuck, yeah Rube," I rasp out, breathless.

A guttural groan rips through me, as my orgasm explodes with a euphoric high almost knocking me out – every single one of my muscles is taut and strained. I feel a burning sensation coursed through my legs from all the exertion. I keep groaning as I slowly come down from my climatic high with each thrust.

Ruby purrs beneath me. Still riding my high, I manage to lower her leg, lifting her up. I take the few steps back and sit down with her sitting on top of me, my cock still lodged up in her. Ruby collapses her head back against my shoulder, trying to catch her breath.

"Goddamn baby. It gets better and better each time with you," Ruby murmurs still breathless.

"Mmm," is all I can manage to get out.

Ruby shifts to the side so she can tilt her head to face me. I smile knowing she's watching me, but my eyes are closed.

"You good baby?" she says softly.

"I'll be better when you have my ring on your finger and my cut on your back," I blurt out.

Ruby's body tenses as I crack open one eye, still smirking at her.

"What?" she says in a gasp.

I open both eyes and look straight into her eyes, letting her know I'm serious and tell her straight up how I feel, "Divorce is done, Rube. I know you're the one. I've already claimed you as my ol' lady, just need your cut. I've been holding off till your shit was sorted." I pause. "And today – it was sorted."

Ruby starts crying as she turns in my arms, smashing her mouth to mine.

"It just keeps getting better and better," she repeats against my lips.

Yes, it does!

23 | The Journey
Ruby

The day I signed my divorce papers and helped make a plan for my aunt's dream club to come true was the day all of our lives changed. Well, everyone's life that was linked to Quick and mine, changed for the better. Being around and seeing Quick with his family was like seeing a whole new Quick. He had a look of complete ease and happiness filling him.

Everyone stayed that following week except Luc and Mia who had to return to New York the following day, leaving their attorney Rick, to handle all their dealings. Luc and Mia said they mostly came down here to support me and make sure I wasn't alone. All the business dealings could be handled over the phone and email.

Both clubs had business they had to take care of up North and would be gone for a few days. They had Quick stay behind to handle the details with Giselle, giving him time to hang out with his family, who had planned to stay another week.

Hanging out getting to know Luis and Sebastian was easy, as they interacted with Bella and me, whereas Malcolm stayed to himself in the distance watching.

Quick and Luis' comradery was like they've never had a day away from each other, let alone years. Just listening to them talk you could tell they've been best friends since birth. Quick was his same ol' self, my biker badass. Sebastian and Luis filled Quick in on all the town gossip, business endeavors, and household changes. When they talked about his home, and the staff, that was the only time I could see Quick still grieved his parents.

Hearing stories about his mom, Mellie, as they called her and his dad, Johnny, there would be flashes of sadness but when he would look over at Bella or me, his expression would soften returning a smile to his face. I asked him about it one night, and he just said his parents would've loved us girls.

Quick promised them we would come to visit so he could show me where he's from. The night before they were all due to leave, Malcolm finally opened up to me. We were in our hotel suite, and I was cleaning up dinner in the kitchen. Malcolm began telling me he was sorry for being so quiet but that he was just trying to take it all in. He loves Jake and only wants what's best for him, but not being able to see him all these years really tore him up. He felt like he lost all three of them. He's been absorbing everything that is Jake's life now and praying he's truly happy. I reassured him I would do everything in my power to make him happy and to get him back home for a visit.

Izzy has called everyday giving me the low down of what's been going on over there. Dallas being good and getting back to normal. She told me about the hot doctor and how he's obsessed with her now. She's been focusing on her song, fucking Gus and taking care of Dallas, and those were her words. I miss her so much, but soon we will all be together, happy.

I kept telling Quick it was too good to be true, that I was waiting for the other shoe to drop. Brody and Sam left two days later back on tour. I spoke with Margret every day, letting her have Bella a couple of hours each day. She told me how she laid into her husband Harold and the boys when she got into the car. She actually giggled when she explained how the boys were so shocked. When she told me she threatened to leave, that was the icing on the cake, and they all fell into line. Margret might have been quiet all these years, but the woman was the glue that kept that family going, so when she finally stood up to them, it was serious.

Of course, I know Harold, and I'm sure it's still not okay between them, but she told me after a long discussion he understood, Brody did need to grow up. He was young, and he could really do something with his life, if he just pulled his self together, and not be such an abusive douche bag. I don't want Bella to *not* have a dad, but I don't want her to know him like he is now.

I told Margret, as long as he doesn't cause problems for Bella or myself, he could see her whenever he wanted too, but I knew in my heart he didn't care about her. I prayed one day he would pull his head out of his ass and see Bella for who she is – his daughter.

No matter what, I know Bella will have a father figure in her life who loves her unconditionally because Quick adores her and her him. Quick is becoming more like a dad every day now. I can see the change in both of us, from having just Bella, Auntie and I, to having so many people that truly love and care about us.

Everything with my aunt fell into place too as Mancini Incorporation and Reeves Corporation went into escrow two days after we met with my aunt. We both learned Luis had started a corporation all those years ago when Jake changed his name to Reeves just in case, he needed it. Once the escrow closes, they will start to push the tenants out so they can begin construction.

My aunt and I as always have a great time. She's like my mom instead of my aunt. My own mother doesn't give a rat's ass about me. So, when Quick asked a few nights ago when he was going to meet my mom, I said you have, Giselle. He gave me a funny look but it's true, I let my mom go a long time ago. When she would fly into town, I would see her for a few hours before she would run off again. Yeah, I let it go a long time ago.

Wolfe and Auntie hung out chatting and getting to know each other for two days until the MC's had to ride out, but he said he would be back. I sat up with her late one night drinking at our hotel while Quick was helping the guys prepare for their ride. She told me he's hot as fuck, scary in a good way that got her lady parts tingling, but she didn't really want to be a reminder of someone's dead wife.

When I explained that to Quick, he seemed kind of worried. I asked why and he told me in a roundabout way that Wolfe doesn't do the let's hang out and have a drink kind of thing. He was worried about him because Wolfe loved Foxy with everything he had and has never-ever dated anyone since. Yeah, he would fuck but never dated, and with Giselle having her life here he didn't see how it would work. So, we both agreed to stay out of it and not ask questions. They were two grown adults.

After his family left, we had a couple of days alone, before the guys were back from a run, so Quick and I got the rest of my shit in order. Quick informed me that Bella and I would be flying home with Wolfe, Bear, Hawk, and Cash. That I wasn't going to be driving my stuff back, instead him, Shy, Tiny, Worm, Blink, Chiv and the two prospects were going to be doing it. I wasn't too happy about this because it was my shit. I should drive it back, but Quick informed me they were going to be doing some club business along the way. He didn't want Bella or me to be stuck in a car for two weeks.

He had a point because having Bella locked in a car seat for two days was a mission, let alone a week or two, so I gave in. What I didn't know or think about was that he would be leaving right when the guys got back. Leaving me...leaving me for two weeks. Jesus, we hadn't even been apart for a week before he came down to Los Angeles to get me. But here I am back in New York with my best friend, in our new beautiful place, back to work and missing my man. It's been six days since I've seen him. Bella misses him too, but she was excited to see Uncle Red when we got back. Until Quick is back home in my arms, my life will not be complete, and I pray that the other shoe doesn't drop while he's away.

Quick

"Did you talk to Mac? Did he pick it up from Storm yet?" Shy asks.

He's talking about Ruby's Wolfeman property cut that I'm having made. I'd called Mac before we left to drive home. Mac's mom, Storm, handles all the lady's cuts. It's been twelve fucking days on the road, and I'm missing my ol' lady real fucking bad, truthfully I have two ladies I'm missing. I didn't know how much that little girl meant to me until I didn't see them each and every day. My heart aches to see them.

"Brother?" Shy questions when I haven't answered.

"Naw, I'll do it closer to home," I reply, not taking my eyes off the road. We've got a couple more days if we're lucky. So far, it's been smooth sailing, with no problems at our first two stops, now only two more to go. Tiny and Worm are in one moving truck, while Chain and Jammer are in the other. Blink and Chiv are on their bikes, lucky bastards, while Shy and I drive Ruby's Mercedes-Benz GLE. At least we have the luxury car since we don't have our bikes.

"What's on your mind, brother?" Shy asks.

"I'm in a fucking cage about ready to lose my fucking mind. My ass hurts from sitting so goddamn much and my dicks depressed it ain't been wet in twelve fucking days. Plus, I'm anxious about driving through Crows' territory and doing a stop in it today."

Shy chuckles. "Brother, I think it's safe to say we all feel that way. Shit, my dicks in mourning because it's been over a fucking month since it was wet by my ol' lady, and we just got engaged too. So, don't bitch to me about your dick's problems. I'm holing up with Snow for a week or until my dick falls off when we get back."

I look over at my brother, one of my best friends and bust up laughing.

We both fall into a comfortable silence after that. The first few days we chatted it up from our ol' ladies to marriage, to the club's future, shit we talked about everything. We've always been close. Shy doesn't hold back what he's thinking, and the man is always thinking. He always has a plan for everything.

I was shocked when he told me they were going to hold off on kids until after the wedding. She didn't want to be pregnant for the wedding or honeymoon. Shy's always wanted her pregnant with his kid, but he loves her too much to take away from her, shining bright as a DJ. I swear to God he's the best man I know, shit I look up to him even though I'm a year older than he is. Crazy how that is because the fucker seems so much older. He's got an old soul and has experienced some hard shit in his life.

I don't think I could be that selfless. I want Ruby pregnant and soon. I want Bella to have a baby brother or sister. I don't give a fuck if people think it's too soon. When we get back, she'll have my cut on her back, a ring on her finger and a baby in her belly right after.

These past few weeks seeing my family, and reconnecting, knowing I can have it all and I don't have to hide anymore has me on the fast track to starting my family.

"Why you anxious about Crows' territory? We all talked about this, and you know the plan," Shy asks.

"It's still in the back of my head, shit I've been hiding for so long it's embedded in me," I answer honestly.

"You need to understand they have so much more shit to worry about with our club than to worry about some punk ass bartender, that they *think* knows something about who killed their men." He pauses to look out the window. "Tommy and I had been fighting each other for years. It was going to come to one of us dead sooner or later. I've told you this already. If anyone should go down for it- it should be me. I would've killed him myself if you hadn't, for what they did to me."

I don't reply. I just keep my eyes straight ahead because I know he's right. They don't have shit to go on to even think it's me. *But it was me.*

Shy turns his upper body to face me, "Do you think for one second either of those two fuckers wouldn't have killed you?" He scoffs, turning straight again. "If you didn't have a gun or draw as quick as you did, brother you wouldn't be here right now. So, fuck them and fuck hiding. We're not fighting with them no more. Haven't been in years but if they do come knocking for *any reason*, best believe we'll be ready to knock back." Shy's voice is filled with hatred.

After these last few weeks, seeing how much I've missed out on because of them I couldn't agree more, fuck them. Let them come.

A few hours later we pull into the shitty hotel, check in and wait for our contact to come so we can do the damn exchange and get the fuck out of here. We could be out of Crow territory by sundown, and I would feel a hell of a lot better.

We get two rooms next to each other one for payment and one for grab or pickup. Wolfe has been transporting shit for years. I always think of the movie transporter. People pay us to transport shit, some things are illegal, and some things aren't.

Most of the time, it usually is illegal. We have guns, money, and marijuana mixed in with Ruby's stuff. We didn't tell her that's what we were doing, but she isn't stupid, seeing as she doesn't have two truckloads of stuff. It's kind of like we're the middleman doing the grunt work, but we get paid a shit ton of money. Shy has been moving our club more toward night clubs and lounges, hoping to get us away from the transporting business but the money is too good to stop doing it.

Shy, Tiny, Worm, and the prospects are inside doing what they are here to do while, Blink, Chiv and I are outside by the trucks. Blink and Chiv are sitting on their bikes smoking next to me, as I lean up against Ruby's SUV drinking a beer. The hotel is on a deserted highway, open wide so we can see who comes in and who goes out. There is a gas station across the street but other than that nothing for a few miles.

Blink lifts his small binoculars to look in both directions, with a cigarette hanging from his lips. We do this every ten minutes because if someone is headed toward us, it will give us time to prepare. Blink pauses in one direction for longer than I like so I step away from the SUV when Blink grunts, "We got company."

I look toward the direction he's looking, casually lifting my beer taking a long swig like nothing's going on. "I got four men can't see colors yet."

Chiv just sits on his bike like it's nothing, but I know he has three guns hiding on his bike. He shouldn't since as he just got out from the big house.

Blink's voice relaxes. "Friendlies."

Meaning we don't have beef with them or don't know them. So, if we just act normal, we shouldn't have a problem. I open the SUV and grab another beer, throwing one to Chiv and handing one to Blink, while he puts his binoculars in his cut.

I pull out my phone and text the guys we have company but friendlies for now. That way they know we got company and to be alert. When the four bikers pull into the gas station, they don't notice us since both the SUV and bikes are between the two moving trucks.

When they start filling up their tanks, they take notice

looking in our direction. Lowering their glasses checking out our colors, that the three of us have on.

The three of us glance over with our sunglasses. We try not to bring attention to ourselves when we're on runs. We never approach others unless we know them. Blink stands up and moves near his brother. "Do you remember the Hernandez brothers? Is that them? I could have sworn they were with the Rockers?"

When the four men start their bikes, we all stand up and turn to face them as they cross the street right for us.

Sonofabitch

Blink moves forward when the two front men smile I somewhat relax.

"Motherfucker, it is you," one of the men says, turning off his engine.

"Well goddamn look who got let out! Chiv," the other man says.

Both my brothers go to greet them with a handshake and shoulder bump.

Blink does the talking, telling them we're moving my ol' lady, stopped to rest but we're getting ready to head out soon. I guess these guys were headed home from another chapter. They shoot the shit about Chiv being out and who's Blink been hunting lately. Obviously, they know each other, so I lean back against the SUV and drink my beer like nothing's going on. I pull out my phone and text the boys to hurry the fuck up.

The four men don't stay long and once they're gone, I take a deep breath and relax. It's time to get the fuck out of here and home to my firecracker.

As soon as we pulled into the compound, our girls along, with our brothers, are there waiting. I notice Dallas' happy ass standing there too but it's my firecracker that I lock eyes with and when I do she starts to run. Her and Ginger high tailing it to us. Shy and I barely get out of the car before they launched themselves at us. With my girl wrapped around me, I throw my keys to Mac, giving him a head nod.

Before I high tail it to my room, I stop in front of Dallas pulling him in for a hug, squishing Ruby between us. She giggles. "Brother, it's good to see you are breathing," I say, gripping him around his neck.

He chuckles. "Me too, brother, me too. Now go get laid, we'll talk when you surface."

Shy and Ginger were already gone by the time I made it to the elevator.

That was Tuesday – it's Friday morning now. I kept my ol' lady in bed naked for three days. I only came out for more drinks and food deliveries that I took right back to my room. I wasn't letting her out of my sight – not until my dick was raw.

But now, I miss my little lady. It's early, and we're hoping to surprise her with breakfast. We bought food so we wouldn't have to make anything. When we open the door, I heard her scream, "An-tee. Qwak's home. Qwak's home." I turn the corner and there comes my beautiful baby girl hauling ass for me. I lift her in the air as she squeals with laughter before giving her a big hug.

"I'm so happy you're home and Momma's home."

Goddamn hearing her say this has my chest constricting, I'm so happy. I pull Ruby in for a family hug. I don't let go as I look up to see Izzy tucked into Gus' side with tears in her eyes. Gus' with a big ass grin, says, "Glad you're home, brother."

I'm so choked up I just give him a head nod and squeeze my girls tighter.

"We're going to head to the clubhouse and help set up for tonight," Gus announces.

Izzy lets go of Gus, rushing over, throwing her arms around all three of us. "I love you guys. Glad your home Quick. See you later tonight."

Once the door shuts, I say to my baby girl, "Miss me beautiful?"

Bella pulls back but doesn't let go of my neck and says with a huge smile, "Yep."

"Hungry?"

She giggles. "Yep."

"Good, we brought breakfast," I tell her giving Ruby a squeeze before letting her go. Bella still doesn't release my neck and to be honest, I don't want to put my baby girl down. So, I shift her to my side and say, "Tell me what's been going on around here? Have your babies been behaving?"

Bella's eyes light up before she begins her rambling about all that has been going on around here.

Yeah, I love this little girl. Besides her momma, she's the best thing in my life. We move around the kitchen, getting stuff ready. When I put her on the island, which seems to be our thing when we hang out in the kitchen, she keeps telling me all about her babies.

Ruby blurts out, "I think you should move in with us?"

Bella claps excitedly. "Yay, Qwak's going to live with us."

I put my fork down, and I look over at Ruby. "Um, I kind of already am."

Because seriously I was here every day and night before we went down to get her stuff. I have my room at the clubhouse which I won't get rid of because when we need adult time, we have that place to go to.

Ruby smiles. "I mean, live here permanently. I know you'll keep your room at the clubhouse, but I want you to move all your stuff here with us."

I chuckle, "Rube, that's only like my clothes. I don't have much besides my truck and bike. I don't need much."

Ruby raises an eyebrow, "Those are the only two things you need?"

Bella chimes in, "He needs us, Momma."

We both look to Bella and smile.

"Yes, baby girl. You two are my girls and are way more important to me than anything in the world."

I then look over at Ruby. "Yes, I'll move all my sh-stuff in," catching myself before I cursed.

I wish I could ask her here and now but it'll have to wait until tonight. God, if I had the ring right now, I would do it but can't. So, instead, I ask the next big question.

"Bella, are you ready to have a little sister or brother?"

Ruby chokes on her food but Bella squeals with excitement yelling, "Yes."

I laugh. *Yeah, tonight is going to be fun.*

24 | Finally Sorted

Ruby

"Izzy, maybe you shouldn't get involved? I mean what if this Dr. Hart really doesn't like him?" I ask Izzy after she texts Dallas' doctor. A doctor I guess Dallas has become obsessed with and can't get to go out with him.

"I'm not doing anything. I'm just inviting her to the lounge this week. Dallas' going nuts that he can't find anything out about her. She won't go out with him, so maybe I can help by inviting her out for drinks with us girls. If she comes, she comes. If she doesn't, then at least I tried," Izzy says with a mischievous smile, that tells me she's in no way going to stop getting involved.

"My bitches!" Maze yells.

We all look up to see a row of shots being set up.

"Girl, I know all you bitches have to be sore from your men being gone for so long but especially you two that were holed up in those rooms of yours for several days. We all took bets who would surface first." Maze says from the other side of the bar.

I laugh. "I'm sure it was me because I do have a kid I had to get home too."

Ginger, Izzy, Storm, Lish, and I line up at the bar getting drinks.

"That's what Dallas said, that it wasn't fair because his money would have been on you two if it wasn't for your kid," Maze replies.

Today we're having a huge cookout and celebration of life for Nick, so the clubhouse is going to be packed. We finally got his ashes back. Almost all of our chapters will be here to honor him. Tomorrow we are doing a ride out, where the whole club will ride together in his honor. We'll be riding to the West

Virginia chapter and have another celebration but that one no kids or outside clubs. It will be just Wolfeman chapters.

We brought Bella with us for part of the cookout, but Eva will be taking her home to watch her overnight. She's hanging out upstairs in the suite, with the other younger kids.

Storm leans forward looking down the bar at me. "Okay, we all need to talk about how your auntie looks identical to my sister-in-law. Bear came home and lost his shit. Telling me how he almost had a heart attack when he looked up and saw her." Storm starts laughing while trying to explain the story, "He-he said, 'baby, it was like looking at Foxy but different.' I was like, 'what the hell. You need to explain.' He said, 'It was our Foxy but like kinkier.'"

Storm has us all laughing, me more so because I know what he was trying to say, she was in her dominatrix gear. Storm catches her breath, wiping her eyes. "I said, 'Bear what the fuck do you mean?' He got all pissed off and yelled, 'I was looking at Foxy, but she was dressed like a kinky bitch.'"

I'm laughing so hard I can't breathe.

"He didn't," I cry.

"I heard every man wanted to bow down when she cracked her whip," Ginger exclaims.

I turn to her and say, "Who told you? Your dad or Shy?"

Ginger tries to control her laughter. "Shy, my dad hasn't told me jack shit. Shy actually snapped a picture of her. Christ, I had to take a couple of glances. He told me I needed to go buy one of those outfits and he was right – she's hot as fuck."

"No, he didn't. I want to see it." I slap her arm. "And, Oh, my God, Quick said the same fucking thing about the outfit, except he would be the one whipping and tying me up," I return, still laughing.

"I want to see," Lish and Storm say at the same time.

"I'll snag his phone from him and show you all later." Ginger snickers.

"What the fuck did I miss? Shit, I leave you bitches alone for two seconds and y'all are crying," Maze yells with laughter in her voice.

"We're laughing at our men and how they reacted to seeing my aunt in Dominatrix gear looking identical to Ginger's mom."

Maze's face goes blank, looking at each one of us. "Um, isn't your mom passed away?"

Ginger's wiping her eyes. "Yeah."

Maze still with a blank face, leans up against the bar. "I don't get it. What would be funny about that."

Storm clears her throat. "It's funny because our men almost shit themselves. Foxy was crazy but nothing close to being a dominatrix. So seeing her dressed in that gear tripped them the fuck out."

Maze looks over our shoulders and straighten.

"What are you all laughing about?" Wolfe says, suddenly behind Ginger.

We all freeze.

Ginger is the only one that turns around. "Hi Daddy! How was your trip?"

"Snow, I was just here. What trip? My trip home?" he answers, irritated.

"Oh, that's right. Never mind. We're headed up to check on the kids." Ginger giggles, turning around to grab her drink.

We all get up with our drinks and walk away following her, saying our hellos to him as we pass.

We're all giggling as we make our way to the elevator.

"Thanks, bitches. See you soon," Maze calls out after us.

When the elevator door opens Quick, who's holding Bella, along with Dallas, Gus, Mac, and Shy exit.

"Momma!" Bella squeals but doesn't move from Quick's arms.

"Where are you all going?" I question.

"We were just headed to find you. We want to show you something," Quick says with a devilish grin.

Mac breaks the silence. "Ma, you ready? Let's go," Mac says loudly.

"Alright, alright, boy. Don't be so bossy," Storm says, grabbing his arm, walking off with Mac.

At that moment, everyone gets weird.

"Momma, Qwak and I are gonna—"

Quick tickles my daughter cutting her off from probably telling me the surprise. I giggle.

"What Bella was going to say is…Ruby, we have a little surprise to show you, but we need to go upstairs to the dance floor," Quick announces, moving to me.

Folding my arms, I smirk. "Dance floor, huh."

Both Quick and Bella yell at the same time, "Yep."

"Oh, I'm coming for this. My little Bug is going to cut up a rug," Izzy exclaims, grabbing Gus' arm dragging him with us, and everyone else seems to follow.

We all make our way upstairs to the second floor where we find Wolfe and the members from both our chapters hanging around the bar. Quick shuffles us over to the front of the stage telling us to sit. Everyone migrates to chairs, pulling them up next to the stage.

"What's going on?" Wolfe asks, walking to us.

"Bella and Quick have a surprise for Ruby, and we all came to watch," Ginger replies to her father.

Quick and Bella walk up to the center of the stage, leaving Bella in the center in front of the pole.

Oh, God.

I'm feeling nervous for my baby girl. Even though Bella's totally excited that she's center stage with everyone watching her. I laugh seeing her smiling big as she twirls around in circles, making her dress fly up, with all eyes on her.

"Yep, that's Firecracker's daughter alright," Worm says under his breath with a chuckle.

I turn around to say something when I see the room filled with more people. Now I'm nervous for my baby girl to be up there, with all these people watching. I stand to approach the stage, but Bella puts her hand up to stop me. "No. Momma."

What the fuck.

She giggles. I hear Quick whistle, and Bella spreads her feet shoulder width apart and crosses her arms over her chest. She looks out at all of us with a funny face, as a voice sounds across the room, "Right about now…"

"Oh. My. God." I breathe as "It Takes Two" by Rob Base & DJ EZ Rock starts playing, and my baby girl stands there all gangster, with a total girlie smile.

Everyone starts to laugh when they say, "hit it," and Quick comes out jumping and bouncing around with Bella's little body trying to mimic his moves.

Izzy jumps up, screaming, "Go, Bella."

I can't help it, and I start laughing and screaming alongside Izzy. Bella is full of smiles now staying in one spot, but still trying to dance like Quick, throwing her little arms around. She does her part through each time he points to her, singing the verse, "It takes two to make a thing go right."

Everyone is on their feet, cheering them on until the music abruptly turned off with a loud scratching sound, and Shy walks out. Everyone boos him. I'm pissed, but a little worried that maybe Bella isn't supposed to be up there or even on this floor. All the what-ifs start firing off in my head as I see Shy, who doesn't look happy staring at me, as he walks to the center of the stage.

I look to Quick, and he looks pissed off as well, picking Bella up into his arms. Shy grabs the mic from Quick, while he whispers something into Bella's ear.

"Alright. Alright." His expression changes as he smiles,

shaking his head. "Christ, I sound like my ol' lady up here. Fuck." He pauses, looking to Bella. "Sorry, I didn't mean to say that."

Bella giggles, putting her face into Quick's neck, hugging him. My heart melts seeing the two of them so close.

"Okay, what I meant was alright calm down. Now, I've got something to say before this continues." He points to me. "Firecracker, you are new to this lifestyle, but, you fit in with our crazy asses. Your man here has claimed you and Bella as his own, and in this lifestyle, that means we claim you too." He stops and snaps his fingers. Quick lets Bella down. She's beaming with excitement, so I don't notice Mac and Storm move to either side of me until Izzy gasps.

When I turn to look at her, I see Storm next to me with a huge grin.

"Ruby this jacket is a symbol of the Wolfeman MC, marking you as Property of our boy Quick here."

Tears fill my eyes as Storm holds up my leather cut and Mac whispers, "Welcome to the family, Firecracker."

"Now, if you put this cut on... you are committed to not just your ol' man here but to the Wolfeman MC too. You will become our family."

Tears are falling from my eyes. I look to my man who's getting just as emotional, holding Bella's hand on stage. Once Mac helps me put the cut on, everyone starts to make howling noises. Shy hands Quick the mic and jumps down, moving toward me, giving me a big hug, whispering, "Thank you for bringing him to life. You're a Wolfeman for life, sweetheart."

I feel hands tapping my shoulder and back, but I don't take my eyes off of my man. "Now, this isn't normal, but I wanted to add a couple of little additions to this ceremony." He walks to the edge of the stage pulling Bella with him. Mac hands him something, and he gets down on his knees, sitting on his heels, looking to Bella.

"Baby girl," Quick says.

Bella who's bouncing around, smiling and squeals when he holds up a little jean jacket. "Now would you like to wear this like your Mama? It means I love you."

I'm moving to the edge of the stage where they are when she nods her head, excited. And, before he puts it on her, he asks, "One more thing. Is it okay if I ask your momma to marry me?"

I freeze.

Bella doesn't. She jumps up and down turning to me. "Momma. Qwak loves me."

I laugh, covering my mouth.

The room has erupted in cheers and laughter.

Quick turns to me, holding Bella around the waist, whispering in her ear again, handing her the mic. She smiles. "Momma, check your pocket."

What?

Storm lifts my hand to the front pocket under where the patch says Firecracker. I feel something in there, so I slide two fingers in and burst into a sob. Inside I can feel a thick ring with what I'm sure is a fat diamond attached to it.

I can't seem to pull it out since I'm a blubbering mess. Quick moves the mic to his mouth. "Ruby-Rue, will you marry me? That is when you pull the damn thing out of the pocket?"

Everyone laughs making comments, but I'm still sobbing and laughing, trying to get the damn ring. Suddenly two strong hands are grabbing my waist, lifting me onto the stage. As he stands up, he lifts my baby girl holding her to him. I'm still trying to pull the damn thing out as I look to them, and say, "yes."

Quick pulls me into a hug with Bella, and I'm smashed to his chest. They both are talking, but I don't listen to anything they are saying. I'm crying, shocked, happy and just overall emotional. I need to get my shit together, wiping my eyes, I hear the music start to play, and Bella is taken from Quick so he can pull me completely to him, giving me a kiss. "I told you I wouldn't stop. It feels good," he sings to me, pulling the ring from the pocket with ease.

With one hand around my waist, he grabs my left hand, slipping a humongous ring onto my finger. I don't have time to admire it because he slips my hand up his chest motioning me to grip his neck before sliding his hand back down my side around to my lower back.

I clasp my hands around his neck and move with him too, "Only You" by 112, The Notorious B.I.G. & Mase.

Quick leans down, kissing my cheek. "Goddamn, Firecracker, you're looking real good in that cut, baby." murmuring in my ear.

"I–I..." I can't finish my sentence as a lump forms in my throat.

"I got you, Rube. I got both of you girls," he says, declaring his love to me. The whistles and catcalls continue, breaking me from my bubble. I look around to see all the members surrounding the stage with Izzy and Gus holding Bella and wearing an adorable little cut of her own.

Yes, he does have my love and the love of my baby girl. I smile, pulling him down for a long deep kiss. *Mine. I guess I finally got my shit sorted*

25 | Skeletons

Quick

My phone beeps.

Ruby's sprawled across me with her leg and arm draped over me, in a deep sleep. I look at the clock and see it's four in the morning.

Fuck me.

But when the phone beeps again, I slowly move to grab the phone off the nightstand, hoping not to wake her.

Unlocking my phone, I see it's a text.

Shy: Clubhouse meeting now.

Knowing he wouldn't text unless it was urgent, I slip the rest of the way out from under her, and as soon as our connection is gone, she stirs awake.

"Is everything okay?" she murmurs, half asleep.

"Sshh...Rube. I have to head to the clubhouse," I whisper in return.

Putting my clothes on in record time, I lean over the bed, placing a kiss on her cheek.

She mumbles, "Be safe. Love you."

"Always, love you too," I reply.

Heading to the front door, I check on my other girl, pulling her blankets up over her, and head out.

Entering the clubhouse, I notice its completely empty, so I head to the clubhouse room and find everyone at the table. Everyone meaning all the officers, and no one looks happy.

"What's up?" I ask, concerned.

Shy looks up exhausted.

"Just got the call from Wolfe. Black Crows want a sit-down," he replies.

My heart skips a beat as everyone around the table looks to me.

Sonofabitch.

I move to sit down at the table. Shy's in his chair at the head of the table with Mac next to him. I move my eyes around the table to Tiny, Worm, Dallas, and then back on Shy.

"What did they say? Is this about me?" I question.

Shy shrugs. "Wolfe didn't say. Just said Knight reached out. Said he needed to meet with us." When no one speaks Shy adds, "He did say it was a friendly meet, that he just needed to have a chat."

"A chat my ass," Mac grunts.

"When? Where?" Dallas asked.

"Next Thursday, which gives us a few days to get our shit together," Shy explains.

All kinds of emotions start to run through me, guilt, fear, irritation, and most of all, nervousness.

"When do we head out?" I ask next.

"We leave tomorrow and head to Wolfe, everyone's going to migrate there. We'll put a plan together and sort our shit before we meet with them."

"Who is everyone?" Tiny asks.

Shy looks to him. "Seems Wolfe called in all chapters." He looks to me before adding, "You, Mac, Dallas, Tiny, and I will head out tomorrow. While Worm holds down the fort with the rest of the club."

Everyone nods, I can see Worm wants to say something. "What?" I ask him.

Worm looks around the table. "What happens if it's a trap or something? Shouldn't we have everyone there close by just in case?"

Shy shakes his head. "We need to have our women and clubhouses covered just in case they try to lure us away only to hit us at home. When we leave, I want eyes on all the women and kids."

We all nod in agreement. Shy hits his fist to the table, and everyone starts to leave the room.

"Quick, a minute," Shy says, standing next to Mac.

When I turn to face them, they both look tired.

"Reached out to our guy inside and he said there's been no word about you from Knight or any Crow, so we don't know for sure what this meet up is about. We don't really know if you should go to the meeting," Shy explains.

"I'm going," I return.

"You sure?" Mac questions.

I nod my head. "Yep. No more hiding. I want this shit done and over with. I'm gonna be getting married."

It's only been a week since I ask Ruby to marry me, but I don't want this shit hanging over my head anymore.

They both look at me with understanding eyes.

"Okay, I'll let Wolfe know, and we'll come up with some plans," Shy says, moving around the table. "Oh, and no word to the women. This is club business. I don't need either of our women going ape shit."

Mac laughs. "Yeah, we don't need Firecracker or my cousin storming into the meeting flipping out."

"Just tell them we're headed to West Virginia for a club meeting," Shy tells me.

Mac scoffs. "That won't work on Snow either. Hello, she'll want to come with you."

I look between the two men waiting for them to figure out what I need to tell my woman when I get home.

Shy looking more irritated barks, "Fucking tell her you're going on a run for club business."

I nod my head and exit the room with my mind going crazy with motherfucking what-ifs.

When I hit the front door to the clubhouse, I'm about ready

to open it, when I hear Shy yell, "Wolfeman for life, brother. Don't worry."

I stop, turn my head and give him a head nod, not saying anything as I head home.

When I got home and crawled back into bed, Ruby didn't wake. When I told her I was leaving for club business, she said okay, but her eyes wanted to ask more but didn't. Thank God. When I didn't give her more, she told me she loved me and to be safe.

Yep, best fucking ol' lady ever. My ol' lady. Mine.

"Everyone shut the fuck up," Wolfe yells from the bar. We're at the compound in West Virginia, and since there are too many men here to fit us all in the clubroom, we're all hanging out in the main club area.

"I want to meet with all officers right now. Once the meeting is done, each chapter president will give the orders. Until then hang out have some drinks," Wolfe explains.

The officers follow Wolfe into the club room. "Presidents and VPs at the table with everyone else behind your chapter," Wolfe instructs as he makes his way to the head of the table.

Once Shy and Mac are seated, I make my way behind him. As the chapters fill in the room, there's no chatter. Everyone's on edge and ready to hear what's going on.

When the door shuts Wolfe leans his forearms onto the table and begins, "Okay, as you all know the Black Crows requested a friendly sit down for a chat. Knight, their founding president, called this meeting and requested all chapters to attend." He pauses to look around the room. When his eyes land on me, he says, "We all know the beef we've had for decades with them and the agreement to stay in our own territories."

Everyone nods their heads. My heart starts to race with all kinds of emotions rushing through me.

"Okay, this is what I wanted to discuss here and now with all of you because it doesn't need to be spoken about outside this room. But, I need you all to know the facts just in case it's the issue they want to discuss. Most of you know about the incident at Bike Week a few years back with Shy getting jumped and a couple of their men being killed."

Again everyone nods their heads. I fist my hands, clenching and unclenching trying to release some of this tension.

"Most of you were with us during the fight with them, over who killed members of their club. They beat Jake, almost to death trying to get answers."

The men that were there at the time look to me, giving me a nodded understanding. But, the ones that weren't there just look around trying to figure out who Jake is.

"Now for those of you who weren't here back then, Jake, who you know as Quick wasn't a member back then. He was just in the wrong place at the right time. He didn't become a Wolfeman until later."

Now every eye in the room is looking at me, with some questioning, some understanding.

"We don't know why they want to meet, but there are a few things we need to understand and have a plan for. One, they don't know Jake is Quick – but they could have found out. Two, we stopped in their territory a few weeks back. I sent a message to Knight telling him we were going to make a stop on our way through from California. Since that's in our agreement. If we ever enter one's territory, we are to make contact before, so there's no misunderstanding. Well, when we stopped we did make an exchange – so it could be regarding that."

"Why would they care if Jake was Quick?" Brick, president of the Chicago chapter, asks.

Wolfe looks to Shy and then to me. Shy stands up. "I was jumped by two Crows and was almost beaten to death. Those two Crows were killed. Quick or back then Jake was bartending that night and was the only one who could have known who the killer was. They either thought it was him or he knew who did it, so they jumped him. They beat him as well, he got away, and we took him, putting him under our protection. That's when he became Quick. We don't know if the Crows are still looking for him but no matter what they don't know shit. If they are coming for Quick, we'll handle it. No one knows what happened that night except for two things – Jake saved me, and he earned his name Quick."

Everyone nods their heads, some hitting the table while some uttering words, but all in acceptance.

"Okay, so needless to say we don't know what they want but what we do know is that beef between our clubs has ended except with the South Carolina chapter, where Ronny, the brother of Tommy who was killed, he's the Enforcer there. Knight, the founder, has no beef with us, and I am hoping to keep it that way. So we need to be smart and have every outcome covered. We need to make a plan for getting in, getting out and keeping eyes on them," Wolfe explains.

"You killed those fuckers, didn't you?" Chiv asks me, taking a drink of his beer two hours later as we sit at the clubhouse bar. As soon as we finalized the plans and relayed them to each chapter member. Everyone starts to party trying to get some pussy before we head out tomorrow. I'm sitting at the bar as the party is in full effect.

"Chiv, you were there, brother, you know what happened. Shit, you went to jail for fuck's sake," Dallas says on my other side.

Chiv leans forward to look over at Dallas. "I know,

motherfucker, but I didn't know Quick that well, and he was in New York. I didn't know shit except they fucked up Shy, two Crow bitches were killed, and they were hot on our asses for it," he hammers.

"As Shy said, you know two things, he saved him, and he got his name Quick. End of the story," Dallas says more demanding.

"I spent my time in jail. Had to be a kiss-ass, pussyfooting motherfucker in there to get out on good behavior. So, I think I deserve more fucking details than that." Chiv glares over at Dallas.

I feel the tension between the two men and I'm honored Dallas' being protective of me, but I lift my beer to my mouth and say, "Yeah, I did it."

No more hiding.

Both men look at me while I take a long swig of my beer, neither one saying a word, so I continue.

I look to Chiv, who looks surprised and say calmly in a low voice, "You saw the photos. You know what I did. You know how I got Shy out. What else do you need to know?"

Chiv looks at me a beat before throwing his head back, raising an arm to grip my shoulder. "Not a goddamn thing, brother. I have been waiting years for you to own up to that shit. Started thinking they made that shit up about you. You were a scrawny little fucker back then too. It was hard to believe before, but the fucker in front of me today, now that I can see." Chiv chuckles, still holding my shoulder.

I laugh.

Dallas laughs.

All tension gone.

Since Knight requested the meet, Wolfe got to pick the place. Wolfe picked a bar on the border of Tennessee, North Carolina, and Virginia. The bar, Shooters Bar and Grill is owned by a big motherfucker name Bristol, who's in good with Wolfe but, he also knows Knight. It was a neutral place for both parties. Bristol welcomes all bikers and only had one rule no fighting in his bar. Whatever the fuck you wanted to do outside was your own dealings, but inside his bar, you kept your shit intact. A place off the beaten path and in the middle of nowhere, that you could see anyone coming for miles and big enough to hold all of us.

When we first got there, Knight was already there. When we pulled in, there were quite a few Crow members lingering around outside with prospects watching the bikes. I didn't see anyone I knew, but then again, I wouldn't remember anyone really except Ronny.

As we followed Wolfe inside, the place was crawling with Crows. Wolfe spotted Bristol walking toward him with a big smile.

"My brother! How was the trip?" Bristol shakes Wolfe's hand, embracing him in a short shoulder bump.

"Good, brother. Good," Wolfe returns.

When Bristol takes a step back, Knight's standing there with no sign of Ronny. Everyone says their greetings as Bristol moves us to the back banquet area, where he usually has live music, that holds a big group of people. He had the room set up how Wolfe requested, a table that held twelve seats on each side with one at each end of the table. If there were more than that, they could stand or find their own chair.

Everyone got a drink and started filtering into the room. Knight and Wolfe taking the end chairs followed by their VP and then whoever their president wanted to be at the table. Wolfe wanted Cash, Shy, Mac, and then four of his oldest chapters at the table with the rest of us behind him.

Once everyone was seated Wolfe gestured for Knight to take

the lead. When Knight clears his throat, everyone goes quiet. There's still no sign of Ronny, he wasn't the president or VP, but he was an officer, so he should be at this meeting.

Knight starts off by saying, "Wolfe, thanks for coming to meet with us on such short notice. I want to cover a few things, and hopefully we can come to an understanding, again so that we can keep the peace that we've kept going for these past few years." When he pauses Wolfe nods his head but doesn't say anything, so Knight continues, "It's come to our attention that you were doing business on our territory a few weeks back. I know you messaged us, letting us know you were traveling through from California, but from what our scouts said you did business here?"

This time when he paused, Wolfe does speak. "We did stop in your territory as I'd told you, but during our twelve-day trip we missed a meet, so we told them to meet us at that stop to exchange money, but no product was exchanged. It saved us two days of backtracking. They aren't from your territory, and we didn't take away or steal any of your business. This was just to save us from spending two more days away from our families. I'm sorry for the miscommunication or misleading," Wolfe says, in a calm voice.

Knight nods his head, and the room is nothing but calm. Some of the Crow men look furious and before Knight can say anything, Wolfe adds, "Knight, I haven't called or retaliated when your men entered into my territory. I've given them the benefit of the doubt. They didn't take away from my business or do any harm."

Knight's face hardens as he looks to his men. Showing us that he knew nothing of his men entering our territories unannounced. He turns his attention back to Wolfe. "Well, I wish you would have informed me, because that's not okay. We have an agreement and if I am to uphold my part of the deal, I need to know when my men are not doing their part."

Wolfe nods his head in understanding but doesn't say anything. The door to the room swings open and in walks Ronny, along with five other men. Knight's face turns from irritated to livid and spits out, "You're late. Again."

Ronny is looking just as pissed off, fires back sarcastically, "Hit traffic."

There are quite a few scoffs at the table because everyone here damn well knows there is no traffic around here and the look on Knight's face shows he knows it too but doesn't say anything. He turns back to Wolfe. "Sorry for the interruption. I guess that covers our first deal of business, seeing as you explained what you were doing and informed me of my men doing the same. I'll speak with you after to get the descriptions of those men," Knight draws out.

Wolfe clears his throat getting everyone's attention. "No need to wait. I know exactly who entered my territory and it was on more than one occasion, but like I said my scouts just watched and waited to see what he was doing. Since he wasn't doing anything wrong, we left him alone." Wolfe explains.

Ronny snaps his head to Wolfe. Wolfe smiles, pissing off Ronny even more as his face turns red with anger.

Knight snaps them out of their stare down by asking, "Who was it?"

Wolfe still not taking his eyes off Ronny returns, "Ronny and the men he just entered the room with."

One of the presidents and VPs snap their heads to the men. I'm taking it they are the president and VP from Ronny's South Carolina chapter.

No words are spoken between them, but murderous glares are definitely exchanged.

Knight replies, "Thank you. We'll deal with the issue and please let us know if this happens again.

Ronny blurts out, "It's going to happen again. If *that* mother fucker doesn't leave my cousin alone." He points to Dallas, standing next to me.

What the fuck? Cousin?

I look to Dallas, who looks just as confused as I am, but Dallas being Dallas fires back, "Um, you're going to have to be more specific because I fuck *a lot* of bitches. Like one or two a day."

This infuriates Ronny. "Motherfucking cocksucker, if you touch Harley, I'll fucking kill you."

Again, both Dallas and I look at each other with confusion. I know Dallas is searching the plethora of bitches he's fucked, trying to remember a Harley when Wolfe speaks up. "Knight, what's this all about?"

Knight looking irritated and put out says, "This was the other business that was to be talked about. Ronny brought to our attention that one of your Wolfs have been pursuing one of our Crows. We wanted to make sure it wasn't in retaliation or anything. I had no idea Ronny had been breaking the agreement going into your territories." Knight looks to Wolfe. "I take it New York is where Ronny's been going too?"

Suddenly, Ronny yells, "Wait a fucking minute," moving toward us.

Blink and Chiv are by Dallas' and my side instantly.

Ronny points. "Rocco said it was you, but I didn't believe it, but it is. This motherfucker is Jake Reeves. The bartender we fucked up because he wouldn't tell us who killed my brother," Ronny practically shouts across the room, stopping his advance as some of his men pull him back.

Knight uses his thumb and forefinger to pinch his nose then stands up. "Ronny back the fuck off, or I will remove you from this fucking bar myself. You've caused us enough drama to last us a fucking lifetime. Christ! Rash, you better lock that fucking down before I strip all of you of those fucking patches," Knight declares.

Ronny charges me, yelling, "You either killed them or you know who did motherfucker. Either way, I'm going to get it from you."

Four large as fuck Crows grab him and haul him out of the room. The four men who came in with him though stay looking like they want to murder me as well. I keep my shit in and don't flinch a muscle. They don't have shit.

Dallas cuts the tension bring us back to his issues. "What bitch am I fucking that is a Crow?"

Knight is looking at me, then the door where Ronny was just dragged and then back to me. "Wolfe you need to explain why you have the bartender in your ranks now."

Wolfe laughs.

The room becomes quiet.

"Felt bad for the kid. Y'all beat the fuck out of him for being a bartender at the wrong bar. Just because he found Shy and your men dead don't mean he knows shit! He told you what he knew. I took him in to protect him from your men killing him. If he didn't take the trash out and find Shy, Shy would be dead too."

Knight looks between Shy, Wolfe, and me. I can see when he decides to let it go because his face softens as he sits down.

"What girl?" Dallas demands even louder.

"She's Ronny's cousin. Her name is Harley Donovan." The guy who was shooting daggers at Ronny, turns and now that I can see his cut, is named Rash and is the president of the South Carolina chapter.

Dallas cuts him off. "I don't know any Crow bitch name, Harley Donovan."

Rash fires back, "You know her as Dr. Lee Hart. She changed her name when she moved away. She has no ties to the Crows, but Ronny's still protective of her."

Dallas looks murderous and like someone took his puppy away. "My doctor, Dr. Hart is Ronny's cousin?"

Rash nods his head.

"Well by the look on your face that tells us you didn't know, and it wasn't a ploy to get back at us," Knight says, sitting back in his chair.

Wolfe, who's still standing, demands, "So, I pulled in all my chapters to come to this meeting just so you could ask me about doing business on your territory and if Dallas was pursuing this bitch to get revenge."

Dallas growls.

Knight sits forward placing his forearms on the table. "Wolfe, I didn't know what to expect. Word was you did business on our territory and my men were mad. Word was your boy was looking into one of our Crows and they wanted to know why. I wanted to make sure we were all on the same page. I have liked these past few years drama free and would like to keep it that way."

Wolfe fires back, "You could have just picked up a goddamn phone, and we could have chatted about it or just had the New York chapter and my chapter meet, instead of involving all chapters."

Knight nods his head in acknowledgment.

Wolfe continues, "So, now that we are all clear. You're not mad we did an exchange, and we're not mad Ronny has been running loose in our territories." Wolfe pauses, waiting for Knight to acknowledge him and when he does, he continues. "You need to put a leash on Ronny. If he keeps coming into our territories and fucks with either Jake or Dallas, we will have problems."

Knight nods his acknowledgment but states, "Dallas needs to leave Harley alone. She's a Crow."

Dallas jaw clenches. "She's my doctor and isn't that up to her to decide?"

Knight darts his eyes to Dallas. "She is Crow's property."

Dallas adds again, "She's my doctor. I have to do follow-ups."

Knight looks at him, "She better just be your doctor and leave it at that."

Dallas' whole body tenses but he doesn't say a word.

"Are we done here? Are we all in agreement?" Wolfe asks, looking around the room. When all heads nod in acknowledgment, Knight stands, along with all his men.

"Thank you, Wolfe for this meeting, and I hope we can keep the peace," Knight states before moving around the table. Wolfe meets him halfway, giving him a handshake before all the Crows file out of the room.

I know in my gut Ronny isn't going to keep any peace, but it's good to know his club isn't behind him. If Ronny comes, he'll be coming alone. But, who will he be coming for Dallas or me?

Dallas growls, "She's a motherfucking Crow. But why change her name?" he asks more to himself than anyone as he's deep in thought next to me.

Yeah, I'm thinking Ronny's going to come for him... Dallas isn't going to stay away from that bitch. *Fuck no.*

THE END

...Stay tuned for more of the Wolfeman MC Series with Dallas' story coming next.

QUICK PLAYLIST

"Simple Man" by Lynyrd Skynyrd
"Chandelier" by Sia
"Another One Bites the Dust" by Queen
"Babe I'm Gonna Leave" by Led Zeppelin
"Rump Shaker" by Wreckx-N-Effect
"Feelin' Myself" by Mac Dre
"Get Ur Freak On" by Missy Elliot
"Just A Lil Bit" by 50 Cent
"Sliding Down the Pole" by E-40 featuring Too Short
"The Hills" by The Weeknd
"Please Me" by Cardi B and Bruno Mars
"Touch Me Tease Me" by Case, Foxy Brown, Mary J Blige
"Anywhere" by 112
"It Takes Two" by Rob Base & DJ EZ Rock
"Only You" by 112, The Notorious B.I.G & Mase

To Follow **Quick** playlist on Spotify click here

ABOUT THE AUTHOR

Crazy, outgoing, adventurous, full of energy and talks faster than an auctioneer with a heart as big as the ocean... that is Angera. A born and raised California native, Angera is currently living and working in the Bay Area. Mom of a smart and sassy little girl, an English bulldog, and two Siamese Cats. She spends her days running a successful law firm but in her spare time enjoys writing, reading, dancing, playing softball, spending time with family, and making friends wherever she goes. She started writing after the birth of her daughter in 2012 and hasn't been able to turn the voices off yet. The Spin It Series is inspired by the several years Angera spent married into the world of underground music and her undeniable love of dirty and gritty romance novels.

FOLLOW AND CONNECT
Email ~ authorangeraallen@gmail.com
Website ~ www.authorangeraallen.com
Facebook ~ www.facebook.com/authorangeraallen
Instagram ~ www.instagram.com/angeraallen
Twitter ~ www.twitter.com/angeraallen
Amazon ~ https://amzn.to/2A6dX8L
Bookbud ~ https://www.bookbub.com/profile/angera-allen?
list=author_books
Goodreads ~ https://www.goodreads.com/author/show/
16200622.Angera_Allen

Available ~ Amazon – iBooks – Nook – Kobo

ALSO BY ANGERA ALLEN

STANDALONE

Firecracker – Click Here

SPIN IT SERIES

Alexandria – Book One – Click Here

Ginger – Book Two – Click Here

Izzy – Book Three – Click Here

WOLFEMAN MC SERIES

Quick – Book One

COMING SOON

Dallas – Book Two – The Wolfeman MC Series

BB Securities – Book One (Brant's Story)

ACKNOWLEDGMENTS

My Wolfeman MC is here! Quick is here! Who thought writing three books at one time would be fun? Me…this stupid fuck. Well, I am glad to say I'm done finally! Thank you, Baby Jesus! Ruby and Quick's story is done but not over. You will be reading more of their story in both my series, seeing as Ruby has become a Spin It girl and of course Quick is one of my Wolfemen so you'll definitely be reading more of him. Here comes Dallas, y'all.

First and foremost, to my beautiful baby girl: Always my biggest fan. Thank you for all the help counting flyers and getting swag bags together for my events. Thank you for understanding Momma has to work on her computer late at night. I cherish our late-night coloring or working on the computer. (her just practicing writing while I write.) The love and support you give to me is the strength I need to keep going. I love you, my little sunshine. To my mom for loving me unconditionally. I hope and pray I will be as good of a mother to my baby girl that you have been to me. You are, and will always be, my best friend.

To my die-hard BETA readers: Jennifer G., Kim H., Jennifer

R., Kari J., Marlena S., Heather H., Tanya W. and Michelle K. All of you ladies have been with me each step of the way, giving me honest advice and unwavering support, even when I didn't want it. Thank you for always dropping what you are doing to read the newest chapters and respond with your advice. I love each and every one of you.

Angie D, Jennifer R, and Michelle K: Thank you for keeping my Angels group going strong with all the planning, building, scheduling of takeovers and daily devotion to the group. I love you girls and thank you for all you do.

Jennifer G, Kim H, and Michelle K. Thank you too for pushing me each step of the way. I just want you ladies to know how much it means to me. For all the phone calls and text messages helping me work through something in my head. Dropping everything to answer my calls to calm me down. For fixing my mixed-up words and just knowing what I'm trying to say. You ladies are very important to me, and I hope you know it. I love your opinion, the ideas, and advice you give me. I really love how you get so excited, push for an idea or even get mad at me with each character. I promise so much more to come. Jen, I promise a baby is coming! Teehee

Heather Coker & Jennifer Ramsey: Thank you, ladies, for designing and making my swag. I love them! Both of you have been by my side through all my books, and I am so grateful to have each of you in my life.

To all my friends who helped in making this book by giving me advice, doing "research" or stating the facts: Cousin Sandy, Amy W., Michelle K., Worm, Baby James, LO and all the men from the MC next door. Thank you so much for all your advice. I love you all.

CT Cover Creations – Clarise Tan, thank you for being patient with me. Girl, you are A-Maze-Ing, and I look forward too many more cover designs from you.

Logan & Wander – Wander thank you for being so talented

and capturing such an amazing shot of Logan. Logan, thank you for being fine as fuck and letting me use your body to put on my cover! Teehee… seriously thank you both for everything.

To my editor, Ellie Mc Love: Thank you for always going above and beyond to make me happy. You saved me with Izzy and now again with Quick. I promise my next one won't be so rushed. I would be dead without you and Petra fixing my shit. My biggest fear is when I hit send that you'll reply with sorry I can't help you. LMAO. All I can say is THANK FUCK for you!

My bloggers: There are too many to name now but know I love each and every one of you. Thank you for loving my books and for helping me promote them.

* Repeat but soooo true. HEA PR and more: First, thank you to Kathy Coopmans for referring them to me. Kathy, I cherish your friendship so much. You are my go-to Mama Bear for everything. I love ya girl! Ladies of HEA PR and more, thank you for taking me on this year. Well, and years to come! LOL For helping me keep it together for my book covers and releases. I would be so fucked if it wasn't for you! Thank you, and I look forward to working with you again soon.

To my Angels, thank you for all your love, support, and helping me build my dream. I love my group, and it just keeps getting bigger… let's keep it going!

To my Angera's Street Crew! I look forward to bouncing my ideas off you and having y'all there to help me make a decision. God knows I need help. Thank you!

To all my friends and family that have pushed me and supported me through these back to back book releases, I just want you all to know I love you and thank God every day for you. Without your love and support, I wouldn't have been able to finish these books. I know I am going to forget people, and I'm sorry for that, but just know I'm so thankful for everyone that had a part in making this dream a reality.

Last, but definitely not least, to my fans. I know it has been

CRAZY with back to back releases, and I hope it was worth it because it ain't happening again... =) Thank you for all the emails, messages, and most of all, reviews. They all mean so much to me.

I love each and every one of you.

With love, Angera